THE PULP HORROR BOOK OF PHOBIAS

VOLUME II

EDITED BY MJ SYDNEY

LVP
PUBLICATIONS

THE
PULP HORROR
BOOK
OF
PHOBIAS
II

EDITED BY MJ SYDNEY

Lycan Valley Press Publications
1625 E 72nd St STE 700 PMB 132
Tacoma, Washington 98404 United States of America

Printed in the United States of America

First Printing, Limited to 600 copies

ISBN-13: 978-1-64562-979-5

This book is dedicated to you — all of you.

"*Fear is pain arising from the anticipation of evil.*" ~ Aristotle

"*There are few monsters who warrant the fear we have of them.*" ~ André Gide

TABLE OF CONTENTS

THE SECOND STORY by Mehitobel Wilson   13

MÖBIUS by Michael Bailey   35

RIGHT-HAND MAN by Donna JW Munro   47

THE PETER PROBLEM by Steve Carr   65

THE ACQUISITION by Kealan Patrick Burke   83

GRAMMA by Stephen King   99

WHAT YOU BELIEVE by JG Faherty   147

THE MAN WHO HATED FOLEY by John Peyton Cooke   165

SIXTY-EIGHT DEGREES by John Palisano   201

MOUSETRAP by Colleen Anderson   217

VERMICULTURE by Nancy Kilpatrick   243

COMPULSION by Jill Hand   259

ANOTHER DOOR OPENS by Sèphera Girón   279

ABOUT THE CONTRIBUTORS   303

THE SECOND
STORY

BY MEHITOBEL WILSON

THE SECOND STORY

BY MEHITOBEL WILSON

AT TEN PAST SIX in the evening, Ivy's phone chimed three times.

Ivy scrambled from the cozy nest she'd arranged on the couch and shook the velvet blanket that had warmed her bare feet. Its bottle-green folds released her phone. She scooped up her device and confirmed the time.

Walking quickly on the balls of her feet, she first went to the patio door. On the other side of the glass, framed by a molten-caramel sunset, a square of cardboard hung from knotted twine. Ivy raised her phone and took a snapshot of the tag, which read BEDROOM in heavy red marker.

Next she moved to her left, to the living room window. Ivy shoved the blackout curtain aside and took a photo of the cardboard square that hung outside of it: MASTER BATH.

The kitchen window was next. The placard outside it, while attached to a string like the others, was also taped to the outside of the glass. It read MY OFFICE.

Ivy snapped her photo, then stepped into the flats she kept by the front door and went outside.

First, she peeled the MY OFFICE cardboard from the window pane. Ivy had to tape that one down, because once the sign had been caught up by the wind and tangled in the bushy magnolia beside the porch. Then she hopped off the concrete slab of the porch and went around to the side of the house, where there were no downstairs windows. She held her phone high and focused on the sign taped in the sole second-floor window: KEVIN'S STUDY.

The clock on her phone read 6:18pm. Ivy pocketed the phone, headed back inside the house, and locked the deadbolt behind her. She thumbed her shoes off and placed them beside the front door again, their toes touching the molding, perfectly even.

The stairs came next.

Ivy switched on the bright stairwell light and clasped the glossy oak handrail that was bolted to the wall. She took a deep breath, exhaled, took another breath.

She mounted the steps, her focus on her feet. The carpet needed to be vacuumed, as always. She hated doing it: no matter how methodically she tried to lay the path, she always got turned around. Had to turn around to get this crevice or move the cord or chase down that ball of dog hair.

After nine stair steps Ivy reached the landing. She moved so that her back was to the wall, pressed her shoulder blades against the plaster. The stairs leading down were to her left. The flight leading up was to her right.

She pointed at each and breathed, "That is down. That is up."

Then she climbed the seven steps to the second floor.

Quickly, quickly—she was going to run out of time. *Tomorrow I'll set the alarm for five past six instead*, she thought, and rushed into her office.

The vinyl blinds chittered as she pulled the string that raised them, and she shoved the sill up, grunting with the effort. Three weeks' worth of daily opening and closing had not loosened the window any, and the candle she had rubbed on the tracks had not eased their slide either. But she only had to make enough of a gap for her sheet of cardboard.

The twine knotted around the leg of her desk anchored the sheet. She grabbed the rough string and reeled the placard up, bouncing it past the projection of the porch roof, over the sill, and into her hands. One side was printed with the toothy cartoon face of a tiger proffering a bowl of golden cereal. She flipped it over and read: MY OFFICE.

Ivy's knees went watery with relief and she braced herself on her desk. *Deep breath, exhale, deep breath.* So far, so good.

A sun-crisped magnolia petal had gotten stuck to the strip of tape that edged her sign. She peeled it free and flicked it back out the window.

From the pocket of her pajama pants, a message notification jingled. Kevin, most likely. She ignored it. If she was lucky, Kevin was stopping by the grocery store on the way home, which would give her a few extra minutes—even more time if she ignored him and he shopped slowly while waiting for her response.

The sign that said KEVIN'S STUDY was indeed in the window of Kevin's own office. Ivy slotted the cardboard into its hiding spot behind his filing cabinet.

The sign that said BEDROOM slipped into her hands through the bedroom window. Her breath shuddered and she forced it steady again as she tucked the sign under their mattress.

The sign that said MASTER BATH was trickier to retrieve; Ivy had to carefully work it through the slit she'd cut in the window screen, her fingers shaking all the while, but once the sign was in her hands, she slid the window closed and lay her burning cheek against the cool white subway tile of the wall.

Nothing had been rearranged. Everything was where it belonged.

Today, at least.

"Carrots are ready," Kevin crowed as he shouldered the patio door open. Ivy could smell the hickory smoke that rolled off the grill. Kevin himself smelled like the woodsmoke, too, and Ivy bounced up from the kitchen table to relieve him of the platter of whole carrots.

"Oooh, perfect char on these," she said, and kissed his cheek. Her lips read his smile in the flex of his muscles. She stepped back and used her thumb to wipe the rosy smear of her lipstick from his skin.

"Five minutes for chicken. We should eat outside, there's a great breeze." Ivy looked past him toward the deck, and he chuckled. "Well, you can't see it, but it's there."

Ivy clenched her jaw, then reminded herself that Kevin was not a mean-spirited man. He wasn't commenting on her anxiety about the house. He couldn't be, because he didn't know about it.

As she finished the carrots—chopped them, then tossed them with olive oil, sazon, and za'atar—she kept her chin tucked to her breastbone, feeling the stretch in the back of her neck.

That way, she wasn't constantly checking the ceiling of the kitchen.

"It's the office," she whispered to herself. "Office is above me."

They loaded their plates with the carrots, bulgur pilaf, and Kevin's grilled chicken, and settled at the deck table to dine. Ivy sat with her back to the house so as not to see the windows.

There was a nice breeze, indeed.

"Did you research smartwatches yet?" Kevin asked, trying to sound casual.

"A little. Bunches of them have onboard GPS and compasses, but we'll have to decide whether I need one with a SIM card so I can use it when I'm not near my phone. I'm not sure if that's overkill."

"Heart rate monitor too, right? For your stress. To manage it."

Ivy pushed her grains of wheat into a buttery little mountain with the back of her fork.

"I just think," Kevin continued, and Ivy could hear a note of appeal in his voice, "that you'd be happier if you weren't so afraid of getting lost. And, hon, I'm not opposed to the watch having a SIM card, don't get me wrong—but will you really be without your phone when you're out of the house?"

He specified *out of the house* because in the house, Ivy and her phone were hardly ever in proximity. She'd plug it in upstairs to charge, come downstairs for coffee and to let Robey outside, and then never make it back upstairs to retrieve it.

Kevin often teased her about it with gentle good humor, thinking she was just forgetful, or lazy.

He didn't know that she was absolutely terrified. He didn't know that she would stand rooted at the foot of the stairs, quaking, her pulse slamming in her ears, her vision dimming and brightening, her thigh muscles hard and heavy as granite as she struggled to force herself to step up, just step up. Up and up, and turn around on the landing, and up some more, and turn at the top of the stairs, and then where the hell would she be? Would she be facing the door to her office, as she should be?

What would be directly below, if her office were where it belonged and she stood just outside the door? She frowned and rubbed the crease between her eyes, trying to visualize it.

"I think it's the coat stand," she muttered.

"What's the coat stand?"

Ivy didn't answer. She twisted in her chair and examined the house. Patio door behind her. White vinyl siding, tinged green by algae in spots. Two windows above the patio door, which should be the bedroom windows.

"Hey," she said, "Come with me. It'll be quick."

Kevin looked pointedly down at his full plate, then up at her, but Ivy had already risen from the table and was holding the door open for him. He sighed, lay down his fork, and followed her inside.

"Okay, go upstairs, please. I'll stay here."

"What are you checking on this time?"

"Just curious," Ivy said. "Humor me. Can you go up and stand outside my office door?"

She didn't ask him to confirm that her office door was where it belonged. Fear gave her heart a brief twist: if her office weren't where it belonged, would he even notice?

Kevin headed upstairs. He turned the corner on the landing and disappeared from view. Ivy fought the urge to run after him and bring him back.

"Okay," he called. "I'm there."

"Can you march in place? Stomp, like?"

Ivy waited.

After a moment, she heard him slam his big boots on the carpet, left, right, left, right. She stared up at the ceiling, trying to locate the spot where her husband was.

Not the coat rack, no. When Ivy approached the entryway to their kitchen, he was overhead.

"Got it, babe," she called, and the stomping stopped. His regular tread returned as he came back downstairs.

"You good? Can we finish dinner now?" Kevin sounded genuinely concerned, which embarrassed Ivy.

"Definitely," she said. "Thanks. Sorry."

She followed him across the house, casting quick glances at the ceiling, trying to track the upstairs rooms in relation to her own location—where would the laundry room be? She made a little dizzy pirouette, scanning the plaster, but it was fruitless—then gasped and involuntarily grabbed Kevin's elbow.

He whirled and caught her shoulders.

"What is it? Are you all right?" He looked down at her feet, clearly thinking she had stepped on something.

"I—fine, it's fine, I stubbed my toe, it's fine," she said, but it was not fine. Out on the deck, two windows upstairs, the bedroom windows, they're supposed to be, two windows, but where had the master bathroom window gone?

Kevin lent Ivy support as she faked a limp all the way back to the deck. She collapsed into her chair and waved a gnat from the lip of her wine glass.

"I hope it didn't get too cold," she said.

"Cold chicken's still great," said Kevin, and meant it.

"The breeze is stronger. I wonder if a storm is coming?" Ivy made an exaggerated show of examining the sky for clouds so she could check the house and count the windows.

Bedroom, bedroom, master bath.

I'll label them all tomorrow, she thought, and ate a cold carrot.

"I know you like older homes," Kevin had said, just months ago, "but let's just see this one. It won't hurt."

Ivy's first thought upon stepping inside the house and greeting their realtor was of vastness. The downstairs had an open floor plan, and it looked to her like a ballroom. She had thought, *I could roller skate in here if I wanted.* The vinyl underfoot was smooth, and though she was used to rental houses with hundred-year-old hardwood floors, the artificiality wasn't a dealbreaker. Robey was a big German Shepherd, and if his nails wore down a pine-look vinyl plank, she could just replace it rather than refinishing nice wood.

"The walls are plumb," Ivy had whispered to Kevin, awed. "The corners are squared!"

"No lead paint, either," he had murmured in response.

"So many outlets!" Ivy had turned to the realtor, unable to suppress her excitement. "Do you think we can run a vacuum without tripping the circuit breaker?"

The realtor, a lovely woman who had shown them every old house they'd asked to see—from tiny Sears catalog bungalows to a tattered and beratted Victorian —had actually guffawed, then winked at them both.

"Why don't you go upstairs and see what's there?" their realtor had said, casting her arm in an expansive gesture toward the stairway. "Just have a look around while I do some paperwork."

Because she had known before they did, hadn't she?

"Stairs!" Ivy had clasped Kevin's hand and squeezed it. He had raised their hands and kissed her knuckle, right above her slim steel wedding band. He knew how she romanticized staircases, how she had always wanted to live in a two-story house.

"Let us ascend, then," he had said, and so they did.

The stairs and the second floor were carpeted. The bedrooms and laundry room were on the second floor, plenty of room for each of them.

"There are doors everywhere! Kevin! Closets! There are closets in every room! Kevin! There's a linen closet! Kevin, there's a walk-in closet here! It has its own light! You could fit a whole other bed in here if you wanted!"

And so, they had bought the house. Moved all their stuff in, with Ivy fretful because the house was so big that they suddenly seemed to not have enough stuff. She had bought a few pieces of furniture from thrift stores, and a few more from internet classifieds, and busied herself refinishing them. Writing desk here, 1920s vanity there, an ottoman with Ivy's own bright upholstery in the living room, and art to at least make a start at filling the blank expanses of the walls.

There came a night when they had felt like they were done doing New House tasks—when all the curtains had been hung, the cabinets organized, the street number freshly repainted, the mail forwarded. Kevin had brought home fatayas from their favorite West African joint and they put their feet up on the ottoman and ate in front of the TV.

Overhead there was an almighty thump.

"How did Robey get in my office?" Ivy had set her plate on the arm of the couch and got up, intending to go fetch the dog.

"That's the bedroom," Kevin said.

Ivy had stopped. "No," she had said, pointing toward the front of the house. "Bedroom's over there. My office is on top of us."

"Hon. I know your sense of direction is abysmal, but can you really not figure out where things are in your own house? We're below the bedroom. Your office is at the front of the house."

"That doesn't make any sense."

Robey, who had needed to be taught how to navigate steps when they had moved in, was already an expert, and proved it by tearing down the stairs and across the vinyl floor at top speed. Ivy had grabbed her plate from the couch before he could snatch her dinner.

"Sure it makes sense," Kevin had said. "What's outside your office window?"

"The driveway."

"And the bedroom window overlooks the deck. Right?"

Ivy had turned slowly on her heels and tried to reconcile what she knew was true with what she felt was true.

"Okay," she had said, slowly, "then what's above the utility room?"

"Laundry room," Kevin answered. He hadn't even had to think about it.

"But the utility room is in the center of the house, and the laundry room is at the edge."

"No it's not!" He had laughed. "Let me ask you this: is it the stairs that throw you off?"

Ivy had sat back down on the couch and waved her foot at Robey, warding him off as she went back to her food.

"I just get turned around on the landing, that's all."

"You do, physically, but the upstairs stays in the same place," Kevin had said, and grinned at her. "I promise."

Ivy stood in the upstairs hallway, curling her toes into the lemon-scented carpet, counting the doors. They were all closed. *Laundry room, linen closet, hall bathroom, my office, Kevin's office, bedroom, laundry room, linen closet, hall bathroom...*

Then, she went from door to door and checked each room. Yes, laundry room. Yes, linen closet. Yes, bathroom. Yes, office. Yes, Kevin's office. Yes, bedroom.

She looked out her office window. Yes, driveway. She looked out of Kevin's office window. Yes, side yard. In the bedroom, she checked the windows—yes, street intersection—and then the subrooms: yes, sinks, yes, walk-in closet, yes, bathroom. Bathroom window: yes, same view as the bedroom.

"I'm not going to dissuade you from getting a laptop," Kevin said, signaling to change lanes, "but I just don't really understand what the goal is. You put so much effort into making your office perfect, rearranged it fifty times until it was just right, and now you want to work down here at the kitchen table instead?"

"I like the light, and the proximity to coffee." Ivy tried to sound blithe but her tone came out more querulous instead. She tried again. "It'll just free me up some, is all."

"You hate freedom. You like everything in its place. If you tried to casually work at the kitchen table, you'd end up building another office around it anyway. Desk organizers, a task lamp, a new desk chair instead of a kitchen chair. Which is absolutely okay, Ivy, you know it is."

If he were to check her desktop computer's browser, he'd see an array of tabs open, each for items just as he'd described. He knew the entire map of her brain.

Kevin slowed the car for a turn and Ivy tightened her grip on her silenced phone. The screen in her hand displayed the route to the new farmer's market, and she watched the colorful map spin on the screen as the GPS tried to calculate a new route.

"Why are we turning?" she asked, even though she knew why.

"I bet I know a back way," he said, and he did. Kevin's innate sense of direction was faultless, and it was dark wizardry to Ivy. She trusted him, but could not bring herself to completely part with the glowing security of her phone's navigator, whether or not Kevin had ever needed it.

"I'm just more comfortable downstairs sometimes," she said, and that was the best she could do, the most she could say.

Ivy forced herself to drop her phone into her canvas messenger bag and pressed her head and shoulders against the seat, hard, trying to release the tension in her muscles. She breathed in time with the slow thud of the windshield wipers and watched as Kevin drove them through the gray: gray rain, gray pavement, gray loading docks and dumpsters along the back of the shopping center.

"Seems to me," Kevin said, "that you would be more comfortable upstairs. I know you get distracted by the spatial thing."

Ivy barked a laugh, so surprised was she by the casual notation of her "spatial thing" and by the severity of the understatement.

"You'd think so, wouldn't you?" she agreed.

She caught Kevin looking over at her, but he turned his attention back to the road—well, the parking lot, she saw—and said, "We'll get you a laptop."

Upstairs should have been the easier place to be. When Ivy was upstairs, with all those doors and rooms and doors in rooms and rooms in rooms—when Ivy was upstairs, she knew what was below her.

Below was downstairs. That's it. Her brain read the open floor plan as a single room, so wherever she was on the second floor, downstairs was always underneath.

When she was downstairs, she didn't know what was overhead.

That should have been the end of it, and she understood that she should therefore be comforted by being upstairs.

Just go up, she told herself. Just go up.

Ivy did.

The doors, all closed to keep Robey out, now bore labels, each room's designation penciled on a thin strip of masking tape that ran vertically alongside the top hinge. Ivy hoped that Kevin wouldn't notice the labels.

Still, she intended to check inside each room to be sure the interior still matched its label.

As her hand touched the brassy knob of the laundry room door, she paused. What if it was wrong in there? What if the wrong room was behind the door?

Think it through, Ivy told herself. She could have misremembered which door was which. That in itself would be cause for concern. Or, Kevin could have played a prank on her by switching the labels, but she doubted such meanness would even occur to him.

Or the house could have twisted and changed itself around. Rearranged itself.

She pulled her hand back and retreated downstairs.

"What did you do to your leg, buddy?" Kevin asked Robey, and Ivy shrunk into the couch.

The shepherd stood patiently as Kevin crouched and examined his rear leg.

"Hon, come look at his leg, tell me what you think this is."

Ivy knew exactly what she would see, but she got up and joined them anyway.

Kevin was gently rubbing his thumb over a spot just above Robey's right rear paw.

Oh, it's something else, then, thought Ivy, her relief so strong it felt like nausea. Or maybe that was the shame.

As she knelt beside them she saw that Kevin was stroking a narrow pink abrasion that ringed Robey's right leg.

"That's not right," she said. "It was on the left leg."

"His left leg is fine."

"No, no." Ivy pressed her hand to her chest and then to her forehead. "I think he's been turned around. I knew it. I was right. It rearranged him."

"What are you talking about?"

"I didn't want him getting lost up there," she said, "so I just put a string on him so I could find him. If I had to. Because I wasn't sure where he might be. But I put it on his *left* leg."

Kevin looked aghast. He pulled Robey's head toward him and began to intently rub the big dog's velvety ears. "You put a string on him?"

"Yes," Ivy said, impatient. "Not tight. I didn't want it on his collar because the string was really long, it had to be long enough to reach downstairs, obviously, and I was afraid he might choke. But he's been turned around! I put it on his left leg!"

"How long have you been doing this to him? Long enough to wear the fur off. Long enough to have trained him to leave your string alone. Long enough to injure his leg, Ivy."

"You're not listening! It's the wrong leg! He's been moved around! Rearranged! His legs aren't where they belong, because he went upstairs!"

Kevin gave Robey a firm pat on the flank, dismissing him, and rose to his feet. The shepherd took the opportunity to avail himself of the vacant couch. Kevin extended his hand to Ivy.

"Let's go get you some help," he said. "I won't make you go upstairs. We'll get an appointment for you and pick up some ointment for the pup. We probably even have time to look at watches. To help manage your stress, like we talked about."

Ivy looked at his outstretched hand. It was his left hand, and his wedding ring was present. He had not been rearranged. She could trust him.

She took his hand and let him pull her to her feet.

"Get your stuff together," he said. "Your shoes are by the door. I'll run up and get mine and then we'll go."

"No!" She gripped his hand tighter and pulled him toward her.

"Ouch, damn, Ivy, let go. I have to get my shoes."

"You are not going upstairs," she said. "Things aren't where they belong. They look like they are, but they aren't. They might go back when they think you're looking, but before that, they're wrong. You'll get turned around like Robey did!"

"Ivy. I am bigger than you are. You can let go of me and wait for me to get my shoes, or you can hang onto me and I'll pull you up the stairs behind me."

"At least wait for me to get the twine, then, just wait so I can tie a lifeline to you," she begged, and the way he looked at her made Ivy drop his hand and stand back. He looked repulsed by her. Revolted.

Her lips went numb.

Kevin turned from her, shook his head once, and went upstairs.

Ivy stood at the foot of the stairs, gripping the oak handrail. Robey tore past her, hip-checking her into the wall, and thundered after Kevin.

She listened.

Ivy could hear Robey's bouncing feet and little whines of excitement. She traced the source of the sound to the kitchen. The tape on the ceiling said BEDROOM. There was no reason for Robey to be in there, and the door had been closed.

Kevin kept his boots in his own office. Ivy crossed the open floor, staring up at the ceiling until she located the strip of tape that said KEVIN, and stopped to listen. Nothing.

Instead, she heard the floorboards squeaking near the tape that said LAUNDRY ROOM.

She followed the sounds from room to room, label to label.

She went to the front door and slipped her feet into her shoes, then took them off again.

She stood at the foot of the stairs and called for them.

Robey didn't come.

Kevin didn't answer.

Ivy did not go upstairs in search of her husband and her dog. She kept the light on the landing turned on, both so she could see if anyone descended the stairs and to guide Kevin and Robey back if they needed help.

She listened to them up there, though. She tracked them. The white plaster of the ceiling downstairs bore hundreds of scraps of tape. At first she had written KEVIN and ROBEY with marker on each piece of tape, dragged her stepladder to the spot where she had heard one of them, and smoothed the tape with great care overhead.

After a few weeks, she switched to color-coded sticky notes, yellow for Kevin and pink for Robey. She labeled some, left some blank.

Once in a while, she found a sticky note on the floor.

Ivy suspected the yellow one in the kitchen that read BEDROOM meant that the bedroom was under the house today. *Probably cooler without the sun hitting the windows*, she thought. *How nice.*

One evening she heard music upstairs and knew that Kevin was in his study, using his turntable. She labeled the ceiling above the ottoman, then dismounted the stepladder and gnawed on her fingertip for a moment.

The music was pretty loud. She needed quiet so she could sleep on the couch.

She climbed back up the ladder and peeled the square of paper from the ceiling. It said KEVIN MUSIC STUDY.

Ivy dragged the ladder out to the front porch and stuck the note on the haint-blue painted ceiling.

She waited.

It hadn't worked. The music had not followed the note out of the house. Kevin and Robey were still inside.

The light bulb in the landing's hanging fixture burned out.

Ivy considered placing an ad in the classifieds, asking someone to come change the bulb for her, but they might get lost upstairs too.

She found a pocket flashlight in the kitchen's junk drawer, inserted fresh batteries, switched it on, and tossed it onto the landing. It should last a couple of weeks.

Ivy curled up on the couch and pulled her velvet blanket to her chin. She would watch the stairs as long as she could before nodding off.

She had to watch closely. She loved them both so much, and wanted them to safely come down to her. She would not leave them while they were lost upstairs.

When she adjusted the blanket, the knives she'd hidden beneath it clicked and slid their blades together.

Some day, Kevin and Robey would come down the stairs, and she would watch them closely too, watch to be sure they had not been turned around.

If they seemed wrong, she would rearrange them herself. She had the knives. She would put them right.

)(

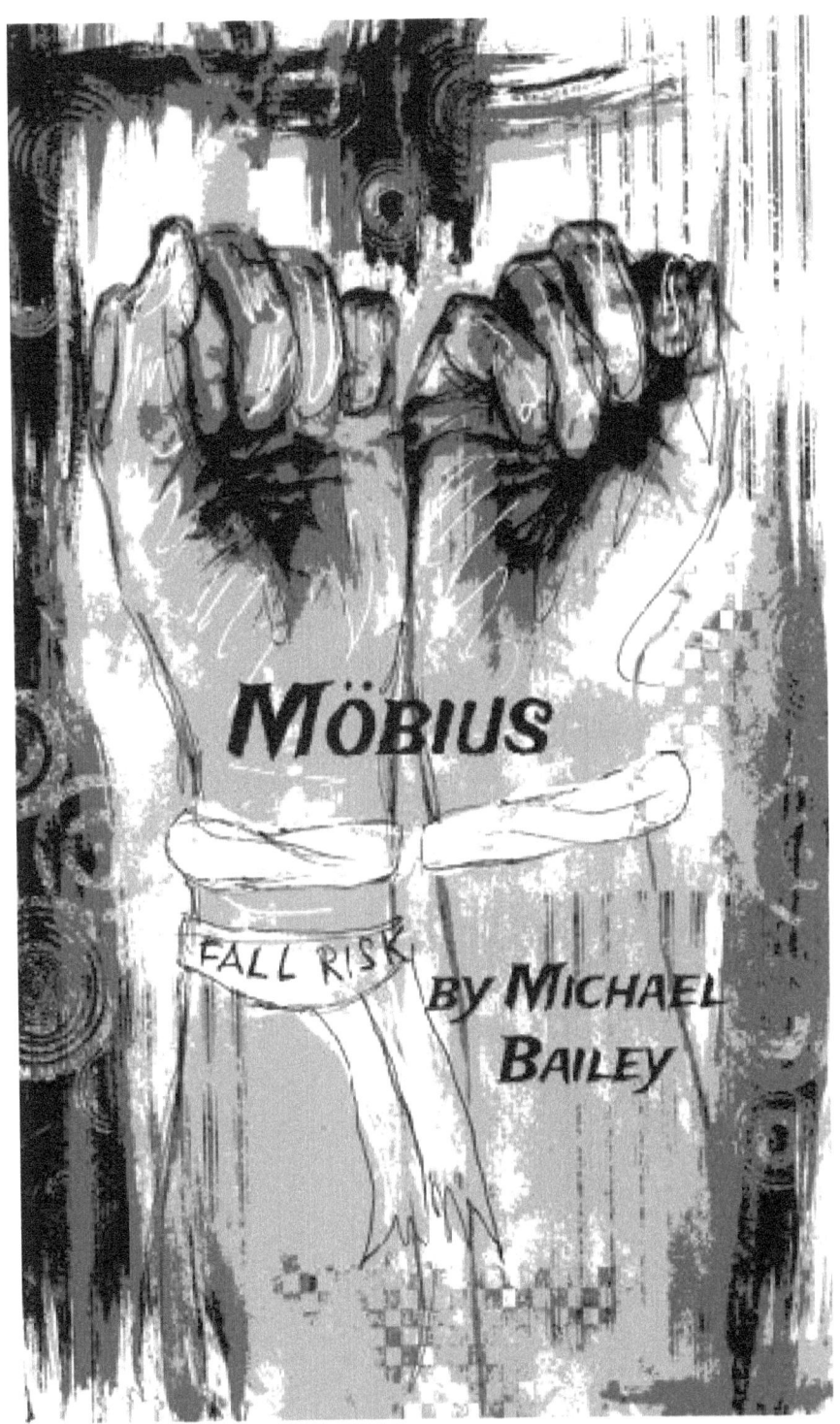

MöBIUS

BY MICHAEL BAILEY

"What's right is what's left if you do everything else
wrong." – Robin Williams

BRACELETS CIRCLE MY WRISTS, Möbius strips of
polished steel to keep me stable. Without them, I
would teeter and fall, bounce off walls. I would walk in
circles if I were capable of standing at all. Where does
this loop of endless confusion begin?

Imagine cutting a flat rubber band, with one of the
two ends flipped and reattached to the other. If the
tiniest of insects were to walk a straight line anywhere
along this band, or if you were to take a pencil and
draw a continuous straight line, either the insect or
your pencil would return to its original starting point,
having traversed both sides of the loop, or two entire
lengths of the band, without ever having to cross an
edge.

I guess that's what I'm doing with these bands:
walking the razor's edge. But I wear them. They keep
me upright in their magic.

"For you," my father had said.

"For you," my mother had said.

The bracelet on my right hand, given to me by my father, is half-twisted clockwise, the one on my left, given to me by my mother, is half-twisted counterclockwise; thus, they are both sentimental and both chiral; in Euclidean space, one exhibits right-handedness while the other left-handedness, albeit their underlying topological spaces are both homeomorphic and the curve in the bands press snugly against pressure points in my wrists.

Why is any of this important?

Without the bracelets my body would otherwise want to rotate one way or the other and fall to the ground because of chronic vertigo. My eyes are telling me one thing and my ears are telling me another, and their argument sends quite a whirling effect to the brain.

The bracelets are prescription, incredibly expensive, and the batteries within send small continuous electric pulses every few microseconds. My health insurance wouldn't cover the cost, so my parents, divorced for as long as I can remember, each paid for a pair. No clue how either afforded them. How they work, I don't know. All I know that every thirty days I need to replace the flat papery batteries, which are small, and also expensive, and if you mishandle the batteries just right, you can short them out. It's never easy swapping the batteries old for new.

Without the bracelets, the very second they come off, I spin, first mentally, then physically as a reaction. Removing the left, I turn clockwise; removing the right, I turn counterclockwise. A confused clock. Removing both, well, it's either summersaults or reverse summersaults with the world flipping around like a movie reel.

Vertigo typically lasts a few minutes in most cases, sometimes fifteen to thirty, coming and going for a few days, a few weeks, months, or in worst cases even up to as long as a year or longer, until the body adapts. Before the bracelets, my vertigo had lasted ten years.

Everything major first starts with something minor, and my something minor was a sinus infection—I used to get them all the time—and a 1500mg prescription of amoxicillin, taken two in the morning / two at night, had cleared my sinuses before the seven-day treatment completed.

The week following the infection I felt great, and then the dizziness came, and a throbbing in my left ear, and then the right, letting me feel each heartbeat. An underwater-like pressure with every step. I managed in this state for a while, until it got so bad that I came home from work one night, my driving impaired as if inebriated. That's the best way I can describe what I felt is that I was flat out drunk... without the alcohol. I'd fallen asleep spinning one direction, and had awoken the next morning spinning the opposite direction, wet with cold sweats, and as soon as I rose from bed the ground wanted me and I stumbled my way into the bathroom, dry heaving into the toilet bowl because I hadn't yet eaten.

My equilibrium was off, and so my emergency room doctor suspected an inner ear infection and scheduled an MRI to scan my head for abnormalities, to rule out a *mass*—a simple but frighteningly complex word—and to get a closer look at what was going on behind my face. They took blood as well, testing for various things, but never found anything.

I could barely walk a straight line without bouncing off walls or having to hold onto someone, my head always wanting to tilt to one side or the other.

The primary responsibility of the inner ear, apparently, is to provide equilibrium, balance, and for orientation in three-dimensional space, and my own equilibrium had my mind walking a perfectly straight line, while unknowingly I was twisting / turning ever so slightly somewhere in the middle, as if I were traversing the 'perceivably' straight line of a Möbius loop.

Going in circles, everyone.

Labyrinthitis was my first misdiagnosis, an inflammation of the labyrinths—usually following sinus infections—that can result in a multitude of balance ailments, including nausea, disorientation, dizziness, and vertigo. This made sense because the previous treatment of antibiotics for the sinus infection, and the symptoms matched *my* symptoms.

The treatment for labyrinthitis: to simply wait it out. Bed rest. Let the inflammation die down. Let the body readjust on its own by pretending it isn't there. Just go with the flow.

My doctor had suggested something called the Brandt-Daroff exercise to help my brain adapt to the vertigo. Basically, you sit on the edge of a couch or bed until the dizziness goes away, and then quickly collapse to one side for thirty seconds or longer—until the dizziness ceases—and then sit back up until the vertigo stops, which it sometimes did and sometimes didn't, and then to repeat on the other side, completing this cycle ten times, twice per day. I can only imagine how strange it looked not from my perspective. She said to do this until I felt sick, then to stop, and then start again, over and over. She had prescribed me 25mg tablets of *meclizine*, to take up to three per day to help control dizziness, as well as 4mg pills of *ondansetron*, these little M-etched tablets that dissolve on the tongue.

In case I felt nauseated, like puking, like when all this first started.

For the next few weeks I never vomited; I simply felt inebriated, *drunk*, all the damn time, which sounds fun, but is entirely not. I even tried alcohol, to see if that would perhaps straighten things out by twisting me the other way—like the childhood rumor that if you were to spin around in one direction, spinning in the opposite would cancel out the dizziness—and so I had a few fingers of whiskey. That only made things worsen. One sip and I was lit.

Since my condition lasted longer than a few weeks— the typical lifespan of labyrinthitis—I was next tested for AIED, or *autoimmune inner ear disease*, mostly because of the obnoxious tinnitus, a constant ringing in my ears. Like someone had struck a tuning fork and had placed one of the tips deep inside my ears.

Rapidly progressive, idiopathic, bilateral sensorineural hearing loss; that was my doctor's concern; I was concerned it was something else: a mass, cancer.

The MRI was pushed up because someone else had cancelled, and I found myself walking into a smallish room that resembled a set from Stanley Kubrick's *2001: A Space Odyssey*, with a giant domed contraption in its center with a bed that hung out like a giant tongue waiting to taste me. After answering a bunch of questions about claustrophobia and piercings and exposure to metal shavings, and removing everything metal from my body, and after dressing into a hospital gown, I was helped onto the bed and handed a panic button. For nearly thirty minutes I lay motionless, staring up at a reflection of my eyes, focusing on the eyes staring back at me while the rest of the world spun round and round, my head held straight despite the spin. And for close to thirty minutes this magnetic resonance imaging machine pulsed radio wave energy through my body, blasting my ears with clicks and beeps and blasts of sound, like robot giants attempting intercourse within the magnetic field that surrounded me.

They were hunting for brain tumors, signs of a stroke, an aneurysm, nerve injuries, bleeding in the brain. They hunted, but found nothing. I imagined my doctor holding up the results to the light later, squinting, but it's all digital now.

MRI results came back clean, despite a spiderweb of inflammation.

Permanent Bilateral Loss of Labyrinthine Function, is now the official diagnosis after months of this hell, or *Perm Bilat Labyrinthine Dysfunction*, according to my doctor.

Permanent: another horrible word.

Yet after another few months of physical therapy and meclizine, the vertigo continued and so I found myself spinning in hospital debt, wondering how I'd ever be able to afford being healthy. It's not being sick or broken that's costly, but getting well and *un*broken.

Walls and other people held me upright until the bracelets.

The loss of vestibular function, in both labyrinths, led to what has been described to me as characteristic dysfunction in my vision and balance, of not having the proper reflexes to see clearly when I'm moving, and the inability to not lose my balance when standing or walking. Why I feel drunk all the time. Why I walk like a drunkard. Why I need the experimental bands.

Oscillopsia, an illusion that my environment is moving with every subtle movement of my head, has rendered me from driving, indefinitely, even when the world's not spinning so bad. Even *being* driven has proven difficult, even if I close my eyes or stare at the dashboard.

Walking in the dark? Nearly impossible.

I'd rather crawl, but at least I have my bracelets now. My parents rarely talked to each other, even while married, but outside of marriage they'd spoken and had found a way to pay for these damn things. They can barely afford rent, afford groceries, but they managed, perhaps dipped into their retirements or sold some things.

"For you," they'd said, handing over their lives.

Balance, apparently, is controlled by the eyes and the ears working simultaneously to send separate signals to the brain, so taking away vision makes the other overcompensate the already false information required to stay balanced. So of course I tire easily. It takes an incredible amount of concentration and mental effort to maintain balance without a labyrinthine sense, and it zaps all energy. Simply going for a short walk on a beautiful day can be extremely fatiguing, even after years of physical therapy to teach my body tricks to cope with the disability.

The body has to overcompensate, and so it wears.

I'm also restricted from swimming in deep or dark waters, as simply going underwater for any length of time can hinder sensory cues required to delineate up from down. A swaying tree can send me toppling over —the swaying of the tree misinterpreted as my body swaying instead—or a moving car, or anything or anyone rushing past. I once fell against a stand of mangos because a woman walked her shopping cart by mine. In my mind I thought *my* cart was the one rolling, and once the mangos started tumbling, so did I. Shopping carts are not the greatest walkers, especially if they pull to one side from a bad wheel.

Last week I read an article from a physician with the initials J.C. called "Living without a Balance Mechanism," published in 1954 in the *New England Journal of Medicine*, a recount of his own loss of labyrinthine function, the result of a toxic side effect of an unfortunate antibiotic, and his inability to even read without the letters moving around the page. To not read, can you imagine such a thing? The simple transmission of pulses from his heart to his head was enough to disable his reading ability. In the article, he suspected toxicity from antibiotics, and so now I can't help but wonder about the amoxicillin I'd first taken for the sinus infection.

This has also rendered me a *fall risk*—which I've sworn to call my rock band if I ever start one—and so I sometimes wear a plastic ribbon around my wrist, with the other bands, stating those words in bold black lettering: fall risk.

Which brings me back to the twin—but not identical —bracelets around my wrists and their Möbius loops. I walk what I believe is a straight line, yet the rest of world around me turns. There's an imbalance between the normally-equal and even flow of sensory signals my faulty labyrinths send to my brain, a bilateral loss of vestibular functions—hence the name of my condition—and thus the asymmetry of what my mind determines as balance is destroyed.

But what if *I* am the stable one?

What if reality is some kind of twisted infinity loop?

Of the billions upon billions of people living in this world, I am one of twenty-three with a "permanent" diagnosis of this condition, one of twenty-three prescribed with these special bracelets that send electric pulses every few microseconds.

The bracelets do not *fix* the problem, no; they alter my *reality* of the problem. They counteract my mind's mixed signals with opposing mixed signals and the two blend into something false my brain interprets as a balanced reality.

But what if I were to take off the bracelets?

What if I were to stop taking the pills, stop the physical therapy, simply allow my body to spin around as it desires?

I haven't taken a pill in nearly a week.

Haven't exercised my mind.

No one's come to check on me.

The words are starting to stumble around the page.

It's time to move forward, to take off these gifts, but if I walk in what my mind perceives is a continuous straight line, will I eventually return to my original starting point, having traversed both sides of the Möbius loop without ever having to cross an edge? ⋊

RIGHT HAND MAN

BY DONNA JW MUNRO

PEOPLE ASK ME about it all the time.

"How'd you hurt your eye?" "Is it a fashion statement?" "Why are you wearing that patch?"

How am I to explain without sounding like a lunatic?

Nothing is wrong with my right eye's physical function. Nothing except that it sees an entirely different world where everything wants to hurt me.

I first began to see the other world when I was just a kid. My Dad, a refugee of the Vietnam service that shaped him before I came, taught me about the other world in a strange game. My first memory is of playing "good hand, bad hand" with him. He explained his left hand was my friend and protector with its soft skin and white fleshy countenance. I imagined it purring with sweetness as it pet my hair and capered our table like some circus dog preforming hoops and flips. Dad narrated its actions with his honeyed, storytelling voice.

"Leftie loves you, Carlie boy. See how he rolls like a pup? He's your best friend."

And I giggled and pet the hand as it played, even with creeping dread over what I knew was coming sure as night must conquer the day. Dad's voice took on an edge of silvered panic, razoring through his words right into my childish glee, sawing away at it.

"Leftie would die for you, Carlie. He'd do anything to save you, because that's what loyal friends do."

"Don't let him die, Daddy," I said, petting the left hand, sheltering it in a nest of my own hands to protect it, even as I knew what would come next. "Noooo," I screamed as the tips of his right hand fingers breached the edge of the table, gripping as if Dad fought with all his strength against it. White-knuckled fingers, thinner, more gnarled and veiny than on his left hand crawled up onto the table top, scuttling like a cretinous crab-thing. Dread knifed through me as the hand moved in seeming random circles, blindly circling the table top. Dad's left hand shuffled over and flattened itself into the pit of my elbow, wobbling up and down like it panted in fear. I curled my own hand around it, and that's when Dad's right hand shuddered to a stop, body of his right hand rigid as the middle finger twitched and turned toward me. Sniffing the air. That's what it looked like. Like some blind bloodhound on a trail only it could smell. Then it rushed over in a jerky gate, clicking across the surface of the table, toward the left hand, clutched against me.

My heart hammered in my little chest and I whined as the right hand clawed and scraped itself nearer, always nearer. I looked up at Dad's unfocused eyes, staring off to his right toward the right hand, but almost through it like it was something else. The slack horror on his features drove me over and I started slapping his clawed right hand, whomping my little fist down on it over and over. His left hand leapt over and joined in, and we two beat the monster hand down until it lay flat on the table top, void of movement. And Dad laughed and said, "Great job, son. You defeated evil claw hand. Gotta watch those things on the right."

And I looked down and realized that I'd killed it with my own left hand. And that my right hand sat off to the side in a strange gnarled posture, turned at an uncomfortable angle seeming to watch the beat down of its righty twin on my Dad's body.

I'll never forget how reality shifted just a little bit that day.

I started to notice that people are two halves, the left and the right. Mathematically, there are differences in the size and alignment of each human feature on the left and the right of their bodies. We are a circus mirror reflecting the reality of our left side with an ugly new world on the right. That's why I've come to cover the right eye. It sees the evil of the right so clearly now. I can't manage my dual reality without the patch.

Marrying what my two different eyes saw made my stomach turn. Trying to make senses of the beauty of someone through my left eye and then the terrifying truths of my right eye paralyzed me as a teen. So many monsters walk among us, the puss filled sores on their skin, the extra limbs and cracked faces made me retreat into books and then into writing. I covered my right eye and dove into the beautiful words. Sure, they often had dualities and double meanings and complex subtexts, but those things seemed so simple, understandable next to the weird world that my periscope of a right eye could see.

That's when the poetry started. It was an acceptable outlet for the horrors in my villainous right eye.

Thank God, I was trained to be a leftie. I can't imagine what would come out of that right claw of mine if I tried to write directly from it. Instead, I clutch my black writing pen with my left hand, scrawling out my metered lines in a handwriting that only I could read. Sure, I had to get it typed up. That's what I hired the lovely Miss Simms to do for me as I dictated the words that sloshed across the unlined paper I used for my poetry.

Ah, Miss Simms. Beautiful brunette with a body that suggested athleticism framed up in the tightest little pencil skirts modesty allowed. She typed for me at ten dollars an hour, decorating my world with some normal prattle and smiles that hung like ornaments in the air of my simple apartment.

"Why don't you use some of your money to take a trip, Carl?" She asked between poems, combing her long, dark hair back behind her left ear with the lovely fingers of her left hand. She had this impression that published poets made big money, especially award-winning ones like me. I couldn't squash that notion for her with the truth that I survived on a small trust fund left to me by my long since passed aunt, Rosie. Aunt Rosie only supported what the rest of my kin called my "artsy-fartsy foolishness" because she'd seen the shadow world all her life. Didn't need a war to make her aware like my Dad. No, Rosie's crossed eyes looked two different ways and that right one had an evil coat of milky yellow filming its surface. Never married, never cared for other people, kept to herself until I'd told her about the creeping shadows that pooled under the Thanksgiving turkey. The others laughed, but she turned her good eye on me and winked. I helped her with the dishes after dinner and that's when she told me that she'd been imprinted by a mouse chased by a cat up her mother's skirts the day she'd been born.

"Poor critter died there in mama's hand. Left me with two things—a lifetime of hating all cats and this poor, all seeing eye." She pointed her pink nail on her left hand at her yellowed eye. "Keeps the bad away from me, but it lets me see everything rotten in the world. The other side of us. You have the same sight, Carl boy, only you got no shielding caul like me. Might drive you insane one day."

She'd been a life saver to me. Left me just enough money that I could stay away from most folks, live frugally and write my poems about the things I couldn't help but see even with my kind left eye. If I avoided people, I wouldn't have to see the darkness under their right eyes, circling there beneath the skin. The bloom of tiny red cracks around the right side of people's noses. The older they were, the more terrible the facade crumbled.

I wore the eyepatch to save me from the demonic sights of blood and gore and broken teeth all lined up in my right eye. But that protection only went so far. I wore a glove over that terrible right hand, blinding it I hoped. I used it for nothing. Not even to wipe my nose. It dangled there at my side like a broken tree branch, but I knew that it wouldn't last. Sometimes, it moved without me moving it, stretching and clasping without my knowledge.

"Does your hand hurt?" Miss Simms asked me after a four-hour streak of typing and retyping a poem about the crawling things that lived in my mattress, held back from my flesh by the sheets I washed in bleach every day.

"Why?" I asked, coming back from the sights inside my right eye, even blocked up as it was.

"Your hand keeps clutching closed and stretching open. Do you have a touch of arthritis? My sister stared getting that young too. Pains her all the time. Turned her fingers into nasty looking claws, so young, too," Miss Simms said, glancing up at me, then rolling another sheet of paper into the typewriter. She wants me to get a computer, but the horrors that live within those screens are dark fantasies woven from the strands of gore, living on the right side of everyone's perception. It is a cancer of the right-side world and I won't have it in my home, seeping its poison into my eye.

I raised my hand up. Covered by a black leather glove, it didn't look so bad to my left eye, but I knew if I laid it bare and opened my right eye, I'd be blinded by the crazing of skin, the knobby bones dancing underneath. It flopped forward just then like a lion lunging behind a glass-walled exhibit. It knew it couldn't reach me, but wanted me scared, all the same. I gasped when I didn't feel its shifting movements in my right-side muscles, as if it floated next to me, a disconnected brother to my left.

"What's wrong, Carl?" she asked, so familiar. Such a dear woman to worry about me. Her gaze skimmed across me, eyes so clear and white with brown, twinkling pupils. If things weren't as they were, I might pursue her. But not with the sight in my eye. Not with the other world. Its corruptions seemed always to destroy the people, the things I loved. My caring about anything led to cancers that metastasized in multiple, painful carcinomas, bubbling across the scanner screens. Or some freak accident—mother's misstep and tumbling down the stair to strike her head on the whimsical boot scraper shaped like a dachshund, something she'd bought that very day. No, love and family were beyond me. Beyond my left-sided reach. Even here, in the safety of my spartan room, my right hand acted like a caged tiger. My right eye itched with the need to see free of its dark prison. That itch, tickling deep in the orb never ceased. In my sleep, I cuffed my right hand to the bed, so that it couldn't free my right eye. In the past, it had. Waking to the demented shifts of the right-side world had frozen me in my bed, locked me in place so that I'd spent a whole weekend at the mercy of the right.

"Nothing's wrong, Miss Simms," I said, lowering my left to clutch my right hand and hold it still. My left hand caught the longer fingers of my right hand in a tangle, though they twitched and jerked against them. It squirmed in my grip until finally it accepted the cage of my hand. "Perhaps we should call it a night, don't you think?"

If I let go, what would those fingers do to my poor, sweet Miss Simms?

"I don't mind staying." She stood and faced me, that beautiful brown hair streaming across her left shoulder and her smile twitching sweetly to the left side of her face. There was so little difference between her left and her right, I'd fallen in love with her face. The purity of it. She reminded me of Aunt Rose's mouse, so sweet and brown and stalked. She didn't know yet. Didn't know about the right side and its villainy. The ugly plans the right side had for this world stalked her perfection. She'd be degraded by it, year by year, and wouldn't know why the left side profile was so much more beautiful than the right. "Let me stay, Carl. We could watch the sunset from your roof. Maybe order some take out."

She smiled again, that shy smile. How could I refuse her?

"Okay, Miss Simms."

"Jena, please."

"Jena."

The local Chinese joint delivered and we took a blanket up to the roof, spread it there and ate silently, enjoying the beauty of the sunset. I'd had so little time for the beauty of this world, what with the threats of the other. Sitting with her was nice. She fanned herself with lazy flicks of her left hand, clutching pages of poetry sent back for approval from the publisher. She'd brought it to the roof with the notion that we might read it together and discuss it. But so far, silence, comfortable and warm, dominated the meal. A companionable silence, though I couldn't help but worry about the frantic itch behind my patch and the twitching of my damned right hand.

Finally, she leaned forward, light of the dying sun catching bright across the chestnut red in her curls.

"Carl," she said, hesitating for a breath of courage, "Carl, I read your poems and... they are beautiful. Disturbing, sure, but so packed with description and tension. Like that other world is waiting to break through. It's in every poem, every line you write. You could be describing a sleeping kitten and you'd give it a sense of wrath and blistering panic. Is that what it's like inside your mind?"

To admit what I saw, what I knew might make her run from me. It might drive her away from me or... Her eyes glittered as she spoke to me. Some kind of magic lay in her fascination with my mind. She leaned in, eyes gazing into mine, lips inches from me, breath washing across my skin.

The itch danced behind my eye patch insisting I notice. I reached with my left hand, pressing the meat of my palm into the socket of my right eye, trying to sooth the maddening dance of nerves and pain behind it. Pressing there soothed it for a moment and in that seconds-long distraction, Jena moaned in my ear.

"Carl! I didn't think you had it in you!" She purred and pressed herself against me.

I shook my head and opened my left eye, only to find my vile right hand had wrapped around her, pulling her into me. It clutched her waist and from the looks of the angle, made its way further south. The idea of those villainous claws cupping her enraged me.

"Miss Simms, I'll need you to leave now," I said, using my left had to pull that vile hand back. I stepped back from her, watching her face as it ran through a gamut of emotions, slack-mouthed shock followed by a tight-lipped, head-tilting flash of anger that reached her eyes, killing that lovely twinkle she'd had. Now she stood tall and distant as a Greek statue on a marble pedestal. I wanted to reach for her, to release that damned claw hand gapping like a fish out of water in my grip. I wanted to say something that would crack the icy facade forming, but it was better to let her go. Let her escape and hire a less lovely, less innocent person to type my warnings to the world.

"Good bye, Miss Simms," I said, stepping back another two feet, trying to look as distant as one can with a raging erection.

Her head tilted to the right a bit and her gaze trailed down my body for a moment, then back up to my own. She bit her lip, softly, not provocatively, but it provoked anyway. I was aching in so many ways. I really wanted her to go.

"Fine," Jena said, gathering up her things. "We aren't done yet, Carl. Not by a long shot."

And she left me there without another glance.

The sound of the door snicking shut released some imaginary strings holding me upright, taut against her onslaught. I sagged back into my disappointment and hurried, round shouldered and slumping to the window facing the street, still cradling that damned hand. She swished away in her long pace, down the street toward the public parking. The air parted for her like she was the Queen Mary cutting the Atlantic and leaving a wake for the rest of us to tumble in.

I couldn't resist. My trembling left hand found my patch, and with a steadying breath I pulled the blinder from my eye to watch her with my full sight for the first time. My bifurcated vision saw layers and on the left was the more normal beauty of the city lights against the deep dusk, the clean street, her flirty calf length skirt swirling in the puffs of wind coming off the gurgling river, her hair dancing. But on the right, her hair whipped in a preternatural wind until each coiling curl looked like snakes seething in a boiling pot. Light, sickening green and yellow that reminded me of comic book corpses, shot through the edges of everything she passed, the jagged brick buildings, the grasping bald tree branches that in my left eye were full of soft green, summer leaves. My chest began to heave as I tried to pull myself away from the view. My left hand struggled to get back to the eye patch, to cover the horror, but my right held it captive in a steely pinch.

Then, before I could drag myself away, my right side froze. Leg like a concrete pier. Arm frozen, my left pinched in the clutch of my right hand. Even my facial muscles did two different things. My left-side mouth tried to cry out, but with the right side caught in a rictus like the stiff lips of the dead, the sound came out a desperate squawk. Even my lungs seemed to breath at different rates, my right so slow it barely moved, my left huffed and heaved trying to make up for the lack of effort on the right.

My gaze still tracked the movements of Miss. Simms as she swam through the swirling vomit of the right-side world's nasty wind. She stopped, turned back toward me, gazing up at my window where I perched, a stuffed turkey with no will of my own. Seeing me watching her, she turned back toward me, a slow twirling, neon-crackling smile rocking on her bright, perfect face like a sweetheart excursion on a glassy pond. Her lips moved and though we were separated by distance and chaos, I read them as clear as if she breathed them into the shell of my ear.

"Let me back in," she mouthed. "Let me in forever."

Electric need shot through both sides of me. It didn't matter that hell swirled around her or that both my halves wanted to have her, perhaps for completely different reasons. I nodded with all of me. Wished for her back with every cell, corrupt or kind. Every hair tensed its salute. My heart pounded on the left, so full of blood and fear. Sucking the desiccated blood back from the right and pushing the oxygen filled blood back into the void. Every function knifed through me, through my awareness as she made her way back to me. My vision kaleidoscoped with the sickening right colors ravaging the still, subtle hues of the left's night. And Miss Simms, Jena, walked in beauty, though she was no night. She radiated golden light as bright as if she'd fallen from the vault of the stars. She left my vision for seconds—not nearly long enough to get up the stairs. Then before me in the fullness of my patio's glass door, she stood as a blinding vision. Stunning Jena.

She strode through the glass as if it were a breath of fog.

Frozen there, the icy fear of the other world turned in to a clutching panic, crushing the air of my lungs. Oh, how terrible her beauty turned in the night of my right eye. Blistering white skin, whipping hair with a wind I didn't feel on my face, fingers long as whips.

Then her mouth on me, soft and burning. Tongue on mine and I was lost, swirling in the worlds.

"Stop!" I screamed. "Stop or I'll lose my mind."

Had I already?

"Your mind is not lost, Carl. You are like me," she purred and wrapped her arms around my shoulders. "We are the silent rulers of our worlds. For too long, we've been kept apart. Divided like our sight."

She leaned closer and I saw that the brown of her left eye deepened in a warm well of color. As it always had. But the right swirled and sputtered with gold flecks and bolts of green, changing as she spoke.

"How? I should have known..."

She smiled and tapped the eye patch that still rode the top of my brow. "You never embraced your sight, love. Never understood what you were seeing. You covered it, like the magic wouldn't build up. Like a bright beacon, it found me. Invited me here."

My right side gave up holding me in place and I sagged into the nearest armchair, grasping the arms as if they'd float above these rapid and carry me to safety. My lovely Jena, a monster. A right-side monster.

"I see how you look at me, now, Carl. I came for you because I saw you through both eyes. Look at me now, love. Look!" She demanded.

So, I did.

She blazed with the power of the other side. She was the other side, all edges and curves that called to my right and my left. All desires and fears wrapped up in the perfection of her body. A queen. Maybe a goddess.

"I can be yours, Carl. We can be each other's. The man of the left and the lady of the right. We were built for each other. Together, we might tear down the walls that separate our worlds. Your little humans and their puerile lives will meet my beings of shadow and teeth. What was dream will become real and we, you and I my love, will rule it all." She pressed against me and kissed again, her exquisite angry mouth and brilliant sharp teeth savored me, left and right. It couldn't go on. The halves of me fought inside for those morsels— the touch of her hand, to nuzzle her neck, to feel her pressing into me. Both hands struggled across her back, feathered touches on her neck, cupped her chin, pressed her skin and kneaded it until she answered my breath with moans. I was two halves on fire and split between her.

It couldn't go on.

"Because of you, I can open the door between our worlds. Your glorious left eye led me here like a lamp." She spoke between acts and dove back into her seduction of my sides, the right knowing and the left surprised by how much it wanted the dame of the right world. "We will conquer both together, love. Together."

I thought of all the children who'd have to live with right handed terror. Screw monsters under the bed! What of the terror on the right that they didn't know? Us together—we'd breed the sight. We'd let all the monsters out.

I couldn't say no to her on either side of me.

I couldn't stop the conquest.

"Would you want me, even if I wasn't the... man of the left?" I asked, leaning in to nibble the left edge of her jaw.

"How can you doubt me, love? I saw you with my open left eye writing the warnings to the world. I saw you and pitied you. Then the pity turned to love. There's little love on the right, Carl. Little pity. That's when I knew my shadow giants and skin knights would never make me whole."

"You just want me—"

"No, love, not when we can have it all." She smiled and lowered herself to my bed. "One act and then we will be together forever. Just one act will open the worlds to each other and make us the rulers of all. Come to me love."

One act. My halves convened a conference committee. We wanted her, loved her. All of her. But my left couldn't rule the birds and the rabbits and the toddlers and the wives. Couldn't dominate the pubescents and the sweepers and the poets. The poets.

A bit of poetry came to me in that moment and the conference committee suddenly swung.

"Jena, my queen, I will go with you. I will be yours but let me give you a gift before we go." My sides had decided and it was unanimous. I would go but there would be no passage for the shadows of the right. I'd be a right-hand man. My left hand joined by the right for more strength lifted to my eye and pressed into it... my left eye. The gateway. "Here's a verse my love. If your eye causes you to stumble, pluck it out and throw it from you. It is better for you to enter life with one eye, than to have two eyes and be cast into the fiery hell."

And my hands, in concert, pressed deep into the ocular socket, slick with blood and jelly, and pulled, loosening. They pulled and the nerves and tissues gave with a rip that brought me to my knees. And then I held it out to her, a gift and a locked door. A tribute that protected the left sides of humanity from the ravages of the right. I would forever be her right-hand man. ✗

THE PETER
PROBLEM

BY STEVE CARR

THE PETER PROBLEM

BY STEVE CARR

THE FLESH OF THE DEAD WOMAN lying next to Pete was icy cold. With his eyes wide open and staring into the dark he was afraid to move. His right arm felt glued to her naked torso. Remnants of her cheap, flowery perfume hung in the still air. Barely moving his head, he shifted his focus to the closed window and watched the flashing of red neon light on the brick wall of the building across the alley. Rivulets of sweat trickled down his side and between his legs. He licked his lips, thinking he had never felt such thirst. Muffled noises of voices and footsteps in the hallway outside the room penetrated the silence.

"You made me do this," he whispered without looking at her. "I told you not to touch it."

He turned his head to the stand next to the bed where he had placed his watch and stared at it with disbelief. The illuminated dial read 5:10. It had been five hours of lying next to the woman's body. As he started to shift away from her, the bed springs squeaked. The hairs on his right arm were matted against his skin. Slowly, he sat up and put his legs over the edge of the bare mattress and placed his feet on the worn, thin carpet. He put on his watch, then stood up.

He turned and looked at the woman's body partially hidden by the darkness. She was skinny and her bright blue tinted blonde hair that had been chopped haphazardly into layers cascaded from a part in the middle of her head. He had chosen her specifically because she didn't appeal to him at all. She was an experiment that went awry.

He turned on the lamp on the bedside stand and blinked several times as his eyes adjusted to the light. It was then that he noticed for the first time that the woman's toenails were painted his favorite color, green. Her's was the first real dead body he had ever seen. Unlike what he had read or heard, she didn't look like she was just sleeping. Despite her lack of weight, her body seemed to be heavily embedded in the stained material of the mattress. Her eyes were open and had the stare of someone who was feeling the worse fear they had ever experienced. Her mouth was shaped into a silent scream. A bright purple and red bruise encircled her neck.

Going to the dresser he stood in front of the cracked mirror and looked at his reflection. At age twenty-six he was in excellent physical shape, thanks to hours spent working out four days a week at the gym. His sandy brown hair hung to his eyebrows but was cut short on the sides and back. Looking into his bright blue eyes, he thought no one would think he was capable of killing someone. His gaze went down his hard chest and his abdominal muscles, then he quickly looked away. Whatever was happening below his waist he didn't want to know.

He turned to the mound of clothes on the chair in the corner of the room and pulled out his white boxers and quickly slipped them on, then put on a pair of loose fitting jeans, a t-shirt and socks. Returning to the bed, he sat on the bed and put on his running shoes and tied the laces. He took the unopened condom from the stand and put it in his pocket. Lastly, he put on a black ball cap.

Surveying the room one last time, he thought nothing in it had been repaired in years. The pale yellow wallpaper was dirty and peeling in spots and there were cracks in the ceiling. Without taking a last look at the dead woman, he opened the door and stepped out into the dingy, dim hallway and closed the door behind him.

Going down the back stairs he left the building, coming out in the alley. It smelled of stale urine and rancid meat. A large rat scuttled by his feet going from one trash can to the next. As he walked out of the alley he pulled the brim of the ball cap down over his eyes and bowed his head. He briskly walked out of the neighborhood.

"What did you do last night?" Jenny said as she braided her long black hair.

Pete ran his hand down Sheba's back. In his lap, the cat arched its back and purred contentedly as it kneaded his leg with her paws. "Just went bowling," he said.

"All by yourself?" she said.

He rubbed the top of Sheba's head. "Yeah, I didn't think you would want to go."

She stretched her legs out on the sofa, her bare feet against his leg. "I would have gone," she said. "Pete, is there something wrong?"

"Wrong?" he said.

"Do I no longer interest you?" she said. "You don't come here as often as you used to."

He picked Sheba up and held the cat close to his chest. "I've just been busy."

She slid her feet up and down the side of his leg.

Pete tossed Sheba into Jenny's lap and jumped up. "I should go," he said. "I have to be at work early tomorrow."

Sheba leapt onto the floor and headed toward the kitchen.

"You could stay over if you'd like," she said.

"I really need a good night's sleep," he said. "I'll call you tomorrow." He kissed her on the top of the head and left her apartment. In the hallway he leaned against the wall, closed his eyes and tried to catch his breath.

"You okay buddy?" a young man in a muscle-t and running shorts who had just came out of his apartment said.

Pete opened his eyes. "Yeah, just catching my breath," he said.

The man placed his hand casually on Pete's shoulder. "You don't look good. You want me to call someone?"

Pete straightened up and slapped the man's hand away. "Don't touch me," he growled. Having a hand, any hand, placed on him was the last thing he wanted. He walked down the hallway and down the stairs. In the lobby he took his ball cap from his back pocket and put it on and went out the door.

Outside in the warm summer breeze he tried to calm his nerves. He tried to not think about what Jenny had almost started inside his jeans. He walked down the crowded sidewalk avoiding rubbing against anyone. His entire body felt like a current of electricity was running through it. At the steps of St. Boniface Church he sat down and watched the people walking by. He looked at the crotches of the men who passed by feeling a renewed burst of anxiety any time he saw an obvious bulge.

When the church door opened, Pete turned to see a middle aged priest with flaming red hair standing in the doorway. He stood up. "Father, can I talk to you for a minute?"

"For a confession?" the priest said.

"Sort of, Father, but it's more about needing some advice," Pete said.

The priest looked at his watch. "Okay, I have a little time. Come in," he said, holding the door open.

There was no one else in the dimly lit church.

"We can talk here," the priest said pointing at the last pew.

Pete sat down on the cushioned pew. As he looked at the semi-nude religious statues behind the altar and on the walls between the stained glass windows a chill went through him.

"I'm Father John," the priest said as he sat down. "I haven't seen you in church services before."

"I'm not Catholic," Pete said.

Father John hesitated briefly then said, "Are you certain I'm the one who should be giving you advice?"

Pete pulled a hymnal from the slot in the back of the pew in front of him and thumbed through the pages. "You're the perfect person." Pete locked eyes with the priest. "Father, how do you keep from getting an erection?"

The benign smile on Father John's face quickly disappeared. "Are you trying to be funny?"

"No Father, I'm serious. My life has become a living hell. As hard as I try not to get erections, I do anyway. They terrify me. You priests must know how to control it," Pete said.

"Erections are normal for most men your age and frequently can't be controlled," Father John said. "What is there to be terrified of?"

"I wish I knew, but it's how I feel," Pete said. "Lately I've been putting myself in sexual situations just to see if I can keep from getting an erection."

Father John ran his fingers down the large silver cross that hung from a chain around his neck. "Perhaps you should see a mental health professional," he said. "This isn't a spiritual matter."

Pete blurted out, "I killed a prostitute who almost caused me to have a hard-on."

Father John stood up. "You shouldn't have told me. I'll have to contact the police since it's not a confession." He turned toward the aisle.

Pete jumped up and hit the back of Father John's head with the hymnal, sending him forward onto the floor. Pete leapt onto Father John's back and pulled the cross around and stabbed it into the priest's carotid artery. Pete climbed off the priest's body and stood over him and watched as his blood spurt out covering the floor, until Father John died.

Pete walked out of the church carrying the hymnal covered with his fingerprints along with Father John's cross with him. A block down from the church he tossed the hymnal and cross into a garbage can.

In the back row of the dark movie theater Pete bit into the knuckle of his index finger trying to stifle a scream. As If watching a horror movie he stared at the images of the naked bodies on the screen engaging in sex. Forcing himself to watch, trying to will himself into not being aroused, he didn't avert or close his eyes, but fixed his gaze on the woman's body parts and what the man was doing to them. As sweat ran from his forehead and soaked his underarms, his entire body trembled. Just as he felt his penis begin to stiffen, he blacked out.

"Hey, you okay?" a man's voice said.

Pete opened his eyes. "Where am I?" he stammered.

The man's eyes were bloodshot and his breath smelled of cheap whiskey. "You're in the Doll's House triple x movie theater," the man said. "I heard you back here and thought you were just enjoying yourself then I saw you had passed out or something. I was just about to contact the management and tell them to get an ambulance."

Pete sat up in the seat and wiped the sweat from his forehead with the back of his hand. "I'll be okay, thanks."

The man took a small bottle from the pocket inside his jacket and held it out. "You want a drink?" he said.

"No thanks," Pete said as he stood. "I need to be getting home. I shouldn't have come here."

The man unscrewed the cap on the bottle and took a quick swig. "Porn's not for everybody," he said.

Pete left the dark auditorium not glancing at the lit movie screen. He walked through the lobby with his head down and stepped out into the cool night air. He looked at his watch: 2:45. The street was quiet. Two blocks down he went into Drisco's Diner.

Inside, the red and white décor was garish. It was mostly empty except for a couple sitting in a booth alongside the plate glass window that looked out on the street. The diner reeked of greasy food and stale cigarette smoke. He sat on a stool at the counter and pulled a menu from a clip that held it to a napkin dispenser, and opened it.

"You want some coffee?" The waitress' voice was in the low tonal range, almost to the point of being husky.

Pete looked up from the menu and stared at her ample cleavage showing between the unbuttoned top part of her pink uniform. Feeling his man parts start to tingle, he threw the menu on the counter and ran out of the diner.

Sitting on a blue plastic chair in the corner, Pete watched the nurse behind the counter as she took the papers he had filled out and read them over before putting them into a file folder. She closed the folder and looked up and gave him an inscrutable smile. He squirmed, trying to ignore the size of her breasts while at the same time forcing himself to look. The name tag above her left breast had the name Tanya printed on it in black lettering. Tanya was very pretty. For the amount of willpower it was taking to keep from getting an erection, he wanted to kill Tanya. When she left the counter and went through a door to the exam rooms he let out a sigh of relief.

A few minutes later Tanya opened the door to the waiting room and stood in the doorway and said to Pete, "Come this way, Peter. The doctor is going to see you in a few minutes."

Pete rose from the chair and walked through the door, careful not to touch any part of Tanya. The subtle fragrance of her peach scented perfume assailed his nostrils. He swore to himself that he couldn't risk looking at her again. As she passed him to show him the way to the exam room her arm brushed against his. He felt an instant stirring in his pants.

"Watch it," he said, averting his eyes.

"Excuse me?" she said.

"Your arm touched mine," he said.

The puzzlement clear in her tone, she said, "I'm sorry. It was an accident."

With Pete behind her but avoiding looking at her, they walked into the exam room. She placed his file on a metal table. "Go ahead and get undressed and have a seat on the exam table. The doctor will be in shortly." She left the room, pulling the door closed behind her.

Other than the metal table and the black pad on the exam table peeking out from under a sheet of white paper, the room was blindingly white. He slowly removed his clothes and placed them on a white plastic chair and sat on the paper on the exam table. The room was cool enough to cause goosebumps to raise on his naked flesh.

When the door opened and a petite blonde in a white lab coat entered, Pete quickly covered his exposed genitalia with his hands. "Who are you?" he said pointedly.

"I'm Dr. Rains. I'm filling in for Dr. Lerner," she said. "Is that okay?"

"No it's not," Pete said. "I need to talk to a male doctor."

She picked up the file and flipped it open and read for a moment, then said, "You're having erectile dysfunction problems? I can help you with that. What is the nature of the dysfunction?"

Pete felt his face redden. The room was suddenly very warm. "I get erections," he said.

She looked at him appraisingly. "Are they painful?" she said.

"No," Pete said, the pitch of his voice rising. "I get them and I want help stopping it. Surely there must be some medication or an operation that can be done."

Dr. Rains hugged his closed file against her chest. "You look like you're healthy. Why do you want to stop getting erections?"

"Can you help me or not?" Pete said, almost shouting.

"No doctor in their right mind is going to take away your ability to have an erection without medical cause," she said, then added, "Please lower your voice."

Pete hopped off the table and grabbed his clothes from the chair and began to dress. "Whatever I do next will be your fault," he said. Before he left the room he put on his ball cap, then walked through the waiting room staring at Tanya, but tried to think about anything else but her.

In the parking garage, Pete sat slouched down in his car and looked out through his bug splattered windshield. It was just a chance that Tanya would be coming out the door into the garage, but he had nothing else to do until later that evening. As people and cars came and went he thought about the way she had smiled at him, her perfume, the way she touched his arm on purpose. The harder his penis got the more his mixture of rage and fear boiled inside him. He was certain she had seen what he had written on the form, *erection problems,* and had purposely set out to take advantage of his vulnerability.

When the door opened and Tanya walked out, Pete couldn't believe his good luck. He turned the key in the ignition and let the motor idle while he watched her begin to cross the aisle between the rows of cars. As she reached the middle of the aisle he stepped on the gas and aimed the car at her. She turned just before he hit her, sending her body up into the air, then falling in the middle of the aisle several feet behind the car. He hit the brake, then put the car in reverse. He bounced in the seat as the tires ran over her. He stopped again, then sped forward, running over her one last time before leaving the garage.

On the street he kept watching in the rear view mirror for police cars. He had seen no cameras in the garage, but he thought maybe he had been seen by someone. Going to prison for murder only worried him for one reason. Getting an erection while in a shower and being naked with other men would mean only one thing, he would have to kill himself.

At the open window of his apartment, Pete stared at the passersby on the sidewalk below lit by the soft glow of streetlights. The warm breeze that flowed in brought with it the worst smells of the city: automobile exhaust fumes, the odor of garbage and the faint scent of stale urine. The pee aroma got him to thinking about his penis and he quickly shut the window. He had begun taking as few trips to the toilet as possible in order to avoid having to touch himself. While he liked his own penis, admired it even, it was like a dangerous snake ready to spring out with the least amount of provocation.

He crossed his living room and glanced at the outline on the wall where Jenny's framed picture used to hang. He blamed her, in part, for what his own penis was doing to him. She was pretty, sexy and sexual, and enjoyed getting him aroused. He had always been slightly fearful of the power of his erections, but since he had begun to know her, those increasing fears had become reality: his penis led to murder. Her picture was in the back of the closet where it no longer posed a threat.

Going into his bedroom he took the jeans he had laid on the bed and slipped them up and over his boxer shorts. He put on a crisp button down shirt, socks, his shoes and finally his ball cap. Before leaving his apartment he looked at his reflection in a full length mirror, avoiding looking at his crotch. Out of sight, out of mind.

Leaving his apartment building, he stepped out into the night air feeling anxious. It was only a short distance to where he was going, but he rubbed his hand over the dent in the hood left by the impact with Tanya's body, and got into his car. He turned the key, rolled down the window and pulled away from the curb. A few minutes later as he passed St. Boniface Church he took only passing notice of the yellow police tape still across the door.

To his surprise there was an available parking space at the curb right in front of Jenny's apartment building. He pulled in and shut off the engine and sat for several minutes staring at the crack in his windshield, also a remnant of his car's encounter with Tanya. When he opened the door, the young man who before had tried to assist him, came out the apartment doors, again wearing running shorts and a muscle-t.

"Sorry..." Pete started to say.

The man glared at him, then began a fast jog down the sidewalk.

Pete went into the building and stepped into the elevator. On the way up to the fifth floor he tried to calm his increasing nervousness. By the time the elevator doors opened on Jenny's floor, he had broken out into a cold sweat. He knocked on her door.

"I'm so glad to see you," Jenny said as she stood in the open doorway. "I'm fixing us a little supper. Come on in."

He didn't want to see what she was wearing, but as he followed her into the apartment, it was almost impossible not to. It was worse than he thought it could be. She had on a short, flared, floral print skirt that showed off her long, silky legs, and a sleeveless white blouse. The outline of her bra was visible through the blouse's thin material. Her hair was pulled back into a ponytail that swung as she walked, like a hypnotist's swinging watch. The subtle scent of her perfume wafted from her like an airborne aphrodisiac. He bit hard into his lower lip as he felt an unwanted sensation stirring in his penis.

In the kitchen doorway she stopped, turned, and put her hands on his shoulders and rose up on her tiptoes and kissed him.

"Why did you do that?" he said.

"I've missed your lips," she said. "When you called and said you wanted to come over it made me very happy."

"Jenny, I have a problem," he said.

"You do?" she said breezily as she went to the table and placed several carrots on a cutting board. "What's the problem? Maybe I can help." She picked up a sharp knife and began chopping a carrot into thin slices.

His face reddened even before he said it. "You give me erections," he said.

Jenny laughed. "Why is that a problem?" She pushed the sliced carrot pieces from the cutting board onto a plate, then put the second carrot on the board.

"I don't want them anymore. The idea of getting one terrifies me and actually getting one drives me insane," he said.

She sliced a piece from the carrot. "Ha ha, very funny," she said. "Men love having a hard dick."

He walked over and placed his hand on her hand that had the knife in it. "This man doesn't," he said gutturally.

"If this is some kind of game, I like it," she said reaching down with her free hand and rubbing his crotch.

"I told you I didn't want an erection," he bellowed as his hand enveloped her hand still grasping the knife and raised it from the cutting board and plunged the blade into the middle of her chest.

She stepped back from the table and fell back against the sink as blood spread out across her blouse. "Why?" she said weakly as she slid to the floor.

"I told you why," he said, still holding onto the knife dripping with blood. He bent down and kissed her on the forehead and felt her last breath on his cheek. He stood up and unzipped his pants and took out his erect dick and laid it on the cutting board and chopped it off. With it in his hand he staggered into the living room. Sheba rubbed against his legs as he stood at the window and saw two police cars with their lights on alongside his car. The man in the running shorts was on the sidewalk talking to several police officers and pointing toward the window. ✗

THE ACQUISITION
BY KEALAN PATRICK BURKE

THE ACQUISITION

BY KEALAN PATRICK BURKE

Carnegie Hill, New York

THOUGH THE DAY HAD BEEN LONG and less than remarkable, from the unexpected wait for his usual table at Le Paris, to the news that his friend Bill Glass's cancer had returned, Julius was nevertheless unable to contain his excitement as he mounted the steps to his townhouse. Ill-tidings aside—and really, if Bill had beaten that foul disease once, there was nothing to suggest he couldn't again; the old man was strong as an ox—this was a day he had been anticipating for weeks, ever since he had received the certificate of authenticity from his man in Manhattan for the Verner piece. That he'd managed to find anyone to authenticate the painting at all was nothing short of a miracle. Once upon a time, he could have had one of the good folks at the Warhol or Noguchi take a peek, but these days fear of litigation from swindled collectors had led even the most qualified experts in the business to strike that particular talent from their resumes. It was an alarming development. Should the day come in which authenticators vanished completely, it would throw the art world into turmoil. Fakes and forgeries would abound and if one could no longer trust in the purity of the water, where would the incentive be to continue drinking from the well? It was a disturbing thought and one Julius was not eager to dwell upon. Besides, art had endured worse challenges. Opposing ideologies had rid France of wide swaths of art during the Revolution. Cubism and surrealism had burned in the flames of Hitler's purge on "degenerate art". George Washington's trek across the Delaware had been halted by air raids during World War II, and there had been countless attempts to disfigure the Mona Lisa. Still, art prevailed because mankind simply could not live without it. Just as creation begets destruction, so too does destruction beget creation.

The old man smiled as he fished his keys from his pocket and opened the front door. He would have to remember that line at MOMA's next fundraiser.

His hands were shaking with anticipation as he hurried inside and shut the outer door on the late evening chill. A pause to consider his reflection in the beveled glass showed a much younger man, rid of the myriad lines and pouches beneath the eyes. Julius nodded his approval. Enthusiasm was a wonderful thing, and nothing enthused him more than the acquisition of a rare work of art. But as he shrugged out of his overcoat, kicked off his shoes and slipped his stockinged feet into the monogrammed slippers Elsa had dutifully left for him by the door, he realized *rare* wasn't the right word at all. The Verner piece was beyond rare, because up until a week ago, nobody even knew it existed. And while he didn't consider himself a greedy man—snide intimations from those hacks in the *Times* aside—it did rather gall him that there were sixteen more pieces out there he would probably never get to see in person, especially if they ended up in private collections, or worse, galleries abroad. No matter what the mirror told him, he was too old to travel like he had back in the day, one of the many realities of age that made his heart ache. Besides, seeing them would only inflame his need to possess them, and he suspected he was lucky he had managed to acquire one at all. In every respect, provenance had delivered it to his door.

"Elsa?"

The house was quiet but for the clucking of the grandfather clock in the hall. He waited a few moments for his housekeeper to appear. When she didn't, he waved a wrinkled hand in the direction of her memory and shuffled off to the living room to fetch his own drink. It was not an evening in which he was content to wait to be attended to, nor did he feel like wasting time hunting her down. She could be chastised in the morning.

In the living room, he was glad to see that the men he had tasked to deliver the painting had, as per his instructions, already unpacked it for him. Ideally, he would have preferred to have been present to oversee its arrival and unboxing for fear the men did not exercise enough care, but alas, the unprecedented delay at Le Paris and the grim phone call from Bill had denied him the luxury. Still, better they took care of the hardest work than leave him to do it himself. His arthritis, a burden on the best days, had started gnawing at his bones with the settling of the autumnal cold, making his joints feel as withered as the leaves. The mere thought of having to pull the crate apart to get to his prize made his knuckles throb.

As he went to the corner bar to pour himself a sherry, he was struck again by a note of irritation that the ordinarily loyal Elsa was in absentia, for he could have used her hands. He supposed she might have gone home, though it was rare for her to do so before his arrival. It was also possible she had informed him of some pressing family business or prior engagement, and he had simply forgot. That seemed to happen more and more these days, his mind not being what it used to be. In such instances, he turned hostile toward the housekeeper, his caustic disposition masking his fear at the steady decline of his faculties. She was no fool, of course. He sometimes suspected she knew him better than he ever would, and thus she accepted his impromptu belligerence with maddening grace. *Yes, Mr. Julius. Will there be anything else, Mr. Julius?* And always with that withering look. The memory of it summoned a touch of a smile. Incorrigible as she was, she was also the closest he had or would ever come to a wife unless he lost his mind and decided to take some gold-digging floozy for a bride for the sake of vanity, like so many of his fellows had done.

Such things did not interest him.

He had Elsa and he had his art and that was company enough. Thus, he would never admit into his sanctum some surgery-enhanced dilettante whose very appearance flew in the face of the collection he had spent a lifetime cultivating, just so he could die and bestow upon her wealth she had not earned. Besides, he had no need of a trophy wife. All his trophies were downstairs in the climate-controlled room he called The Vault.

Although his body quaked with the need to unveil the painting, which the delivery men had left still encased in foam and brown paper on the mahogany table in the middle of the room, Julius went instead to the large ornate fireplace and stared down into the flames, content to wring from the occasion a few more moments of suspense. After all, once the painting was unveiled and hung in its carefully selected place in The Vault, he would never be able to recapture this moment, the precious time in which he got to carefully tear away the wrapping and see it up close for the first time. The intoxication of discovery, the thrill of the unveiling, the rush of knowing he held in his hands a rare treasure nobody else could see unless he allowed them the privilege, which undoubtedly, he would, assuming they were connoisseurs, people he wished to impress. Art like this was not intended to be squandered on the uninitiated and would be valueless to ignorant eyes.

In whatever time remained to a man of his years, there would be other treasures, other paintings, each one accompanied by its own moment of intoxication, but with the Verner, as with all the others, each occasion was different in subtle ways. With this one, which the artist had titled "The Womb", the fact that its existence had only come to light a few weeks ago made it a very special acquisition indeed. Though the collection had yet to be made public, the art-world was already abuzz. If he picked up the phone and called his dealer, Julius fully expected to hear that all the remaining pieces had sold. And why not? There are few things more exciting than the revelation that a deceased creator left previously undiscovered work in their wake. The news is a salve on the wound their passing leaves behind.

He drained the sherry and carefully set the glass down on the mantel. Rubbing his hands together briskly, his face spread in a smile, he made his way to the table where the painting awaited him.

As he'd instructed, Elsa had left a pair of blue nitrile gloves on the table next to the package. He removed his jacket and laid it over the top of the wingback chair behind him, rolled up his shirt sleeves, and put on the gloves. He could get as touchy feely as he liked once he'd inspected the piece, but it wouldn't do to damage it during the unwrapping, or before he had verification that everything was in order.

Gently, he undid the tape on the front seam of the brown paper and pushed the flaps to the side. He could just about make out the dark square of the painting beneath the protective plastic sheeting. Hands trembling, palms moist beneath the gloves, he ever-so-carefully removed the plastic and set it aside. Now the picture was revealed to him, the brown paper spread out on both sides of it like the wings of a mummified bird.

The old man felt the breath rush from his lungs. Tears pricked his eyes.

It was so very easy to forget the power of Elizabeth Verner's work, and he felt a tiny stab of shame that he had been so critical of it in her heyday. If he remembered correctly, his issue was that her work had always been too derivative of the past masters. While mimicry was common, even among the greats, to Julius, there was never enough of *her* in her work to think of them as anything other than homages. While he'd acknowledged her talent, it irritated him that she seemed determined to hide herself from the viewer. Reticence in a painter's work was hardly uncommon, but where an artist like Pollock could reveal his true self on the canvas and *then* go to great lengths to obscure it, Verner's just had a vacancy where her truth should have been, an absence that forced the critical eye to pay more attention to her flaws and appropriations. That there was more honesty, more of the woman in the work toward the end of her life was the real tragedy because by then her name had already fallen out of favor. There were newer, bolder, more exciting talents, and the name Elizabeth Verner became just another footnote in New York's long history of passing fancies. The assumption was that she'd either given up painting, or simply stopped selling them. That she'd appeared only briefly to reinvent herself as some kind of feminist witch did not even bear comment, though it did make him marvel at the lengths to which people were willing to go to destroy their reputations once they realized the time had passed to recapture them. Her death, it seemed, was something of a blessing, then. Not only did the mad old woman finally find some peace, the art world saw the removal of the sole obstruction to her private works. Thank God he had had the wherewithal to bring her work to an appraiser or they might have ended up hawked for a pittance at some yard sale.

He shuddered at the thought.

Before him on the table, was a painting few people knew much about other than the name on the list the artist's ex-husband had submitted to Julius's dealer: "The Womb."

And it was breathtaking, the kind of work of which he had always assumed the artist capable, hence his frustration at her inability to deliver it. But here it was, a surrealist portrait of darkness that made his stomach quiver and intensified the trembling in his hands. Electric with excitement and moved nearly to tears, his hands unsure where to go, he hurried back to the bar, poured himself another sherry and quickly downed it, then returned to the table, and "The Womb".

Still wearing the gloves, he reached down, grabbed the upper corners of the painting's gilded frame, and raised it upright so that it was standing on the table in front of him.

In the light, it was even more magnificent and affecting, and now the tears did come, trickling down his face. He moved back a step so they would drip to the floor and not onto the table, or worse, the art, then wiped his eyes and returned to his appraisal, a trembling hand before his face.

The painting depicted an antiquated drawing room, much like his own, but crowded with hundreds of books, all their covers red. They'd been crammed into the lofty bookshelf to the left of the frame and crowded the floor on all but one side. In the center of the picture, a white-framed window showed absolute darkness through its panes, with the faintest suggestion of the artist's reflection, though he would need a magnifying glass to confirm it was more than just a pale smudge. To the right of the frame, more shelves, more books. Under the window—and yes, that was a face in the glass, wasn't it?—was a wooden table with clawfoot legs. There were more books, none of which bore titles, stacked atop it. And in the shadows beneath the table was a pregnant woman. She was sitting naked with her back against the wall, arms to her side, legs splayed, and though her face was but a cream thumbprint unmarred by features, it was somehow clear that she was in pain. If a child had produced itself, however, any suggestion of it was lost in the dense shadow cloaking her sex.

Julius nodded his appreciation. It was a dark piece, that was for sure, but then Verner had never been known for her light, even in person. Indeed, she was better remembered as a sad creature with clear mental issues and questionable hygiene, which to be fair, only verified her as a bona fide artist in the eyes of the connoisseurs. As Bill liked to say: "Show me a sane artist and I'll show you a fraud." The smell, he would quip, was simply unfermented money.

In the coming days, Julius planned to research as much as possible about the artist's life in the hope of decoding a possible meaning from this painting. Was the figure meant to represent the agony of childbirth? Why was the woman hidden? Shame? Was the child the product of an illicit tryst? Given what he knew of Verner's politics, could it be a feminist piece? And who was the woman? A deceased mother or sister or a figure from her imagination? Was it the artist herself? Van Gogh's work had always in some way depicted his feelings of estrangement, of alienation from his father, from the world, and then, toward the end, served as a veritable road map of his insanity and impending self-destruction. His entire life, both the good and the bad, could be found in his paintings. Therein the demons lay. For Julius, part of the fun was solving the mystery behind the images. It invigorated him, made him feel like a detective. Plus, it would increase the value of the piece, if only in cachet, if he had a good tale to accompany it.

After fetching himself another sherry—he reminded himself to be careful not to let his senses get too dull—he returned to the painting and found, after some untold amount of time, and much to his surprise, that he was laughing uncontrollably. Perhaps it was the sherry that made him feel giddy all of a sudden. Perhaps it was the shifting of the light—whether real or imagined—that made it seem as if the figure beneath the table in the picture had raised its head and was staring straight at him with eyes that were tiny red sparks in the black. He found this only moderately odd. The abrupt pain in his temples was worthier of note, and yet he couldn't stop the laughter from bubbling up out of him long enough to give it the proper consideration. The more he tried to stop, the worse it got, until he abandoned the idea entirely and took his hand from his mouth.

The glove came away soaked in blood.

Some small faraway part of his mind notified him that this was a matter of great concern, but he disregarded the voice and returned his attention to the painting, where quite curiously now, the woman was gone. Guffawing still, tears streaming from his eyes, he squinted and leaned in closer to the painting to see if he could divine the figure after all.

"It's fine," he told himself, despite that voice deep down inside him screaming in panic. "It's all in order. She just moved further back into the shadows, that's all. Probably to be away from the mad old man."

At the precise moment that he realized the painting was standing upright without anything to support it, and had been for quite some time, he sensed movement beneath the table. Not the one in the painting, but his own. Blood running freely from his nose, he looked down, his belly still jiggling with mirth that refused to abate and saw the flash of a pale white arm withdrawing into the shadows, like a fish catching the sun in shallow water before returning to the deep.

"There you are," Julius said, unconsciously wiping his sleeve across his nose.

Twin sparks hovered just beneath the hem of the tablecloth, the fire reflected in a glassy stare.

"You builders of the sky made it an uneven weight," said a voice. "It presses so much harder on our shoulders."

The old man nodded at the voice, which sounded like someone speaking through the blades of a fan. "Yes," he said aloud as the tears obscuring his vision turned red. "Yes, of course we did. It was never made clear that we should care."

The room smelled like fresh paint.

"You drove us into the ground to keep us clawing for air. Why build the world at all if you'd rather we didn't see it?"

He turned and staggered toward the opposite side of the room, toward the fireplace. And although he chewed through his tongue before he had a chance to express aloud his absolute joy at having the true meaning of the painting explained, thereby saving him weeks of research, it was enough to know.

A privilege to know.

And it was so much more than he'd expected, than he'd been ready to learn.

As he dropped to his knees before the fire, Julius was glad they didn't hurt anymore. The cold weather had made them stiff as boards lately. Now, he wept with gratitude that they would never bother him again. *She* had promised him that, and so much else.

Thank you, Mother, he thought.

On hands and knees, the old man crawled into the fireplace, his palms crunching into the burning logs, feet kicking embers out behind him onto the carpet. He was still holding the glass in one hand, but it shattered in short order, the sherry igniting and sending a mixture of blue and red flame racing up his arm.

There, on the coals, he lay on his side, knees drawn up, head bowed, and waited in the flames.

The room began to burn and before the heat burst his eyes, he saw the artist standing before him, watching, shimmering in the heat. She appeared to be smiling, as any artist will when their work is finally understood. X

GRAMMA

BY STEPHEN KING

GRAMMA

BY STEPHEN KING

GEORGE'S MOTHER WENT to the door, hesitated there, came back, and tousled George's hair. "I don't want you to worry," she said. "You'll be all right. Gramma, too."

"Sure, I'll be okay. Tell Buddy to lay chilly."

"Pardon me?"

George smiled. "To stay cool."

"Oh. Very funny." She smiled back at him, a distracted, going-in-six-directions-at-once smile. "George, are you sure—"

"I'll be *fine.*"

Are you sure what? Are you sure you're not scared to be alone with Gramma? Was that what she was going to ask?

If it was, the answer is no. After all, it wasn't like he was six anymore, when they had first come to Maine to take care of Gramma, and he had cried with terror whenever Gramma held out her heavy arms toward him from her white vinyl chair that always smelled of the poached eggs she ate and the sweet bland powder George's mom rubbed into her flabby, wrinkled skin; she held out her white-elephant arms, wanting him to come to her and be hugged to that huge and heavy old white-elephant body: Buddy had gone to her, had been enfolded in Gramma's blind embrace, and Buddy had come out alive... but Buddy was two years older.

Now Buddy had broken his leg and was at the CMG Hospital in Lewiston.

"You've got the doctor's number if something *should* go wrong. Which it won't. Right?"

"Sure," he said, and swallowed something dry in his throat. He smiled. Did the smile look okay? Sure. Sure it did. He wasn't scared of Gramma anymore. After all, he wasn't *six* anymore. Mom was going up to the hospital to see Buddy and he was just going to stay here and lay chilly. Hang out with Gramma awhile. No problem.

Mom went to the door again, hesitated again, and came back again, smiling that distracted, going-six-ways-at-once smile. "If she wakes up and calls for her tea—"

"I know," George said, seeing how scared and worried she was underneath that distracted smile. She was worried about Buddy, Buddy and his dumb *Pony League,* the coach had called and said Buddy had been hurt in a play at the plate, and the first George had known of it (he was just home from school and sitting at the table eating some cookies and having a glass of Nestlé's Quik) was when his mother gave a funny little gasp and said, *Hurt? Buddy? How bad?*

"I know *all* that stuff, Mom. I got it knocked. Negative perspiration. Go on, now."

"You're a good boy, George. Don't be scared. You're not scared of Gramma anymore, are you?"

"Huh-uh," George said. He smiled. The smile felt pretty good; the smile of a fellow who was laying chilly with negative perspiration on his brow, the smile of a fellow who Had It Knocked, the smile of a fellow who was most definitely not six anymore. He swallowed. It was a great smile, but beyond it, down in the darkness behind his smile, was one very dry throat. It felt as if his throat was lined with mitten-wool. "Tell Buddy I'm sorry he broke his leg."

"I will," she said, and went to the door again. Four-o'clock sunshine slanted in through the window. "Thank God we took the sports insurance, Georgie. I don't know what we'd do if we didn't have it."

"Tell him I hope he tagged the sucker out."

She smiled her distracted smile, a woman of just past fifty with two late sons, one thirteen, one eleven, and no man. This time she opened the door, and a cool whisper of October came in through the sheds.

"And remember, Dr. Arlinder—"

"Sure," he said. "You better go or his leg'll be fixed by the time you get there."

"She'll probably sleep the whole time," Mom said. "I love you, Georgie. You're a good son." She closed the door on that.

George went to the window and watched her hurry to the old '69 Dodge that burned too much gas and oil, digging the keys from her purse. Now that she was out of the house and didn't know George was looking at her, the distracted smile fell away and she only looked distracted—distracted and sick with worry about

Buddy. George felt bad for her. He didn't waste any similar feelings on Buddy, who liked to get him down and sit on top of him with a knee on each of George's shoulders and tap a spoon in the middle of George's forehead until he just about went crazy (Buddy called it the Spoon Torture of the Heathen Chinee and laughed like a madman and sometimes went on doing it until George cried), Buddy who sometimes gave him the Indian Rope Burn so hard that little drops of blood would appear on George's forearm, sitting on top of the pores like dew on blades of grass at dawn, Buddy who had listened so sympathetically when George had one night whispered in the dark of their bedroom that he liked Heather MacArdle and who the next morning ran across the schoolyard screaming *GEORGE AND HEATHER UP IN A TREE, KAY-EYE-ESS-ESS-EYE-EN-GEE! FIRSE COMES LOVE AN THEN COMES MARRITCH! HERE COMES HEATHER WITH A BABY CARRITCH!* like a runaway fire engine. Broken legs did not keep older brothers like Buddy down for long, but George was rather looking forward to the quiet as long as this one did. *Let's see you give me the Spoon Torture of the Heathen* Chinee with your leg in a cast, Buddy. Sure, kid—EVERY day.

The Dodge backed out of the driveway and paused while his mother looked both ways, although nothing would be coming; nothing ever was. His mother would have a two-mile ride over washboards and ruts before she even got to tar, and it was nineteen miles to Lewiston after that.

She backed all the way out and drove away. For a moment dust hung in the bright October afternoon air, and then it began to settle.

He was alone in the house.

With Gramma.

He swallowed.

Hey! Negative perspiration! Just lay chilly, right?

"Right," George said in a low voice, and walked across the small, sunwashed kitchen. He was a towheaded, good-looking boy with a spray of freckles across his nose and cheeks and a look of good humor in his darkish gray eyes.

Buddy's accident had occurred while he had been playing in the Pony League championship game this October 5th. George's Pee Wee League team, the Tigers, had been knocked out of their tournament on the first day, two Saturdays ago *(What a bunch of babies!* Buddy had exulted as George walked tearfully off the field. *What a bunch of PUSSIES!)...* and now Buddy had broken his leg. If Mom wasn't so worried and scared, George would have been almost happy.

There was a phone on the wall, and next to it was a note-minder board with a grease pencil hanging beside it. In the upper corner of the board was a cheerful country Gramma, her cheeks rosy, her white hair done up in a bun; a cartoon Gramma who was pointing at the board. There was a comic-strip balloon coming out of the cheerful country Gramma's mouth and she was saying, "REMEMBER *THIS,* SONNY!" Written on the board in his mother's sprawling hand was *Dr. Arlinder, 681-4330.* Mom hadn't written the number there just today, because she had to go to Buddy; it had been there almost three weeks now, because Gramma was having her "bad spells" again.

George picked up the phone and listened.

"—so I told her, I said, 'Mabel, if he treats you like that—'"

He put it down again. Henrietta Dodd. Henrietta was always on the phone, and if it was in the afternoon you could always hear the soap opera stories going on in the background. One night after she had a glass of wine with Gramma (since she started having the "bad spells" again, Dr. Arlinder said Gramma couldn't have the wine with her supper, so Mom didn't either— George was sorry, because the wine made Mom sort of giggly and she would tell stories about her girlhood), Mom had said that every time Henrietta Dodd opened her mouth, all her guts fell out. Buddy and George laughed wildly, and Mom put a hand to her mouth and said *Don't you EVER tell anyone I said that,* and then *she* began to laugh too, all three of them sitting at the supper table laughing, and at last the racket had awakened Gramma, who slept more and more, and she began to cry *Ruth! Ruth! ROO-OOOTH!* in that high, querulous voice of hers, and Mom had stopped laughing and went into her room.

Today Henrietta Dodd could talk all she wanted, as far as George was concerned. He just wanted to make sure the phone was working. Two weeks ago there had been a bad storm, and since then it went out sometimes.

He found himself looking at the cheery cartoon Gramma again, and wondered what it would be like to have a Gramma like that. *His* Gramma was huge and fat and blind; the hypertension had made her senile as well. Sometimes, when she had her "bad spells," she would (as Mom put it) "act out the Tartar," calling for people who weren't there, holding conversations with total emptiness, mumbling strange words that made no sense. On one occasion when she was doing this last, Mom had turned white and had gone in and told her to shut up, shut up, *shut up!* George remembered that occasion very well, not only because it was the only time Mom had ever actually *yelled* at Gramma, but because it was the next day that someone discovered that the Birches cemetery out on the Maple Sugar Road had been vandalized—gravestones knocked over, the old nineteenth-century gates pulled down, and one or two of the graves actually dug up— or something. *Desecrated* was the word Mr. Burdon, the principal, had used the next day when he convened all eight grades for Assembly and lectured the whole school on Malicious Mischief and how some things Just Weren't Funny. Going home that night, George had asked Buddy what *desecrated* meant, and Buddy said it meant digging up graves and pissing on the coffins, but George didn't believe that... unless it was late. And dark.

Gramma was noisy when she had her "bad spells," but mostly she just lay in the bed she had taken to three years before, a fat slug wearing rubber pants and diapers under her flannel nightgown, her face runneled with cracks and wrinkles, her eyes empty and blind—faded blue irises floating atop yellowed corneas.

At first Gramma hadn't been totally blind. But she had been *going* blind, and she had to have a person at each elbow to help her totter from her white vinyl egg-and-baby-powder-smelling chair to her bed or the bathroom. In those days, five years ago, Gramma had weighed well over two hundred pounds.

She had held out her arms and Buddy, then eight, had gone to her. George had hung back. And cried.

But I'm not scared now, he told himself, moving across the kitchen in his Keds. *Not a bit. She's just an old lady who has "bad spells" sometimes.*

He filled the teakettle with water and put it on a cold burner. He got a teacup and put one of Gramma's special herb tea bags into it. In case she should wake up and want a cup. He hoped like mad that she wouldn't, because then he would have to crank up the hospital bed and sit next to her and give her the tea a sip at a time, watching the toothless mouth fold itself over the rim of the cup, and listen to the slurping sounds as she took the tea into her dank, dying guts. Sometimes she slipped sideways on the bed and you had to pull her back over and her flesh was *soft*, kind of *jiggly*, as if it was filled with hot water, and her blind eyes would look at you...

George licked his lips and walked toward the kitchen table again. His last cookie and half a glass of Quik still stood there, but he didn't want them anymore. He looked at his schoolbooks, covered with Castle Rock Cougars book-covers, without enthusiasm.

He ought to go in and check on her.

He didn't want to.

He swallowed and his throat still felt as if it was lined with mitten-wool.

I'm not afraid of Gramma, he thought. *If she held out her arms I'd go right to her and let her hug me because she's just an old lady. She's senile and that's why she has "bad spells." That's all. Let her hug me and not cry. Just like Buddy.*

He crossed the short entryway to Gramma's room, face set as if for bad medicine, lips pressed together so tightly they were white. He looked in, and there lay Gramma, her yellow-white hair spread around her in a corona, sleeping, her toothless mouth hung open, chest rising under the coverlet so slowly you almost couldn't see it, so slowly that you had to look at her for a while just to make sure she wasn't dead.

Oh God, what if she dies on me while Mom's up to the hospital?

She won't. She won't.

Yeah, but what if she does?

She won't, so stop being a pussy.

One of Gramma's yellow, melted-looking hands moved slowly on the coverlet: her long nails dragged across the sheet and made a minute scratching sound. George drew back quickly, his heart pounding.

Cool as a moose, numbhead, see? Laying chilly.

He went back into the kitchen to see if his mother had been gone only an hour, or perhaps an hour and a half—if the latter, he could start reasonably waiting for her to come back. He looked at the clock and was astounded to see that not even twenty minutes had passed. Mom wouldn't even be *into* the city yet, let alone on her way back out of it! He stood still, listening to the silence. Faintly, he could hear the hum of the refrigerator and the electric clock. The snuffle of the afternoon breeze around the corners of the little house. And then—at the very edge of audibility—the faint, rasping susurrus of skin over cloth... Gramma's wrinkled, tallowy hand moving on the coverlet.

He prayed in a single gust of mental breath:

PleaseGoddon'tletherwakeupuntilMomcomeshomefor Jesus'sakeAmen.

He sat down and finished his cookie, drank his Quik. He thought of turning on the TV and watching something, but he was afraid the sound would wake up Gramma and that high, querulous, not-to-be-denied voice would begin calling *Roo-OOTH! RUTH! BRING ME M'TEA! TEA! ROOOOOOOOTH!*

He slicked his dry tongue over his drier lips and told himself not to be such a pussy. She was an old lady stuck in bed, it wasn't as if she could get up and hurt him, and she was eighty-three years old, she wasn't going to die this afternoon.

George walked over and picked up the phone again.

"—that same day! And she even *knew* he was married! Gorry, I hate these cheap little corner-walkers that think they're so smart! So at Grange I said—"

George guessed that Henrietta was on the phone with Cora Simard. Henrietta hung on the phone most afternoons from one until six with first *Ryan's Hope* and then *One Life to Live* and then *All My Children* and then *As the World Turns* and then *Search for Tomorrow* and then God knew what other ones playing in the background, and Cora Simard was one of her most faithful telephone correspondents, and a lot of what they talked about was 1) who was going to be having a Tupperware party or an Amway party and what the refreshments were apt to be, 2) cheap little corner-walkers, and 3) what they had said to various people at 3-a) the Grange, 3-b) the monthly church fair, or 3-c) K of P Hall Beano.

"—that if I ever saw her up that way again, I guess I could be a good citizen and call—"

He put the phone back in its cradle. He and Buddy made fun of Cora when they went past her house just like all the other kids—she was fat and sloppy and gossipy and they would chant, *Cora-Cora from Bora-Bora, ate a dog turd and wanted more-a!* and Mom would have killed them *both* if she had known that, but now George was glad she and Henrietta Dodd were on the phone. They could talk all afternoon, for all George cared. He didn't mind Cora, anyway. Once he had fallen down in front of her house and scraped his knee—Buddy had been chasing him—and Cora had put a Band-Aid on the scrape and gave them each a cookie, talking all the time. George had felt ashamed for all the times he had said the rhyme about the dog turd and the rest of it.

George crossed to the sideboard and took down his reading book. He held it for a moment, then put it back. He had read all the stories in it already, although school had only been going a month. He read better than Buddy, although Buddy was better at sports. *Won't be better for a while,* he thought with momentary good cheer, *not with a broken leg.*

He took down his history book, sat down at the kitchen table, and began to read about how Cornwallis had surrendered up his sword at Yorktown. His thoughts wouldn't stay on it. He got up, went through the entryway again. The yellow hand was still. Gramma slept, her face a gray, sagging circle against the pillow, a dying sun surrounded by the wild yellowish-white corona of her hair. To George she didn't look anything like people who were old and getting ready to die were supposed to look. She didn't look peaceful, like a sunset. She looked crazy, and...

(and dangerous)

...yes, okay, and *dangerous*—like an ancient she-bear that might have one more good swipe left in her claws.

George remembered well enough how they had come to Castle Rock to take care of Gramma when Granpa died. Until then Mom had been working in the Stratford Laundry in Stratford, Connecticut. Granpa was three or four years younger than Gramma, a carpenter by trade, and he had worked right up until the day of his death. It had been a heart attack.

Even then Gramma had been getting senile, having her "bad spells." She had always been a trial to her family, Gramma had. She was a volcanic woman who had taught school for fifteen years, between having babies and getting in fights with the Congregational Church she and Granpa and their nine children went to. Mom said that Granpa and Gramma quit the Congregational Church in Scarborough at the same time Gramma decided to quit teaching, but once, about a year ago, when Aunt Flo was up for a visit from her home in Salt Lake City, George and Buddy, listening at the register as Mom and her sister sat up late, talking, heard quite a different story. Granpa and Gramma had been kicked out of the church and Gramma had been fired off her job because she did something wrong. It was something about *books*. Why or how someone could get fired from their job and kicked out of the church just because of *books*, George didn't understand, and when he and Buddy crawled back into their twin beds under the eave, George asked.

There's all kinds of books, Señor El-Stupido, Buddy whispered.

Yeah, but what kind?

How should I know? Go to sleep!

Silence. George thought it through.

Buddy?

What! An irritated hiss.

Why did Mom tell us Gramma quit the church and her job?

Because it's a skeleton in the closet, that's why! Now go to sleep!

But he hadn't gone to sleep, not for a long time. His eyes *kept straying to the closet door, dimly outlined in moonlight, and he kept wondering what he would do if the door swung open, revealing a skeleton inside, all grinning tombstone teeth and cistern eye sockets and parrot-cage ribs; white moonlight skating delirious and almost blue on whiter bone. Would he scream? What had Buddy meant, a skeleton in the closet? What did skeletons have to do with books? At last he had slipped into sleep without even knowing it and had dreamed he* was six again, and Gramma was holding out her arms, her blind eyes searching for him; Gramma's reedy, querulous voice was saying, *Where's the little one, Ruth? Why's he crying? I only want to put him in the closet... with the skeleton.*

George had puzzled over these matters long and long, and finally, about a month after Aunt Flo had departed, he went to his mother and told her he had heard her and Aunt Flo talking. He knew what a skeleton in the closet meant by then, because he had asked Mrs. Redenbacher at school. She said it meant having a scandal in the family, and a scandal was something that made people talk a lot. *Like Cora Simard talks a lot?* George had asked Mrs. Redenbacher, and Mrs. Redenbacher's face had worked strangely and her lips had quivered and she had said, *That's not nice, George, but... yes, something like that.*

When he asked Mom, her face had gotten very still, and her hands had paused over the solitaire clock-face of cards she had been laying out.

Do you think that's a good thing for you to be doing, Georgie? Do you and your brother make a habit of eavesdropping over the register?

George, then only nine, had hung his head.

We like Aunt Flo, Mom. We wanted to listen to her a little longer.

This was the truth.

Was it Buddy's idea?

It had been, but George wasn't going to tell her *that.* He didn't want to go walking around with his head on backwards, which might happen if Buddy found out he had tattled.

No, mine.

Mom had sat silent for a long time, and then she slowly began laying her cards out again. *Maybe it's time you did know,* she had said. *Lying's worse than eavesdropping, I guess, and we all lie to our children about Gramma. And we lie to ourselves, too, I guess. Most of the time, we do.* And then she spoke with a sudden, vicious bitterness that was like acid squirting out between her front teeth—he felt that her words were so hot they would have burned his face if he hadn't recoiled. *Except for me. I have to live with her, and I can no longer afford the luxury of lies.*

So his Mom told him that after Granpa and Gramma had gotten married, they had had a baby that was born dead, and a year later they had another baby, and *that* was born dead, too, and the doctor told Gramma she would never be able to carry a child to term and all she could do was keep on having babies that were dead or babies that died as soon as they sucked air. That would go on, he said, until one of them died inside her too long before her body could shove it out and it would rot in there and kill her, too.

The doctor told her that.

Not long after, the *books* began.

Books about how to have babies?

But Mom didn't—or wouldn't—say what kind of books they were, or where Gramma got them, or how she *knew* to get them. Gramma got pregnant again, and this time the baby wasn't born dead and the baby didn't die after a breath or two; this time the baby was fine, and that was George's Uncle Larson. And after that, Gramma kept getting pregnant and having babies. Once, Mom said, Granpa had tried to make her get rid of the books to see if they could do it without them (or even if they couldn't, maybe Granpa figured they had enough yowwens by then so it wouldn't matter) and Gramma wouldn't. George asked his mother why and she said: "I think that by then having the books was as important to her as having the babies."

"I don't get it," George said.

"Well," George's mother said, "I'm not sure I do, either... I was very small, remember. All I know for sure is that those books got a hold over her. She said there would be no more talk about it and there wasn't, either. Because Gramma wore the pants in our family."

George closed his history book with a snap. He looked at the clock and saw that it was nearly five o'clock. His stomach was grumbling softly. He realized suddenly, and with something very like horror, that if Mom wasn't home by six or so, Gramma would wake up and start hollering for her supper. Mom had forgotten to give him instructions about that, probably because she was so upset about Buddy's leg. He supposed he could make Gramma one of her special frozen dinners. They were special because Gramma was on a salt-free diet. She also had about a thousand different kinds of pills.

As for himself, he could heat up what was left of last night's macaroni and cheese. If he poured a lot of catsup on it, it would be pretty good.

He got the macaroni and cheese out of the fridge, spooned it into a pan, and put the pan on the burner next to the teakettle, which was still waiting in case Gramma woke up and wanted what she sometimes called "a cuppa cheer." George started to get himself a glass of milk, paused, and picked up the telephone again.

"—and I couldn't even believe my eyes when..." Henrietta Dodd's voice broke off and then rose shrilly: "Who keeps listening in on this line, I'd like to know!"

George put the phone back on the hook in a hurry, his face burning.

She doesn't know it's you, stupe. There's six parties on the line!

All the same, it was wrong to eavesdrop, even if it was just to hear another voice when you were alone in the house, alone except for Gramma, the fat thing sleeping in the hospital bed in the other room; even when it seemed almost *necessary* to hear another human voice because your Mom was in Lewiston and it was going to be dark soon and Gramma was in the other room and Gramma looked like

(yes oh yes she did)

a she-bear that might have just one more murderous swipe left in her old clotted claws.

George went and got the milk.

Mom herself had been born in 1930, followed by Aunt Flo in 1932, and then Uncle Franklin in 1934. Uncle Franklin had died in 1948, of a burst appendix, and Mom sometimes still got teary about that, and carried his picture. She had liked Frank the best of all her brothers and sisters, and she said there was no need for him to die that way, of peritonitis. She said that God had played dirty when He took Frank.

George looked out the window over the sink. The light was more golden now, low over the hill. The shadow of their back shed stretched all the way across the lawn. If Buddy hadn't broken his dumb *leg,* Mom would be here now, making chili or something (plus Gramma's salt-free dinner), and they would all be talking and laughing and maybe they'd play some gin rummy later on.

George flicked on the kitchen light, even though it really wasn't dark enough for it yet. Then he turned on lo heat under his macaroni. His thoughts kept returning to Gramma, sitting in her white vinyl chair like a big fat worm in a dress, her corona of hair every crazy which-way on the shoulders of her pink rayon robe, holding out her arms for him to come, him shrinking back against his Mom, bawling.

Send him to me, Ruth. I want to hug him.

He's a little frightened, Momma. He'll come in time.
But his mother sounded frightened, too.

Frightened? Mom?

George stopped, thinking. Was that true? Buddy said your memory could play tricks on you. Had she really sounded frightened?

Yes. She had.

Gramma's voice rising peremptorily: *Don't coddle the boy, Ruth! Send him over here; I want to give him a hug.*

No. He's crying.

And as Gramma lowered her heavy arms from which the flesh hung in great, dough-like gobbets, a sly, senile smile had overspread her face and she had said: *Does he really look like Franklin, Ruth? I remember you saying he favored Frank.*

Slowly, George stirred the macaroni and cheese and catsup. He hadn't remembered the incident so clearly before. Maybe it was the silence that had made him remember. The silence, and being alone with Gramma.

So Gramma had her babies and taught school, and the doctors were properly dumbfounded, and Granpa carpentered and generally got more and more prosperous, finding work even in the depths of the Depression, and at last people began to talk, Mom said.

What did they say? George asked.

Nothing important, Mom said, but she suddenly swept her cards together. *They said your Gramma and Granpa were too lucky for ordinary folks, that's all.* And it was just after that that the books had been found. Mom wouldn't say more than that, except that the school board had found some and that a hired man had found some more. There had been a big scandal.

Granpa and Gramma had moved to Buxton and that was the end of it.

The children had grown up and had children of their own, making aunts and uncles of each other; Mom had gotten married and moved to New York with Dad (who George could not even remember). Buddy had been born, and then they had moved to Stratford and in 1969 George had been born, and in 1971 Dad had been hit and killed by a car driven by the Drunk Man Who Had to Go to Jail.

When Granpa had his heart attack there had been a great many letters back and forth among the aunts and uncles. They didn't want to put the old lady in a nursing home. And she didn't want to *go* to a home. If Gramma didn't want to do a thing like that, it might be better to accede to her wishes. The old lady wanted to go to one of them and live out the rest of her years with that child. But they were all married, and none of them had spouses who felt like sharing their home with a senile and often unpleasant old woman. All were married, that was, except Ruth.

The letters flew back and forth, and at last George's Mom had given in. She quit her job and came to Maine to take care of the old lady. The others had chipped together to buy a small house in outer Castle View, where property values were low. Each month they would send her a check, so she could "do" for the old lady and for her boys.

What's happened is my brothers and sisters have turned me into a sharecropper, George could remember her saying once, and he didn't know for sure what that meant, but she had sounded bitter when she said it, like it was a joke that didn't come out smooth in a laugh but instead stuck in her throat like a bone. George knew (because Buddy had told him) that Mom had finally given in because everyone in the big, far-flung family had assured her that Gramma couldn't possibly last long. She had too many things wrong with her—high blood pressure, uremic poisoning, obesity, heart palpitations—to last long. It would be eight months, Aunt Flo and Aunt Stephanie and Uncle George (after whom George had been named) all said; a year at the most. But now it had been five years, and George called that lasting pretty long.

She had lasted pretty long, all right. Like a she-bear in hibernation, waiting for... what?

(you know how to deal with her best Ruth you know how to shut her up)

George, on his way to the fridge to check the directions on one of Gramma's special salt-free dinners, stopped. Stopped cold. Where had that come from? That voice speaking inside his head?

Suddenly his belly and chest broke out in gooseflesh. He reached inside his shirt and touched one of his nipples. It was like a little pebble, and he took his finger away in a hurry.

Uncle George. His "namesake uncle," who worked for Sperry-Rand in New York. It had been his voice. He had said that when he and his family came up for Christmas two—no, three—years ago.

She's more dangerous now that she's senile.

George, be quiet. The boys are around somewhere.

George stood by the refrigerator, one hand on the cold chrome handle, thinking, remembering, looking out into the growing dark. Buddy *hadn't* been around that day. Buddy was already outside, because Buddy had wanted the good sled, that was why; they were going sliding on Joe Camber's hill and the other sled had a buckled runner. So Buddy was outside and here was George, hunting through the boot-and-sock box in the entryway, looking for a pair of heavy socks that matched, and was it *his* fault his mother and Uncle George were talking in the kitchen? George didn't think so. Was it George's fault that God hadn't struck him deaf, or, lacking the extremity of that measure, at least located the conversation elsewhere in the house? George didn't believe that, either. As his mother had pointed out on more than one occasion (usually after a glass of wine or two), God sometimes played dirty.

You know what I mean, Uncle George said.

His wife and his three girls had gone over to Gates Falls to do some last-minute Christmas shopping, and Uncle George was pretty much in the bag, just like the Drunk Man Who Had to Go to Jail. George could tell by the way his uncle slurred his words.

You remember what happened to Franklin when he crossed her.

George, be quiet, or I'll pour the rest of your beer right down the sink!

Well, she didn't really mean to do it. Her tongue just got away from her. Peritonitis—

George, shut up!

Maybe, George remembered thinking vaguely, *God isn't the only one who plays dirty.*

Now he broke the hold of these old memories and looked in the freezer and took out one of Gramma's dinners. Veal. With peas on the side. You had to preheat the oven and then bake it for forty minutes at 300 degrees. Easy. He was all set. The tea was ready on the stove if Gramma wanted that. He could make tea, or he could make dinner in short order if Gramma woke up and yelled for it. Tea or dinner, he was a regular two-gun Sam. Dr. Arlinder's number was on the board, in case of an emergency. Everything was cool. So what was he worried about?

He had never been left alone with Gramma, that was what he was worried about.

Send the boy to me, Ruth. Send him over here.

No. He's crying.

She's more dangerous now... you know what I mean.

We all lie to our children about Gramma.

Neither he nor Buddy. Neither of them had ever been left *alone with Gramma. Until now.*

Suddenly George's mouth went dry. He went to the sink and got a drink of water. He felt... funny. These thoughts. These memories. Why was his brain dragging them all up now?

He felt as if someone had dumped all the pieces to a puzzle in front of him and that he couldn't quite put them together. And maybe it was *good* he couldn't put them together, because the finished picture might be, well, sort of boogery. It might—

From the other room, where Gramma lived all her days and nights, a choking, rattling, gargling noise suddenly arose.

A whistling gasp was sucked into George as he pulled breath. He turned toward Gramma's room and discovered his shoes were tightly nailed to the linoleum floor. His heart was spike-iron in his chest. His eyes were wide and bulging. *Go now,* his brain told his feet, and his feet saluted and said *Not at all, sir!*

Gramma had never made a noise like that before.

Gramma had *never* made a noise like that before.

It arose again, a choking sound, low and then descending lower, becoming an insectile buzz before it died out altogether. George was able to move at last. He walked toward the entryway that separated the kitchen from Gramma's room. He crossed it and looked into her room, his heart slamming. Now his throat was *choked* with wool mittens; it would be impossible to swallow past them.

Gramma was still sleeping and it was all right, that was his first thought; it had only been some weird *sound,* after all; maybe she made it all the time when he and Buddy were in school. Just a snore. Gramma was fine. Sleeping.

That was his first thought. Then he noticed that the yellow hand that had been on the coverlet was now dangling limply over the side of the bed, the long nails almost but not quite touching the floor. And her mouth was open, as wrinkled and caved-in as an orifice dug into a rotten piece of fruit.

Timidly, hesitantly, George approached her.

He stood by her side for a long time, looking down at her, not daring to touch her. The imperceptible rise and fall of the coverlet appeared to have ceased.

Appeared.

That was the key word. *Appeared.*

But that's just because you are spooked, Georgie. You're just being Señor El-Stupido, like Buddy says— it's a game. Your brain's playing tricks on your eyes, she's breathing just fine, she's—

"Gramma?" he said, and all that came out was a whisper. He cleared his throat and jumped back, frightened of the sound. But his voice was a little louder. "Gramma? You want your tea now? Gramma?"

Nothing.

The eyes were closed.

The mouth was open.

The hand hung.

Outside, the setting sun shone golden-red through the trees.

He saw her in a positive fullness then; saw her with that childish and brilliantly unhoused eye of unformed immature reflection, not here, not now, not in bed, but sitting in the white vinyl chair, holding out her arms, her face at the same time stupid and triumphant. He found himself remembering one of the "bad spells" when Gramma began to shout, as if in a foreign language—*Gyaagin! Gyaagin! Hastur degryon Yos-soth- oth!*—and Mom had sent them outside, had screamed *"Just GO!"* at Buddy when Buddy stopped at the box in the entry to hunt for his gloves, and Buddy had looked back over his shoulder, so scared he was walleyed with it because their mom *never* shouted, and they had both gone out and stood in the driveway, not talking, their hands stuffed in their pockets for warmth, wondering what was happening.

Later, Mom had called them in for supper as if nothing had happened.

(you know how to deal with her best Ruth you know how to shut her up)

George had not thought of that particular "bad spell" from that day to this. Except now, looking at Gramma, who was sleeping so strangely in her crank-up hospital bed, it occurred to him with dawning horror that it was the next day they had learned that Mrs. Harham, who lived up the road and sometimes visited Gramma, had died in her sleep that night.

Gramma's "bad spells."

Spells.

Witches were supposed to be able to cast spells. That's what made them witches, wasn't it? Poisoned apples. Princes into toads. Gingerbread houses. Abracadabra. Presto-chango. *Spells.*

Spilled-out pieces of an unknown puzzle flying together in George's mind, as if by magic.

Magic, George thought, and groaned.

What was the picture? It was Gramma, of course, Gramma and her *books,* Gramma who had been driven out of town, Gramma who hadn't been able to have babies and then had been able to, Gramma who had been driven out of the *church* as well as out of town. The picture was Gramma, yellow and fat and wrinkled and slug-like, her toothless mouth curved into a sunken grin, her faded, blind eyes somehow sly and cunning; and on her head was a black, conical hat sprinkled with silver stars and glittering Babylonian crescents; at her feet were slinking black cats with eyes as yellow as urine, and the smells were pork and blindness, pork and burning, ancient stars and candles as dark as the earth in which coffins lay; he heard words spoken from ancient books, and each word was like a stone and each sentence like a crypt reared in some stinking boneyard and every paragraph like a nightmare caravan of the plague dead taken to a place of burning; his eye was the eye of a child and in that moment it opened wide in startled understanding on blackness.

Gramma had been a witch, just like the Wicked Witch in the *Wizard of Oz.* And now she was dead. That gargling sound, George thought with increasing horror. That gargling, snoring sound had been a... a... a *"death rattle."*

"Gramma?" he whispered, and crazily he thought: *Ding-dong, the wicked witch is dead.*

No response. He held his cupped hand in front of Gramma's mouth. There was no breeze stirring around inside Gramma. It was dead calm and slack sails and no wake widening behind the keel. Some of his fright began to recede now, and George tried to think. He remembered Uncle Fred showing him how to wet a finger and test the wind, and now he licked his entire palm and held it in front of Gramma's mouth.

Still nothing.

He started for the phone to call Dr. Arlinder, and then stopped. Suppose he called the doctor and she really wasn't dead at all? He'd be in dutch for sure.

Take her pulse.

He stopped in the doorway, looking doubtfully back at that dangling hand. The sleeve of Gramma's nightie had pulled up, exposing her wrist. But that was no good. Once, after a visit to the doctor when the nurse had pressed her finger to his wrist to take his pulse, George had tried it and hadn't been able to find anything. As far as his own unskilled fingers could tell, he was dead.

Besides, he didn't really want to... well... to *touch* Gramma. Even if she was dead. *Especially* if she was dead.

George stood in the entryway, looking from Gramma's still, bedridden form to the phone on the wall beside Dr. Arlinder's number, and back to Gramma again. He would just have to call. He would—

—get a mirror!

Sure! When you breathed on a mirror, it got cloudy. He had seen a doctor check an unconscious person that way once in a movie. There was a bathroom connecting with Gramma's room and now George hurried in and got Gramma's vanity mirror. One side of it was regular, the other side magnified, so you could see to pluck out hairs and do stuff like that.

George took it back to Gramma's bed and held one side of the mirror until it was almost touching Gramma's open, gaping mouth. He held it there while he counted to sixty, watching Gramma the whole time. Nothing changed. He was sure she was dead even before he took the mirror away from her mouth and observed its surface, which was perfectly clear and unclouded.

Gramma was dead.

George realized with relief and some surprise that he could feel sorry for her now. Maybe she had been a witch. Maybe not. Maybe she had only *thought* she was a witch. However it had been, she was gone now. He realized with an adult's comprehension that questions of concrete reality became not unimportant but less *vital* when they were examined in the mute bland face of mortal remains. He realized this with an adult's comprehension and accepted with an adult's relief. This was a passing footprint, the shape of a shoe, in his mind. So are all the child's adult impressions; it is only in later years that the child realizes that he was being *made; formed;* shaped by random experiences; all that remains *in the instant* beyond the footprint is that bitter gunpowder smell which is the ignition of an idea beyond a child's given years.

He returned the mirror to the bathroom, then went back through her room, glancing at the body on his way by. The setting sun had painted the old dead face with barbaric, orange-red colors, and George looked away quickly.

He went through the entry and crossed the kitchen to the telephone, determined to do everything right. Already in his mind he saw a certain advantage over Buddy; whenever Buddy started to tease him, he would simply say: *I was all by myself in the house when Gramma died, and I did everything right.*

Call Dr. Arlinder, that was first. Call him and say, "My Gramma just died. Can you tell me what I should do? Cover her up or something?"

No.

"I *think* my Gramma just died."

Yes. Yes, that was better. Nobody thought a little kid knew anything anyway, so that was better.

Or how about:

"I'm pretty sure my Gramma just died—"

Sure! That was best of all.

And tell about the mirror and the death rattle and all. And the doctor would come right away, and when he was done examining Gramma he would say, *"I pronounce you dead, Gramma,"* and then say to George, *"You laid extremely chilly in a tough situation, George. I want to congratulate you."* And George would say something appropriately modest.

George looked at Dr. Arlinder's number and took a couple of slow deep breaths before grabbing the phone. His heart was beating fast, but that painful spike-iron thud was gone now. Gramma had died. The worst had happened, and somehow it wasn't as bad as waiting for her to start bellowing for Mom to bring her tea.

The phone was dead.

He listened to the blankness, his mouth still formed around the words *I'm sorry, Missus Dodd, but this is George Bruckner and I have to call the doctor for my Gramma.* No voices. No dial tone. Just dead blankness. Like the dead blankness in the bed in there.

Gramma is—

—is—

(oh she is)

Gramma is laying chilly.

Gooseflesh again, painful and marbling. His eyes fixed on the Pyrex teakettle on the stove, the cup on the counter with the herbal tea bag in it. No more tea for Gramma. Not ever.

(laying so chilly)

George shuddered.

He stuttered his finger up and down on the Princess phone's cutoff button, but the phone was dead. Just as dead as—

(just as chilly as)

He slammed the handset down hard and the bell tinged faintly inside and he picked it up in a hurry to see if that meant it had magically gone right again. But there was nothing, and this time he put it back slowly.

His heart was thudding harder again.

I'm alone in this house with her dead body.

He crossed the kitchen slowly, stood by the table for a minute, and then turned on the light. It was getting dark in the house. Soon the sun would be gone; night would be here.

Wait. That's all I got to do. Just wait until Mom gets back. This is better, really. If the phone went out, it's better that she just died instead of maybe having a fit or something, foaming at the mouth, maybe falling out of bed—

Ah, that was bad. He could have done very nicely without *that* horse-pucky.

Like being alone in the dark and thinking of dead things that were still lively—seeing shapes in the shadows on the walls and thinking of death, thinking of the dead, those things, the way they would stink and the way they would move toward you in the black:

thinking this: thinking that: thinking of bugs turning in flesh: burrowing in flesh: eyes that moved in the dark. Yeah. That most of all. Thinking of eyes that moved in the dark and the creak of floorboards as something came across the room through the zebra-stripes of shadows from the light outside. Yeah.

In the dark your thoughts had a perfect circularity, and no matter what you tried to think of—flowers or Jesus or baseball or winning the gold in the 440 at the Olympics—it somehow led back to the form in the shadows with the claws and the unblinking eyes.

"*Shittabrick!*" he hissed, and suddenly slapped his own face. And hard. He was giving himself the whim-whams, it was time to stop it. He wasn't six anymore. She was dead, that was all, dead. There was no more thought inside her now than there was in a marble or a floorboard or a doorknob or a radio dial or—

And a strong alien unprepared-for voice, perhaps only the unforgiving unbidden voice of simple survival, inside him cried: *Shut up Georgie and get about your goddam business!*

Yeah, okay. Okay, but—

He went back to the door of her bedroom to make sure.

There lay Gramma, one hand out of bed and touching the floor, her mouth hinged agape. Gramma was part of the furniture now. You could put her hand back in bed or pull her hair or pop a water glass into her mouth or put earphones on her head and play Chuck Berry into them full-tilt boogie and it would be all the same to her. Gramma was, as Buddy sometimes said, out of it. Gramma had had the course.

A sudden low and rhythmic thudding noise began, not far to George's left, and he started, a little yipping cry escaping him. It was the storm door, which Buddy had put on just last week. Just the storm door, unlatched and thudding back and forth in the freshening breeze.

George opened the inside door, leaned out, and caught the storm door as it swung back. The wind—it wasn't a breeze but a wind—caught his hair and riffled it. He latched the door firmly and wondered where the wind had come from all of a sudden. When Mom left it had been almost dead calm. But when Mom had left it had been bright daylight and now it was dusk.

George glanced in at Gramma again and then went back and tried the phone again. Still dead. He sat down, got up, and began to walk back and forth through the kitchen, pacing, trying to think.

An hour later it was full dark.

The phone was still out. George supposed the wind, which had now risen to a near-gale, had knocked down some of the lines, probably out by the Beaver Bog, where the trees grew everywhere in a helter-skelter of deadfalls and swamp-water. The phone dinged occasionally, ghostly and far, but the line remained blank. Outside the wind moaned along the eaves of the small house and George reckoned he would have a story to tell at the next Boy Scout Camporee, all right... just sitting in the house alone with his dead Gramma and the phone out and the wind pushing rafts of clouds fast across the sky, clouds that were black on top and the color of dead tallow, the color of Gramma's claw-hands, underneath.

It was, as Buddy also sometimes said, a Classic.

He wished he was telling it now, with the actuality of the thing safely behind him. He sat at the kitchen table, his history book open in front of him, jumping at every sound... and now that the wind was up, there were a lot of sounds as the house creaked in all its unoiled secret forgotten joints.

She'll be home pretty quick. She'll be home and then everything will be okay. Everything

(you never covered her)

will be all r

(never covered her face)

George jerked as if someone had spoken aloud and stared wide-eyed across the kitchen at the useless telephone. You were supposed to pull the sheet up over the dead person's face. It was in all the movies.

Hell with that! I'm not going in there!

No! And no reason why he should! *Mom* could cover her face when she got home! Or *Dr. Arlinder* when he came! Or the *undertaker!*

Someone, anyone, but him.

No reason why he should.

It was nothing to him, and nothing to Gramma.

Buddy's voice in his head:

If you weren't scared, how come you didn't dare to cover her face?

It was nothing to me.

Fraidy-cat!

Nothing to Gramma, either.

CHICKEN-GUTS fraidy-cat!

Sitting at the table in front of his unread history book, considering it, George began to see that if he *didn't* pull the counterpane up over Gramma's face, he couldn't claim to have done everything right, and thus Buddy would have a leg (no matter how shaky) to stand on.

Now he saw himself telling the spooky story of Gramma's death at the Camporee fire before taps, just getting to the comforting conclusion where Mom's headlights swept into the driveway—the reappearance of the grown-up, both reestablishing and reconfirming the concept of Order—and suddenly, from the shadows, a dark figure arises, and a pine-knot in the fire explodes and George can see it's Buddy there in the shadows, saying: *If you was so brave, chicken-guts, how come you didn't dare to cover up HER FACE?*

George stood up, reminding himself that Gramma was *out of it*, that Gramma was *wasted*, that Gramma was *laying chilly.* He could put her hand back in bed, stuff a tea bag up her nose, put on earphones playing Chuck Berry full blast, etc., etc., and none of it would put a buzz under Gramma, because that was what being dead was *about*, nobody could put a buzz under a dead person, a dead person was the ultimate laid-back cool, and the rest of it was just dreams, ineluctable and apocalyptic and feverish dreams about closet doors swinging open in the dead mouth of midnight, just dreams about moonlight skating a delirious blue on the bones of disinterred skeletons, just—

He whispered, "Stop it, can't you? Stop being so—"

(gross)

He steeled himself. He was going to go in there and pull the coverlet up over her face, and take away Buddy's last leg to stand on. He would administer the few simple rituals of Gramma's death perfectly. He would cover her face and then—his face lit at the symbolism of this—he would put away her unused tea bag and her unused cup. Yes.

He went in, each step a conscious act. Gramma's room was dark, her body a vague hump in the bed, and he fumbled madly for the light switch, not finding it for what seemed to be an eternity. At last it clicked up, flooding the room with low yellow light from the cut-glass fixture overhead.

Gramma lay there, hand dangling, mouth open. George regarded her, dimly aware that little pearls of sweat now clung to his forehead, and wondered if his responsibility in the matter could possibly extend to picking up that cooling hand and putting it back in bed with the rest of Gramma. He decided it did not. Her hand could have fallen out of bed any old time. That was too much. He couldn't touch her. Everything else, but not that.

Slowly, as if moving through some thick fluid instead of air, George approached Gramma. He stood over her, looking down. Gramma was yellow. Part of it was the light, filtered through the old fixture, but not all.

Breathing through his mouth, his breath rasping audibly, George grasped the coverlet and pulled it up over Gramma's face. He let go of it and it slipped just a little, revealing her hairline and the yellow creased parchment of her brow. Steeling himself, he grasped it again, keeping his hands far to one side and the other of her head so he wouldn't have to touch her, even through the cloth, and pulled it up again. This time it stayed. It was satisfactory. Some of the fear went out of George. He had *buried* her. Yes, that was why you covered the dead person up, and why it was right: it was like *burying* them. It was a statement.

He looked at the hand dangling down, unburied, and discovered now that he could touch it, he could tuck it under and bury it with the rest of Gramma.

He bent, grasped the cool hand, and lifted it.

The hand twisted in his and clutched his wrist.

George screamed. He staggered backward, screaming in the empty house, screaming against the sound of the wind reaving the eaves, screaming against the sound of the house's creaking joints. He backed away, pulling Gramma's body askew under the coverlet, and the hand thudded back down, twisting, turning, snatching at the air... and then relaxing to limpness again.

I'm all right, it was nothing, it was nothing but a reflex.

George nodded in perfect understanding, and then he remembered again how her hand had turned, clutching his, and he shrieked. His eyes bulged in their sockets. His hair stood out, perfectly on end, in a cone. His heart was a run away stamping-press in his chest. The world tilted crazily, came back to the level, and then just went on moving until it was tilted the other way. Every time rational thought started to come back, panic goosed him again. He whirled, wanting only to get out of the room to some other room—or even three or four miles down the road, if that was what it took—where he could get all of this under control. So he whirled and ran full tilt into the wall, missing the open doorway by a good two feet.

He rebounded and fell to the floor, his head singing with a sharp, cutting pain that sliced keenly through the panic. He touched his nose and his hand came back bloody. Fresh drops spotted his shirt. He scrambled to his feet and looked around wildly.

The hand dangled against the floor as it had before, but Gramma's body was not askew; it also was as it had been.

He had imagined the whole thing. He had come into the room, and all the rest of it had been no more than a mind-movie.

No.

But the pain had cleared his head. Dead people didn't grab your wrist. Dead was dead. When you were dead they could use you for a hat rack or stuff you in a tractor tire and roll you downhill or et cetera, et cetera, et cetera. When you were dead you might be acted *upon* (by, say, little boys trying to put dead dangling hands back into bed), but your days of *acting* upon—so to speak—were over.

Unless you're a witch. Unless you pick your time to die when no one's around but one little kid, because it's best that way, you can... can...

Can what?

Nothing. It was stupid. He had imagined the whole thing because he had been scared and that was all there was to it. He wiped his nose with his forearm and winced at the pain. There was a bloody smear on the skin of his inner forearm.

He wasn't going to go near her again, that was all. Reality or hallucination, he wasn't going to mess with Gramma. The bright flare of panic was gone, but he was still miserably scared, near tears, shaky at the sight of his own blood, only wanting his mother to come home and take charge.

George backed out of the room, through the entry, and into the kitchen. He drew a long, shuddery breath and let it out. He wanted a wet rag for his nose, and suddenly he felt like he was going to vomit. He went over to the sink and ran cold water. He bent and got a rag from the basin under the sink—a piece of one of Gramma's old diapers—and ran it under the cold tap, snuffling up blood as he did so. He soaked the old soft cotton diaper-square until his hand was numb, then turned off the tap and wrung it out.

He was putting it to his nose when her voice spoke from the other room.

"Come here, boy," Gramma called in a dead buzzing voice. "Come in here—*Gramma wants to hug you.*"

George tried to scream and no sound came out. No sound at all. But there were sounds in the other room. Sounds that he heard when Mom was in there, giving Gramma her bed-bath, lifting her bulk, dropping it, turning it, dropping it again.

Only those sounds now seemed to have a slightly different and yet utterly specific meaning—it sounded as though Gramma was trying to... to get out of bed.

"Boy! Come in here, boy! Right NOW! Step to it!"

With horror he saw that his feet were answering that command. He told them to stop and they just went on, left foot, right foot, hay foot, straw foot, over the linoleum; his brain was a terrified prisoner inside his body—a hostage in a tower.

She IS a witch, she's a witch and she's having one of her "bad spells," oh yeah, it's a "spell" all right, and it's bad, it's REALLY bad, oh God oh Jesus help me help me help me—

George walked across the kitchen and through the entryway and into Gramma's room and yes, she hadn't just *tried* to get out of bed, she *was* out, she was sitting in the white vinyl chair where she hadn't sat for four years, since she got too heavy to walk and too senile to know where she was, anyway.

But Gramma didn't look senile now.

Her face was sagging and doughy, but the senility was gone—if it had ever really been there at all, and not just a mask she wore to lull small boys and tired husbandless women. Now Gramma's face gleamed with full intelligence—it gleamed like an old, stinking wax candle. Her eyes drooped in her face, lackluster and dead. Her chest was not moving. Her nightie had pulled up, exposing elephantine thighs. The coverlet of her deathbed was thrown back.

Gramma held her huge arms out to him.

"I want to hug you, Georgie," that flat and buzzing dead-voice said. *"Don't be a scared old crybaby. Let your Gramma hug you."*

George cringed back, trying to resist that almost insurmountable pull. Outside, the wind shrieked and roared. George's face was long and twisted with the extremity of his fright; the face of a woodcut caught and shut up in an ancient book.

George began to walk toward her. He couldn't help himself. Step by dragging step toward those outstretched arms. *He would show Buddy that he wasn't scared of Gramma, either. He would go to Gramma and be hugged because he wasn't a crybaby fraidy-cat. He would go to Gramma now.*

He was almost within the circle of her arms when the window to his left crashed inward and suddenly a wind-blown branch was in the room with them, autumn leaves still clinging to it. The river of wind flooded the room, blowing over Gramma's pictures, whipping her nightgown and her hair.

Now George could scream. He stumbled backward out of her grip and Gramma made a cheated hissing sound, her lips pulling back over smooth old gums; her thick, wrinkled hands clapped uselessly together on moving air.

George's feet tangled together and he fell down. Gramma began to rise from the white vinyl chair, a tottering pile of flesh; she began to stagger toward him. George found he couldn't get up; the strength deserted his legs. He began to crawl backward, whimpering. Gramma came on, slowly but relentlessly, dead and yet alive, and suddenly George understood what the hug would mean; the puzzle was complete in his mind and somehow he found his feet just as Gramma's hand closed on his shirt. It ripped up the side, and for one moment he felt her cold flesh against his skin before fleeing into the kitchen again.

He would run into the night. Anything other than being hugged by the witch, his Gramma. Because when his mother came back she would find Gramma dead and George alive, oh yes... but George would have developed a sudden taste for herbal tea.

He looked back over his shoulder and saw Gramma's grotesque, misshapen shadow rising on the wall as she came through the entryway.

And at that moment the telephone rang, shrilly and stridently.

George seized it without even thinking and screamed into it; screamed for someone to come, to please come. He screamed these things silently; not a sound escaped his locked throat.

Gramma tottered into the kitchen in her pink nightie. Her whitish-yellow hair blew wildly around her face, and one of her horn combs hung askew against her wrinkled neck.

Gramma was grinning.

"Ruth?" It was Aunt Flo's voice, almost lost in the whistling wind-tunnel of a bad long-distance connection. "Ruth, are you there?" It was Aunt Flo in Minnesota, over two thousand miles away.

"*Help me!*" George screamed into the phone, and what came out was a tiny, hissing whistle, as if he had blown into a harmonica full of dead reeds.

Gramma tottered across the linoleum, holding her arms out for him. Her hands snapped shut and then open and then shut again. Gramma wanted her hug; she had been waiting for that hug for five years.

"Ruth, can you hear me? It's been storming here, it just started, and I... I got scared. Ruth, I can't hear you—"

"Gramma," George moaned into the telephone. Now she was almost upon him.

"George?" Aunt Flo's voice suddenly sharpened; became almost a shriek. "George, is that *you?*"

He began to back away from Gramma, and suddenly realized that he had stupidly backed away from the door and into the corner formed by the kitchen cabinets and the sink. The horror was complete. As her shadow fell over him, the paralysis broke and he screamed into the phone, screamed it over and over again: *"Gramma! Gramma! Gramma!"*

Gramma's cold hands touched his throat. Her muddy, ancient eyes locked on his, draining his will.

Faintly, dimly, as if across many years as well as many miles, he heard Aunt Flo say: "Tell her to lie down, George, Tell her to lie down and be still. Tell her she must do it in your name and the name of her father. The name of her taken father is *Hastur.* His name is power in her ear, George—tell her *Lie down in the Name of Hastur—tell her—*"

The old, wrinkled hand tore the telephone from George's nerveless grip. There was a taut pop as the cord pulled out of the phone. George collapsed in the corner and Gramma bent down, a huge heap of flesh above him, blotting out the light.

George screamed: *"Lie down! Be still! Hastur's name! Hastur! Lie down! Be still!"*

Her hands closed around his neck—

"You gotta do it! Aunt Flo said you did! In *my* name! In your *Father's* name! Lie down! Be sti—"

—and squeezed.

When the lights finally splashed into the driveway an hour later, George was sitting at the table in front of his unread history book. He got up and walked to the back door and opened it. To his left, the Princess phone hung in its cradle, its useless cord looped around it.

His mother came in, a leaf clinging to the collar of her coat. "Such a wind," she said. "Was everything all —George? *George, what happened?*"

The blood fell from Mom's face in a single, shocked rush, turning her a horrible clown-white.

"Gramma," he said. "Gramma died. Gramma died, Mommy." And he began to cry.

She swept him into her arms and then staggered back against the wall, as if this act of hugging had robbed the last of her strength. "Did... did anything happen?" she asked. *"George, did anything else happen?"*

"The wind knocked a tree branch through her window," George said.

She pushed him away, looked at his shocked, slack face for a moment, and then stumbled into Gramma's room. She was in there for perhaps four minutes. When she came back, she was holding a red tatter of cloth. It was a bit of George's shirt.

"I took this out of her hand," Mom whispered.

"I don't want to talk about it," George said. "Call Aunt Flo, if you want. I'm tired. I want to go to bed."

She made as if to stop him, but didn't. He went up to the room he shared with Buddy and opened the hot-air register so he could hear what his mother did next. She wasn't going to talk to Aunt Flo, not tonight, because the telephone cord had pulled out; not tomorrow, because shortly before Mom had come home, George had spoken a short series of words, some of them bastardized Latin, some only pre-Druidic grunts, and over two thousand miles away Aunt Flo had dropped dead of a massive brain hemorrhage. It was amazing how those words came back. How *everything* came back.

George undressed and lay down naked on his bed. He put his hands behind his head and looked up into the darkness. Slowly, slowly, a sunken and rather horrible grin surfaced on his face.

Things were going to be different around here from now on.

Very different.

Buddy, for instance. George could hardly wait until Buddy came home from the hospital and started in with the Spoon Torture of the Heathen Chinee or an Indian Rope Burn or something like that. George supposed he would have to let Buddy get away with it —at least in the daytime, when people could see—but when night came and they were alone in this room, in the dark, with the door closed...

George began to laugh soundlessly.

As Buddy always said, it was going to be a Classic.

X

WHAT YOU BELIEVE

BY JG FAHERTY

WHAT YOU BELIEVE

BY JG FAHERTY

Molly Campbell let out a gasp as she saw the corpse's face.

Black, empty slits stared up at her from the casket. The corpse's eyelids had rolled up part way. Not all the way. Just a tiny bit. But it was enough.

They were open.

If a dead person's eyes are left open, they'll find someone to bring with them to the other side.

On the heels of that came another thought: *On Samhain, the spirits of the dead can walk among us.*

Lord have mercy. A wake on Halloween, bad enough. And now the eyes... an open invitation for something to get out.

Or get in.

Molly crossed herself, murmured a quick "Amen" and hurried away from the casket. She wanted to shout for someone to do something, warn them of the danger. But they wouldn't understand. Instead, she set off in search of Scott. Maybe she could make him listen, get him to do something before it was too late.

"I think he's in Uncle Ted's office," Scott's mother

told her.

Molly didn't hesitate. Grammy Shaila's long list of admonitions about death rang in her head as she pushed her way through the crowded parlor. Viewing him on Halloween? What had Scott's family been thinking? And why hadn't someone checked the eyes?

I told them this was a bad idea. No one should be near the body, not tonight.

"Scott?" She knocked once and then entered the funeral director's office.

"Molly?" Her fiancé turned away from inspecting himself in the mirror and gave her a grin. "Just in time. I need your help." He flapped his half-knotted tie at her.

"Scott, you've got to do something. His eyes are open."

"What are you talking about?"

"Cousin Tommy. Something's gonna happen for sure if you don't fix it right away."

Scott raised an eyebrow. "I know he was a real bastard, but I doubt he's come back from the dead."

"It's bad luck. Especially today. His spirit... he could..."

The last of Scott's smile faded away and his normally thin lips tightened even further. He turned back to the mirror, started working on the tie.

"I should have guessed. Another of your superstitions?"

"Yes, but..."

"But what? Want me to go out there, tell my uncle he should fix Tommy's eyes in the middle of a wake? Get real. It's the twenty-first century." He stepped back to view himself.

Molly shook her head. As usual, he'd done an awful job. "Let me."

She got on her toes behind him and re-tied the knot. In contrast to Scott's rugged, weather-tanned face, brown eyes, and tousled hair, her pale appearance seemed almost ghostly. Despite being fourth-generation Tennessee born and bred, there was no mistaking her Scotch-Irish roots, thanks to a corona of red curls and her freckled cheeks

"Not Irish, Welsh, you silly thing," she could almost hear her grandmother say. *"Our clan came here 'afore Columbus' grandsires ever laid eyes on each other and you should be proud of that."*

Those roots went much deeper than flesh, thanks to an extremely old-fashioned extended family still led by Grammy Shaila, who dispensed advice with equal parts frequency and acerbity, no matter if people asked or not.

"Thanks, hon." Scott gave her that half grin she loved so much. "Sorry I snapped. Just been a bad day, you know?"

"That's okay. I guess I went overboard." She stopped as a sudden thought hit her. "Doesn't your uncle live upstairs?"

"Yeah? So what?"

"The mirrors! He left them all uncovered while there's a dead body in the house." She looked around for something to place over the rectangle of glass.

"Molly, ease up." Scott placed a gentle hand on her shoulder. "You're being ridiculous."

"If you look in a mirror while there's a corpse in the

house, you'll be the next one to die," she said, but it was Grammy Shaila's voice she heard in her head.

"Oh, for Pete's sake. There's *always* a dead body here—it's a funeral home. Uncle Ted would have died a hundred times over by now. That just shows how silly those superstitions are."

"But did he ever have one here on Halloween? It's different. Everyone knows that on Samhain the spirits can—"

"The spirits can kiss my ass. Now, let it go, okay?" He gave her a smile to take the sting out of his words. "C'mon. It's time to go act like anyone gave a damn about Tommy when he was alive."

Molly gnawed at her lip as she let Scott lead her out to the parlor. He had a way of crushing her beliefs under the weight of common sense. And it did seem like Ted would have been the first one to die—years ago—if the mirror thing was true. As for Halloween... he'd been in business almost thirty years. Surely this couldn't be the first time there'd been a dead body in the building on Samhain night.

But as they mingled with relatives and friends at the wake, Grammy Shaila's voice kept returning.

Superstitions are just truths that ignorant folk don't believe in 'til it's too late.

The day of Tommy McCloud's funeral started badly for Molly and grew progressively worse.

They'd come out of their apartment the morning after the wake to find six fat crows sitting on Scott's truck. The past two days had been awful for her;

everywhere she looked, she saw harbingers of evil. And now this. Scott was already on edge because of the funeral, so she did her best not to overreact at the sight of the birds.

Scott wasn't fooled. He gave her one of his 'looks' before shooing them away. They'd taken off with raucous, laughing cries that remained in her head all the way to the cemetery.

Six crows. A sure sign of death. That's why they call a flock of crows a murder.

Scott stayed silent the entire drive, and Molly did the same, not wanting to risk an argument. But things came to a head when they arrived at Whispering Hills and she refused to get out of the car. Scott's face grew red and he leaned his head on the roof of the car before leaning in to ask why.

"I can't. Don't you see that dog?" She pointed out the back window. A few yards away, a nondescript black dog sat by the side of the roadway, tongue lolling, staring at their car.

"That mutt? What about it? It's probably the caretaker's."

"Being followed by a black dog is bad luck." She knew how lame it sounded but the words, handed down from grandmother to mother to daughter, still held power.

"Oh, for... Can we stop with the old wives' tales for one day? I just want to get this over with and go home." He got out and headed for the gravesite, not even bothering to wait for her.

She gritted her teeth and managed to keep silent when the dog followed them down the path, but her stomach twisted and churned until the dog finally wandered off.

Throughout the funeral, Molly kept an eye out for any other signs of bad luck. It seemed like there were more spirits than usual lurking in the shadows and peering out from behind gravestones—to be expected with the veil between the worlds at its thinnest—but none of them acted overtly menacing. Even the black dog remained pleasantly absent. By the time the ceremony ended, she'd relaxed enough to hold Scott's hand on the way back to the car.

By then, the melancholy whispers of the spirits didn't seem so bad. Certainly not as awful as Tommy's biker friends, standing around in their leather vests, reeking of beer and pot and making everyone uncomfortable just by their presence. She could almost believe she'd let her imagination get away from her. Nothing but coincidences and the usual presence of the dead. Maybe Scott had been right, they had nothing to worry about.

As they drove past the stone wall surrounding Whispering Hills, a sparrow flew into the windshield of the truck.

"Oh!" Molly let out the breath she'd been holding for protection.

It's bad luck to kill a sparrow. They carry the souls of the dead.

"Damn thing flew into us."

"Go see if it's dead."

"What?" Scott shook his head. "I'm not—"

"Please!"

"Fine." He gave an exasperated sigh and pulled over.

She didn't complain. She knew the day-actually, the whole week-had been bad for him, and the fact that he was willing to stop even though he just wanted to get home made her love him even more.

She rolled down her window, letting in chilly November air. "Is it dead?"

Faces peered over the cemetery's stone wall, translucent and wavering. Curious about the outside world? Or perhaps saddened by the interrupted departure of a fellow spirit? She was too far away to see their expressions clearly.

Scott stood up, blocking her view of the nebulous onlookers. He held the tiny body by one wing, wiggled it as proof of death, then tossed it unceremoniously into the weeds.

"Sorry, he's gone to sparrow heaven."

He got back into the truck and pulled away from the curb. As Molly rolled up her window, a dog bayed from deep in the cemetery.

A dog howling for no reason means unseen spirits are near.

"Oh, no," she whispered. She'd forgotten to hold her breath until they were past the cemetery's boundary. She turned and looked back. Four spirits stared at her. The hairs on her arms rose up.

Try as she might, she couldn't remember if there'd been four or five originally.

Molly sprang up in bed, lips pressed tight to hold back a scream. Cold, clammy sweat covered her body and her heart pounded way too fast.

She looked over at Scott. His chest rose and fell in a slow, regular rhythm, unlike the stiff, motionless body she'd dreamed of. The graphic nightmare had been so real, driving a knife into Scott's stomach while he pleaded with her to let him live. When she pulled it out, a brown sparrow flew from the hole.

A warning from beyond? Or just her subconscious sorting through the stressful events of the day?

After the funeral, she'd tried to avoid thinking about the spirits at the graveyard, but her thoughts kept returning to her moment of carelessness.

Had she accidentally opened herself to one of them? And what if she had? Would she feel different if possessed by a ghost? Grammy Shaila could probably tell her. First thing tomorrow she'd stop by and ask.

Decision made, she closed her eyes, thinking she might be able to sleep.

Somewhere in the distance, the mournful cry of a rooster sounded three times.

A rooster's crow between midnight and dawn brings misfortune.

Sleep remained elusive for the rest of the night, leaving Molly staring at the ceiling in a cold sweat, wondering what troubles the next day would deliver.

"Gram, I don't know what to do. Scott don't believe in the old ways, thinks I'm a fool 'cause I do. And now I'm afraid there might be somethin' inside me that don't belong there."

Molly felt her control slipping and hated herself for it. All day she'd been dropping things and losing her place during the simplest of tasks, sure signs she'd reached her breaking point. Even her voice showed it, the way she'd fallen back into the country dialect of her childhood, which only happened in moments of extreme stress.

Shaila Campbell clucked her tongue. "Get hold of yerself, girl. You ain't doin' yerself no favors flying off the handle."

"But the signs! I've never seen so many. Death, misfortune, possession. This morning Scott knocked over the salt and pepper shakers—"

"Drop 'em both, bad luck be doubled."

"And when I said he should be careful at work, he told me to 'stop with the hillbilly bullshit.' He's never talked to me like that before. I'm afraid I might be drivin' him away, but I can't help myself."

Grammy Shaila's eyes narrowed. "Tell me about this dream you had."

"It was horrible. Scott tried to kill me. Then he was saying he was sorry, it wasn't his fault, but it was too late, I already stuck a knife in his belly." Molly shivered and hugged herself. "I ain't never had a dream so real."

"Eh, don't be all surprised and what, my dear. All us Campbell womenfolk has the gift of dead speak. 'Cept your mama, God rest her soul. Mayhaps you're a dream-seer as well."

"You mean I'm really gonna kill Scott?" The very thought set her heart racing and her stomach churning.

"Dreams is funny things. Sometimes their meanings are clear as day, other times they're murkier than a river after a rainstorm. Could be yours is sayin' you're killing his love. Or..." she raised a gnarled, stick-thin finger, "maybe your lover ain't your lover at all."

"What do you mean?" Molly tried to hide her frustration. Speaking with Shaila often led to confusion; part and parcel of dealing with someone who'd been born in another century.

"A great sin can enter through a small door."

"Grammy, I don't have time for riddles. I want to get back before Scott gets home."

"Ah, young 'ns today. No patience. I'm only saying, be careful. Samhain's a dangerous time."

"Samhain's over and done. Why—"

"Don't be a fool! Listen to your *nain*, now. I know what I speak of. Samhain ain't just one night. The old clans measured it in days, not hours. What you call Hallowe'en might be the time we choose to honor our gods, but in the olden days folks knew better. The veil is weak before and after. And the *Aos Sí* can move freely any of those nights. They'll take advantage if you let them."

"So you think I'm right, then? A spirit's got into me?" Molly bit her lip. What would she do? How did one drive out a spirit?

"You? No, child, I doubt that. Maybe not in no one. I'm only saying it's just best if you keep a sharp eye now and after, and come see me if things seem amiss."

With a short nod of her head, Grammy Shaila faded back into her grave, her wispy red hair and sunken blue eyes the last things to disappear.

Molly left Whispering Hills with her thoughts whirling worse than when she'd arrived. Was she just imagining things, or was something hiding inside her?

Or in someone else?

By the time she got home from the cemetery, Molly had decided to put her fears aside and make up to Scott for being so out of sorts the past few days. She spent the rest of the afternoon preparing his favorite dinner, her way of apologizing. She lit candles throughout the house, dimmed the lights, and opened a bottle of his favorite wine.

The moment he walked in the door, her world died.

From the kitchen, she had a clear view of the living room. As Scott passed through, the yellow-orange of each flame shifted to an ice-cold, pale blue in his wake.

If a candle's flame suddenly turns blue, there's a ghost nearby.

Cold truth hit her belly like a fist. Grammy Shaila had been right. It wasn't *her* who'd been possessed at the cemetery.

"Don't come any closer." Molly held up the knife she'd been using, hoping the low light would hide her shaking hand. Memories of her nightmare rushed back. This was it. She was going to have to kill him. Kill *Scott.*

Scott glanced at the candles. His eyes were emotionless voids, frosty companions to the cool azure of the flames. The corner of his mouth twitched up.

"Not bad, Molly. Guess Cousin Scott finally found himself a chick with brains." He walked toward her. "Let's you and me go for a drive. I met a girl on the other side who needs a new home. Told her I knew just the body."

Tommy. I should have guessed.

"Get away!" Molly swung the knife as she backed up.

Scott/Tommy grabbed her wrist and twisted it. The knife fell to the floor. "Nice try. But you're comin' with me."

"Let go!" She slapped his face with her free hand.

"Stupid bitch. I ain't got time for games." He slammed her into the counter. The edge dug into her back and her breath exploded in a sharp gasp.

Something hard smashed into her mouth and the world went gray. Dazed, she had no strength to fight as picked her up and carried her out the door.

Outside, daylight had relinquished its hold on the sky. Streetlights illuminated empty sidewalks. Scott's truck sat in its usual spot, a chariot waiting to take her to her death.

Molly forced her protesting limbs to move, trying to squirm from his grasp.

"Keep still, dammit!" He held her tighter.

She moaned and struggled as he descended the front steps of their building. On the last step, he suddenly stumbled to his knees. There was a moment where she seemed suspended in mid-air. Then she hit the cold cement and stars exploded around her.

A streak of white flashed by, and she realized he must have tripped over Mrs. Henderson's cat, who liked to nap on the stairs.

A white cat means good luck.

Using a parking meter for support, Molly pulled

herself to her feet and ran into the road. A car raced past, its angry horn shouting a warning. She caught a glimpse of the driver's face, eyes wide as saucers.

"Molly!" Scott/Tommy charged around the front of his truck. "Don't make this harder!"

She reached the other sidewalk and stopped. Where could she go? The neighborhood was too safe to have a cop walking the streets, and there were no stores nearby.

Another horn sounded, a deeper, bellowing honk. She turned around in time to see her fiancé frozen in the headlights of a delivery truck.

"Scott!"

The headlights cast a glowing circle around him. Moments before the impact, a wispy face appeared over his head, Cousin Tommy's hard features contorted in a mask of fury.

Then the truck was past, taking Scott's body with it.

"What did you tell the police, dear?" Grammy Shaila patted an ethereal hand on Molly's knee.

Although there was no sense of contact, the comfort behind it still came through, and Molly appreciated the gesture.

"Well, I sure couldn't say he'd been possessed, so I told them somebody broke in. He and Scott fought, and then we ran outside and the truck hit him."

"That's good. No sense having people think bad of your man."

Molly rose. "I have to go to the wake now. But we'll see you real soon." She started back toward the path.

"*We?* Molly, wait."

Ignoring her grandmother's voice, Molly kept walking.

Molly arrived at the funeral home thirty minutes before the second viewing. Dozens of wreaths and bouquets filled the small room. Scott's silver-colored casket lay amid the colorful arrangements, a piece of modern art in a tropical jungle. She shut the door behind her and hurried to the coffin, knelt down by Scott's waxen, artificially calm face.

Taking a deep breath of the cloying air, she grasped one eyelid between two fingers and lifted it, separating the lid from the plastic cap Uncle Ken had used to keep the eye closed. She repositioned the eyelid and pressed down on it, so it caught on the cap's ridges. Then she repeated the process on the other eye.

Now they were both open a fraction of an inch.

"I love you, Scott," she whispered. "Wait for me by the south wall."

She kissed his hard lips. A tear fell onto his cheek, and she patted it away, careful not to smudge the rouge.

Behind her, the door opened. "Molly, people are starting to arrive."

She nodded. "Thank you. I'm going to freshen up real quick."

In the bathroom, Molly dabbed on some lipstick and then regarded herself in the mirror.

Somewhere outside, a dog howled, and another joined in.

She glanced at her watch. Seven o'clock. It had been dark for at least twenty minutes.

Dogs howling in the night, howl for death before daylight.

Molly smiled and put her makeup away.

Time to say goodbye.

For now.   X

THE MAN WHO HATED FOLEY

BY JOHN PEYTON COOKE

THE MAN WHO HATED FOLEY

FOLEY

BY JOHN PEYTON COOKE

"Hyperacusis," said Doctor Sipple. "Ear pain caused by a heightened sensitivity to various frequencies. A collapsed tolerance for what the rest of us take for granted as the background noise of daily life."

"But I don't have ear pain," Rick protested. "Not really. You're damned right about my tolerance. My tolerance for just about everything has definitely collapsed."

"On a scale of one to ten, how much do you feel it's impacting your life?"

"You shouldn't say 'impacting'," Rick said, and instantly regretted himself shifting into schoolmarm mode, but he couldn't stop himself. "I mean, not as a verb. It's a lousy verb. You should say 'having an impact on' and yes, it is."

"On a scale of one to ten," Doctor Sipple repeated, pencil raised above his aluminum clipboard, grey eyes poised upon his note-to-be.

"Are we talking about the real world, or the movies?"

Doctor Sipple raised his eyebrows. "Real world."

"The real world's probably a five or a six."

"Which is it, a five or a six?"

"Let's say a six. But the movies are a nine or a ten."

"Maybe you should stop."

"Excuse me?"

"Stop going to the movies."

"I'm a movie critic, doc. I thought I mentioned that."

"So you did. Perhaps you can try earplugs? Dampen the volume?"

"Volume's not the problem." Rick wasn't entirely getting through to him. "It's the sound design, the sound effects, the Foley work."

"Right." Sipple shook his head. "I'm referring you to a specialist."

And with that Doctor Sipple scribbled out the name of an otorhinolaryngologist at a nearby clinic, handed the scrap to Rick, and clicked the end of his retractable ballpoint pen, thus signaling the end of the discussion.

The pen click so annoyed Rick that he was grateful to Doctor Sipple for prematurely concluding the consult. It was clear he was going to get nowhere with Sipple and would have to start all over with this Doctor Rhyndelboume, or whatever name this was so childishly scrawled in such a sickeningly slanted script.

Rick had loved the cinema all his life, but recently this had begun to change. He pinpointed it to the day when he sat there in the local critics' screening room staring up at the giant visage of Beryl Staines playing a villainess smoking a long cigarette. When she took a drag, the tobacco crackled at a rather high decibel level. The crackling drew elaborate attention to itself. It seemed to say, "Look how clever we are, how we inserted this sound effect to give you, the viewer, this incredible auditory perception that you are right there in the room with Beryl Staines playing the role of Helga Moffat as Helga puffs away with her dry, crackling tobacco." And then after one more line of dialogue, she was at it again, crackling and crackling with every puff.

Rick was thrown out of the movie's previously magical spell. It was as distracting as if someone's phone had vibrated next to him. He found himself simply sitting in a darkened room with a bunch of strangers, staring up at an actress playing a part and not very convincingly, because the Foley artist had made a stick of tobacco crackle twenty times louder than one would ever encounter it in real life, unless one were to be two centimeters away from it. He was unable to enjoy the rest of the film and couldn't bear to come back and watch it again the next day, though he forced himself to do so, because he owed his editor a review and the deadline was upon him. The second viewing was no better, and was in fact worse, as Rick noticed all the Foley effects from the very start and waited in dread of the upcoming cigarette scene. Not exactly the type of suspense the director had intended.

On his next appointment at the screening room, to see a classy new British import called *Sanderton,* the trouble started with water being poured from a pitcher. Miss Lucy Darley, played by the young up-and-comer

Mamie Maddox, found herself alone in her nineteenth-century bedchamber and poured some water out from an enameled pitcher into the basin on her dresser. The sound of the water pouring and trickling from the pitcher, then of Miss Lucy splashing about as she scooped handfuls of it onto her face, then of her shaking off the last noisy droplets and reaching for a stiff linen rag and wiping her hands scruffily against the coarse fabric, sent Rick spiraling back out of the movie and into his uncomfortable seat. Throughout the rest of the film, he missed most of the dialogue and plot, as his ears were bombarded with the sounds of creaky floorboards, clopping footsteps, bed linens being shifted about, drapes being drawn, horses' hooves squelching in the mud, handbrakes being yanked on carriages, a lover's caress across a layer of taffeta, lips smacking, long hair being brushed out by a servant at the lady's dressing table, candle wicks being snuffed, gas lanterns being turned up, coalfires smoldering, roast goose being carved up, cutlery clinking against china, dinner guests gulping claret, various characters sighing and belching heavily, pipe tobacco crackling, whiskey being poured from a decanter, a dog scratching his ruff, a cat padding across the Persian rug, the skittering of a beetle across a floorboard, the creaking of a leather chair as a portly old uncle sat squarely upon it...

No, this was not ear pain. But it was indeed a nine or a ten on the impact scale. When Rick was finished with *Sanderton*, he had no idea what he had seen. He begged his editor to assign the review to someone else, along with reviews of a few other new releases, and took a couple of sick days to stay at home and lie in with a book.

"Earbuds?" asked Doctor Rhyndelboume, two months later, which was the earliest Rick had been permitted to meet this esteemed specialist. Rick liked him, if only because his rubbery face and wild shock of grey hair reminded Rick of silent-movie actor Emil Jannings, who no one in the world but Rick was likely to remember nowadays.

In the time between Sipple and Rhyndelboume, his issues had worsened. It wasn't only the sound effects in the cinema that annoyed him; increasingly it was the noises in the world outside. One might think it would be the sirens, honking, and car alarms, but no, it was the little things. The women walking behind him talking nonstop about the most banal subjects... he would actually stop and pretend to look at his watch to let them pass. The barista at a café scooping a mountain of ice cubes into a plastic venti cup. The bursts of steam and the drowning, gurgling sound of milk being frothed for a latte-in-progress. The electronic groan of an automatic door opening at the pharmacy. The high-pitched beep of the supermarket barcode scanner. The clip-clop of a lady in heels speeding up behind him on the sidewalk. The incessant jabbering of everyone speaking into their cellphones and headsets as if they were schizophrenics talking to themselves.

"Pardon me?" It wasn't that Rick was hard of hearing, naturally, but he didn't quite comprehend the intent of the question.

"Earbuds. Do you listen to music very often on earbuds?"

"Of course," Rick said. "Music, movies. No audiobooks. No podcasts." No, not for Rick, he was a bit of a snob, and if he were listening to anything, it would be a Shostakovich symphony or a Bernard Herrmann movie score.

"Well, it's hardly relevant what you listen to. At what volume, would you say?"

"Max. Listen, I'm sure there's bound to be a danger associated with that. I am getting older. I take it for granted I might suffer some hearing loss. But I've always assumed *that* was the danger from earbuds, not hyperacuteness."

"Hyperacusis. Let's think about what we can do, ways to help you avoid these painful noises."

"They're not painful, I keep telling you. Just annoying."

"And that's why you need to find strategies to avoid them."

"I don't see how. It's a part of my job. Trying to avoid a sound effect at the movies is like trying to avoid a trite cliché. My whole life has been devoted to movies. I'm watching movies nearly every day, in small screening rooms with massive sound systems. But so much these days is on the small screens, and I do use my earbuds a lot for privacy. I might be in a coffee shop or on the subway."

"I'd recommend you cut your usual volume by half."

"I hear you," said Rick, "to coin a phrase! But where's the enjoyment in that?"

"You may have to temper your hedonism if you want to return to normal hearing."

"Hedonism?" Rick repeated. Was Doctor Rhyndleboume judging him? But he let it slide. "Is it *possible* to return to normal?"

Doctor Rhyndleboum shrugged. "Possible? Anything is possible. The brain is a funny thing."

"Brain? We're talking about my ears."

"Your ears function much as they always have, I am sure. I can see no structural issues. The problem is how your brain is interpreting the input. It's possible you may be able to retrain it."

"How likely?"

"As I said, it's possible."

"So not very likely."

"Possible."

"That is not exactly reassuring."

Rick thought about it. He could continue to be a stubborn ass and insist on behaving as before, or he could take the good doctor's advice and alter his ways, and perhaps have the chance to return to those halcyon days when every noise came and went as a matter of course.

"OK, I'll cut the volume to half. What else do you recommend?"

"Noise-cancelling headphones. The kind that fully encase your ears. Just put them on, flip the switch, don't listen to any music or movies, just spend some quality time each day in complete silence."

"How much time?"

"A few hours each day. Use them as you walk outside. Use them at home. Sleep in them, if they're comfortable enough."

"I'll do that," Rick affirmed. He was determined to take some action to halt his downward slide. "Even though I'll feel like an utter geek walking around the city with headphones on my head."

"Everyone else is doing it." The doctor shrugged again. "No one will give it a second thought."

"But what about my job?"

"I'm not saying to use them twenty-four hours a day. Just to give yourself a timeout. You may find it modulates your aural responses."

"What else do you recommend?"

"You could also consider going on a mild antidepressant."

"Not ready for that. I may be annoyed, doc, but I'm not suicidal."

At first, Rick found that using the noise-cancelling headphones helped, especially at home in his apartment. He could drink tea again, as the whole ritual of filling the tea kettle from the faucet, letting the water boil and whistle on the stove, shutting off the gas flame, and pouring the water into the teapot was so much more pleasant in complete silence. Then waiting quietly for five minutes as it steeped, pouring it out into the teacup, and taking that first tentative sip over the rim—all of which would have been gratingly audible under normal conditions. How wonderful it was to enjoy a cup of tea without the odious sounds of himself puttering about!

He stared out the window of his fifth-floor walkup, sipping his tea, gazing out over the treetops, leaves rustling gently in the wind, birds flitting to and fro, a kid on a skateboard tearing up the sidewalk far below, a delivery driver zooming past insanely fast on a scooter. All of it in blessed silence.

Rick lived alone and always had. He had tried dating various persons over the years, but since his college days he had always had a litmus test when it came to a prospective mate: they had to love Kubrick's *Barry Lyndon*. A date who sighed or squirmed or looked at their watch during a revival of *Barry Lyndon* was an immediate reject not worthy of an after-movie drink, much less a second date. One who sat through it to the end and then said they "liked" it or that "it was okay" was cause to end the after-movie drink and go home alone. Only a total *Barry Lyndon* enthusiast could possibly have a chance for a future with Rick, and the slim number of those had run up against other litmuses after having passed the *Barry Lyndon* one. There was the *8½* test, the *Lawrence of Arabia* test, the *What's Up Doc* test, the *Greed* test, the *Miracle of Morgan's Creek* test, the *Touch of Evil* test, and the *Vertigo* test. That no one had passed the full array could hardly be ascribed to any fault of Rick's.

His relationships, rather, were with the stars. And while he could be said to be an "old movie" buff, he had also loved modern cinema until the last decade or so, when the sound design started to get out of control. Moviemakers now took sound to the extreme, for no rational reason other than that they could. They depended on the accuracy of digital sound reproduction to push the limits. They assumed that an audience trapped in a stadium-seating movie theater with full-on Dolby or THX would have no trouble catching every whispered word, every mumbled chat, every breathy speech. But Rick often had to rewatch these movies on Blu-Ray at home with the subtitles turned on to find out what the characters were saying. And this had spilled over onto the small screen, even the TV commercials. So that now, at the height of his latest crisis of hyperacuity, while Rick was watching TV lazily at home with his tea mug at hand and without his noise-cancelling headphones on, onto the screen pops a commercial for an organic beer in which the young woman pitching the beer whispers every word of her script, then proceeds to pour the bubbly, fizzy drink ever-so-slowly out of the bottle with a wicked grin on her face, with the sounds of the pouring amplified louder than her hideous whispers.

Rick stood up and screamed at the TV, knocking over his tea: "*Stop it! Stop it!*"

He found himself in a state, shivering and sweating. He heard the sound of his spilled tea getting sucked into his carpet—one Foley effect he had never encountered before. He was about to turn off the TV, but the commercial was mercifully short. He sat back down and told himself to be calm.

The next commercial was not much better, for a certain grind of coffee, from a director clearly enamored with the new trend of micro-quick edits accompanied by lightning-flash sound effects: ripping open the vaccuum pack with a whoosh, tumbling out the coffee beans into the grinder, pulse-grinding the beans from the bird's-eye view, spilling them out into a French press, pouring the boiling water, stirring vigorously, pouring it tricklingly into a coffee mug, up to the actor's mouth and a big slurpy sip, and a quick shot of the actor's eye becoming dilated with pleasure (though nonsensical). Rick blamed *Requiem for a Dream.*

He grabbed his remote and turned it off angrily, grabbed his noise-cancelling headphones, switched them on, and sat there on the sofa stewing, trying to get his heart to return to a normal resting rate. With the headphones on, he was sealed in silence and was able to get back to something like normal again in about ten minutes. He looked around for a book, picked up *Great Expectations*, and turned to the first page. He had never before read so many good books as when he started using his noise-cancelling headphones, and he was rather enjoying it... but nothing could replace a truly great film. Movies were his life, and he couldn't imagine a world without them.

His apartment buzzer vibrated via an app on his phone. He pressed the "speak" button and said, "Yes?" but there was nobody there. Probably today's FedEx delivery, but it would be five floors down with no elevator, so whatever it was could wait for now.

He had an appointment a few hours later at the local critics' screening room, to catch what amounted to a triple feature. On his way out of his building, he noted a package had been left on the sorting table for him. He would pick it up on his return, later. Looked like another package of complimentary Blu-Rays for preview. On the way to the screening, wearing his headphones, navigating the sidewalks and the subways, he kept hoping that his self-enforced silence therapy would indeed "modulate" his "aural responses" such that he might be able to tolerate today's showings.

On arrival, he nodded at his fellow critics, three in number, who all worked for competing media outlets. None of them were anything close to being extroverts, so this was not an unusual greeting on the part of any of them, and they each sat far removed from each other in the otherwise empty, stale-smelling, darkened old box of a room. He was doubly grateful that he was able to find a seat far away from Herbie Fleischer, who always wore the same cloying body spray and stinky hair gel. He had made the mistake of sitting behind him before.

The first film of the day was *Barnacle 2*, sequel to *Barnacle*, the surprise hit of three years ago starring Nevil Wilkins, a previously washed-up RADA-trained "serious actor" who had stumbled on box-office gold portraying rogue vigilante anti-hero Jake Barnacle. After failed attempts at spinning his *Barnacle* success into his other "serious" work, Wilkins was now back in front of the lens and with executive-producer credit on this big-budget sequel, which found Jake Barnacle once again trying to save a female family member (last time daughter, this time mother) from a gang of British-accented terrorists. The opening scene had Jake swirling a tumbler of Scotch with two tinkling ice cubes, filmed with a tight macro lens. He kicked back the last of the Scotch and set the glass down heavily, swirling the ice around. The noise of the cubes was all Rick could focus on during the scene, although Jake apparently was on the phone with his mother (pre-kidnapping) mumbling all kinds of incoherent mumble-twaddle while the cameraman did the shaky-cam thing for no good reason. When the ice cubes stopped their astonishing performance, we were already cutting to an airport scene and a suspicious-looking swarthy man in an ill-fitting suit clomping around a busy terminal, with chatter and PA announcements in the background, as he finds a quiet spot to sit down and pop open the clasps on his leather briefcase: amplified *pa-pow*! Looking around furtively and then noisily shuffling papers from inside the case, selecting one page and creasing it with a *flittttt* sound before placing it in his inner breast pocket, where it scrapes past the scratchy woolen fabric before disappearing from sight. Cut to elsewhere in the airport, where Jake Barnacle and his mother are buying lattes at Starbucks (frothy noises), when the sound of machine-gun fire rings out...

Rick took his noise-cancelling headphones out of his backpack, placed them over his ears, and turned on the switch. He watched the rest of *Barnacle 2* as a silent movie, interpolating his own intertitles for what was extremely predictable dialogue, for the quiet scenes and likely inappropriate wisecracks in between the car chases, plane crashes, car explosions, gang-style executions, surprise-betrayal-stabbings, runaway elevators, and the final climactic scene when Barnacle's mother (played inexplicably by Beryl

Staines) having been freed by her "Barnacle-I-thought-you-were-dead" son gets to turn on the cowardly terrorist leader and call him a "son-of-a-bitch" (Rick's lip-reading) before shooting him full in the face with a 9mm Glock her son had deftly thrown her. If anything, Rick found that deleting the sound from this motion picture probably made him enjoy it more. As he sat through the closing credits, he wondered at the list of fifty or more sound engineers, Foley artists, sound effects editors, and dialogue loopers who had slaved over this garbage. Were any of them really needed? What was the point of all this high-tech, multimillion-dollar noise, when the end-product plainly sucked?

After a bio break, the critics all came back to the screening room for film number two, some comic-book adaptation about a superhero Rick had never heard of. He kept his headphones off in an attempt to see if his hearing might have been tempered by watching the previous one in silence. Although he kept them in his lap at the ready, just in case. As usual, he found that the volume was not the issue. His ears were not in pain. He could tolerate the overall noise. It was when the individual audio components stood out that he wanted to climb the walls. This superhero had a habit of cracking his knuckles before a fight, and the Foley artist had amped up the knuckle-cracking to ten times louder than was humanly possible. The fight sounds, the squishings and squelchings and slammings, the groans and the grit and the gnashing of teeth, the whooshing through the air, the electrostatic buzzing of the superhero's superpowers, the clinging and clunking and clanging as he and the villain careened from skyscraper to skyscraper, smashing windows, bending flagpoles, throwing I-beams, slinging manhole covers...

Rick was using his willpower to try to keep the headphones at bay. The movie was an intolerable mess. The sound effects were driving his face into a rictus-like expression, as if he were battling 4x G-forces, and he was sliding upwards along the back of his stadium chair, tucking his knees beneath his chin as his feet found purchase on the seat cushion. Finally, for the last twenty minutes of the film, he could resist no more and threw the headphones over his ears. He began to calm down at once, though in his mind he could still imagine all the noises his ears would have been hearing. By the end credits, Rick was drenched in a pool of sweat. He had taken no notes and was unsure how he would be expected to write a review. He couldn't even remember the name of the superhero or the title of the movie itself without referring to the promotional materials.

"You all right?" Herbie Fleischer asked him during the next break. He withdrew a whisky flask from his pocket and said, "Here."

Rick grabbed the flask and was grateful for a swig, feeling himself as macho as Jake Barnacle as he knocked it down his gullet.

"Thanks."

"You look a fright," said Herbie in his affected faux-British pseudo-accent. Rick was thankful that the whisky on his tongue somewhat covered up the odor of Herbie's trendy body spray.

"I guess I can't handle these comic-book movies anymore."

"Occupational hazard."

"No, I really can't."

"Maybe *Sanderton* is more your style."

The blinking red light told them it was time to go back inside.

Rick couldn't bring himself to tell Herbie that *Sanderton* had been just as annoying. If he were honest with himself, he would soon have to face the fact that all of his own future movie reviews were going to read like that: "Annoying. Annoying. Annoying. Annoying. *Annoying. Annoying.* ANNOYING."

The third film of the afternoon was some indie flick called *Enigmas of Cleveland* about a young woman returning home after dropping out from college, and the crazy love-hate relationship between her and her mother, and all the crazy siblings, aunts, uncles, and grannies. Rick could somewhat tolerate all the shouting. But the film was filled with extended scenes of Instagram-inspired cinematography—gritty scenes of post-industrial Cleveland in the warm glow of sunset or the dim blue of twilight. The moments of absolute quiet were compelling and enjoyable. Except the quiet was never absolute. Before you knew it, the heroine was walking alone through the detritus (followed everywhere by a shaky-cam), climbing over crumbling piles of concrete, knocking over stray rebar, smashing old beer bottles, taking out a joint and lighting it up with a *crackle-crackle-crackle* and exhaling the putrid smoke with a highly audible exhalation. Wind whooshing through the weeds. Some dude walking up to her out of nowhere and saying "Hey," and she passes him the joint so he can engage in some crackling and heavy breathing of his own. Mumbly, whispery dialogue Rick would never get to know, because there was no chance in hell he would ever watch this turkey again on Blu-Ray with subtitles. Life was too short.

He was proud of himself for sitting through all eight-eight minutes of *Enigmas of Cleveland* without resorting to his headphones. But he did wear them with all the noise in the world switched off for his journey home, where, instead of writing up a single review, he sat down for one minute and typed out an email to his editor, saying, "I quit!"

After that, he took a hot soaking bath, trying to keep his ears below the waterline while keeping his nose above it. He felt this was the closest approximation he could find in nature to having no ears at all. This required keeping the water perfectly still. He lay there as still as a rock, like a predator awaiting his prey, arms akimbo and floating like dead weight. When he could stand this position no longer, he sat up in the tub, dried off his head, and put his headphones on for the remainder of the bath.

The box he had picked up from the vestibule now lay on his kitchenette table. Wrapped in his bath towel, Rick glanced at it and ripped it open. In it were three new Blu-Rays from Warner Brothers—*Mildred Pierce, The Letter,* and *Casablanca*—"remastered in

4K," with "rerecorded music soundtrack" and "re-engineered sound design."

"I quit, I quit, I quit," he said to himself.

He threw the Blu-Rays straight into the trash. Then out of curiosity he glanced through the promo mats the studio had sent along, with quotes from young executives about their new strategy to *redo our whole library for today's demanding viewers... We start this quest for perfection by presenting three of our perennial favorites, now with pristine digital visual reproduction to rival an old nitrate print, with state-of-the art sound effects replacing the primitive radio-show quality of yesteryear, and newly rerecorded musical scores to capture these masterpieces of composition the way Max Steiner intended them to be heard.*

Rick was highly doubtful of this scheme, but the perverse side of his brain wanted to know how completely the studio might have ruined what he considered to be unrivaled masterpieces of the cinematic art. So he delved back into the trash bin, scraped the coffee grounds off the plastic cases, and considered which one he should sample. Why not go for broke: *Casablanca.*

He switched into a terrycloth bathrobe and sat down to watch, connecting his Bluetooth noise-cancelling headset to his sound system to block out all outside disturbances, though he was cautious to temper the volume at least a tad, out of deference to Doctor Rhyndelboume.

It started out okay. The rerecorded score with its echoes of "La Marseillaise" may have eliminated the limitations of monaural analog, but replaced it with inferior modern-day studio musicians and a remix by some hotshot sound engineer that sounded unmistakably out of balance, heavy on the bass and too bright in the treble. The dialogue had clearly been remastered as well, with an odd effect of smoothing out the imperfections in the actors' voices, such that Humphrey Bogart's cigarette-scratchy timbre was replaced with a honey-smooth vocalization as if he had been put through an autotune, and Ingrid Bergman's vague European accent, though unmistakably in her own voice and from the original recording, had been homogenized and apparently made more palatable to "today's demanding viewers."

But the real crime was that the entire film had been re-Foleyed. Every sound effect had been replaced, and new ones added where none had been before. Whenever anyone sat up from a chair in Rick's Café, an elaborate explosion of chair-leg scooting erupted. Every lit cigarette crackled devilishly loud. The clicking of Nazi boot heels took over whenever the Nazis were moving about on screen. The incessant whirring of the ceiling fans provided a constant droning backdrop to the remixed and newly mumbly dialogue. The gunshots no longer had that old car-backfire quality but rang out like we were in *Saving Private Ryan*. And when Rick and Ilsa kissed, it was lingeringly wet and sloppy and smacky and gross.

Rick ejected it and flung it back into the bin, and considered the other two. He knew he could never watch them. He couldn't bring himself to do it. He could imagine what they were like, with newly rerecorded hand-slappings of mother and daughter in

Mildred, and cacophonous nighttime jungle noises from a real authentic tropical rainforest overtaking *The Letter*. He dumped them into the garbage, plastic wrap uncracked.

He felt trapped in his apartment. He got dressed and went out for a walk. He knew better than to remove his headphones now. He could no longer tolerate being outside without them on. All the little noises were killing him. It was so much better to stride around the city in perfect silence.

He knew, for example, what the sound of the bus braking at the bus stop would sound like. No need to hear it. He knew what sound that barking dog across the street was making. He knew how the front door to the little cupcake shop would squeal as he opened it. The young woman drumming her lacquered fingernails impatiently on the countertop as she dithered over which cupcake to buy—no need for Rick to subject himself to that! The *ka-ching* of the old-fashioned cash register as the fingernail girl was rung up. The clerk was clearly now asking him which cupcake he wanted. Rick pointed at the red velvet one, held up two fingers, and she knew right off what he wanted. Where was the need for any dialogue? He could make himself understood. He did not have to listen as she took out a little flattened box, opened it up and assembled it, tucked in the flaps, grabbed the skittery-sounding parchment paper, inserted the two cupcakes, folded the lid of the box, pulled a screeching stretch of cellophane tape from the dispenser, ripped it off, and slapped the tape across the closed box. No need to listen as she clearly asked whether he wanted a bag, and he nodded yes, and she flung open a paper bag with petite little handles and dropped his box into it.

As he left the cupcake shop, he began wondering whether his noise-cancelling headphones were working properly. As he came to think of it, he had actually heard all those noises in his head, or maybe he was imagining things. He wasn't sure. He tapped the headphones on both sides, as if this would make them behave. He wondered if the battery charge was running down. But he had been vigilant about that, no, it couldn't be that.

He stood there on the street corner and tried to figure out whether he was really hearing anything or if it was all in his imagination. There was a policeman at the intersection directing traffic and blowing a whistle. Surely Rick hadn't heard that. But he felt that he did. Women in high heels were clip-clopping across the intersection. A taxicab came to a sudden halt with a squeal of its brakes. The ice-cream truck was rolling down the street with its calliope music blaring.

It can't be, he thought. He risked it and pulled the headphones away from his ears. Yes, the calliope music was precisely the same as what he'd been hearing a moment ago, headphones or no. The battery light showed green and fully charged. The damn things just weren't working. But they were his security blanket, so he put them back on.

He needed to get back home to the safety of his apartment.

Walking home, he heard the sound of his own footfalls. He heard the birds in the trees. He heard the elderly lady who was sticking herself halfway out the window on the second story of a townhouse, yelling at a man on the front stoop for him to go get her some eggs. He could hear the wind that swirled through the leaves overhead. The booming bass from the car speakers of a BMW cruising by blasting hip-hop. The low whir of an electric scooter whizzing past with a bearded hipster balanced precariously on it.

He tried again removing the headphones to see if they just weren't working. Everything was louder without them and had a more realistic character, more surround-sound in nature, like real noise should be. Whenever he plopped the headphones back on his ears, he found he was still hearing things, but what he was hearing was more selective. He realized he was hearing whatever he was looking at, but nothing more.

The brain is a funny thing, Doctor Rhyndelboume had said.

Right, Rick thought, very funny. He realized his brain was providing all the sound effects he would ever need. It was a Foley library at his fingertips, to match up the right sound with whatever he saw, smelled, tasted, or touched. If he lost his hearing today, he realized, he would still never be without the appropriate effect.

It reminded him of one of the strangest paradoxes about the brain and the eyes: the pseudo-three-dimensional effect. He remembered first reading about it in the advice column of the old *TV Guide* digest... a reader had written in asking why, when watching television or a movie projecting in 2D, you could turn it into 3D by placing a hand over one eye and viewing it through monovision. The columnist confessed he never realized this was true, but that trying it out had convinced him of it. Rick himself had tried it out then, and repeated the experiment many times over the years. There was something in the brain that tried to correct for your lack of stereoscopic vision, if you were to cut off the input from one of your own eyes. Your brain wanted to turn your view of a 2D projection into a full 3D world. The longer you held your hand over your one eye, the more intense the effect became.

Rick figured this was the same thing happening with his hearing, though he wondered why him and presumably no one else. Maybe it was because of his lifetime of movie watching. He was armed with all the sound effects in the world. His brain was intent on deploying them.

"How is it going?" asked Doctor Rhyndelboume at his follow-up visit. Rick was wearing his headphones, but he could tell from his lip-reading what the doctor was saying.

"I want you to cut off my ears," Rick said.

"Pardon me?" the doctor mouthed.

"Just cut them off. I don't need them anymore."

He described his recent experiences, and his conclusion that his brain had already stored up all the noises he could ever want to hear. Therefore, what was the point of retaining his ears?

"Perhaps you want to keep them at least for esthetic reasons." Doctor Rhyndelboume was humoring him now.

"No," Rick said emphatically.

"You do realize cutting off your ears won't make you deaf. Not entirely."

"I don't care. I want them removed. You could perform the surgery, couldn't you? I realize it's an elective procedure, but I've got enough money in savings to handle it, I think."

Doctor Rhyndelboume glared admonishingly and said something Rick was unable to lip-read. Gingerly, Rick pried open his headphones just a tad.

"It goes against my Hippocratic oath. No doctor would do such a thing. At the very least, we would need a full psychiatric evaluation before it could even be considered, perhaps a long period of extended observation..."

"So you won't do it," Rick said.

There was a moment's hesitation, as Rhyndelboume was considering something arcane in his own head, before he said, "No, I'm sorry, Rick, I can't ever do such a thing."

"I'm sorry as well," said Rick. "I'm sorry to hear it."

And he put his headphones back on, swearing to himself that the doctor's refusal would be the last thing he ever heard, if he had anything to say about it.

He had set up a small operating theater in the bathroom of his apartment. A fifth of bourbon, a liter of vodka, some rubbing alcohol, a bottle of aspirin, some heavy-duty carpet thread, a panoply of upholstery needles, and a straight razor. He took alternating swigs of bourbon and vodka, staring straight into the mirror and thinking of Van Gogh.

If he *could do it...*

He tried to buck up his courage.

Rick was not too appalled by gore. He was one of the few mainstream critics who enjoyed a good horror movie. The wizards who created extreme makeup effects had come up with so many convincing ways of making you think you were watching someone get their head split open, their heart pierced with an arrow, their limbs chopped off... as long as you reminded yourself it was "only a special effect" it was quite easy to trick your brain into stifling its normal human visceral revulsion.

Just keep telling yourself, it's only a movie!

Rick stared at himself and held the straight razor above his right ear. He saw he was breathing heavily, chest heaving, sweat pouring off his brow. He set the razor down and drank more vodka. Then he poured some rubbing alcohol over his ear, as prep.

He tried another psychological trick he had used many times in the past, such as when he had his wisdom teeth pulled. *This is the only time in your life this is ever going to happen to you, so you might as well just lie back and enjoy it.*

What he was mostly concerned about was passing out and bleeding to death on the floor of his bathroom. He wasn't suicidal. He only wanted to get rid of his ears. He would have to remain awake after severing his right, so he could stitch everything up and do his left.

Van Gogh, Van Gogh, Van Gogh, he thought to himself, and tried to visualize Kirk Douglas in Lust for Life.

He held the straight razor again above his right ear. *No time like the present.* If he was going to succeed, it would have to be done in one clean, swift stroke.

Just lie back and enjoy it, he thought, and brought his arm down.

He did not go outside for several days. He had stockpiled various canned foods and mac-and-cheese kits in his apartment and was able to subsist quite adequately while he recovered. His rudimentary stitching had served its purpose and everything was healing decently, although grotesquely. Whenever he looked in the mirror, he reminded himself of Lon Chaney as Erik in *The Phantom of the Opera*. This made him realize that he might frighten people out on the street when he returned, so he went online and had no trouble at all locating a few attractive sets of ear prosthetics to wear on the outside.

He remembered the doctor had said that cutting off his ears wouldn't render him totally deaf, and this was true. But here in his apartment, at least, most noises were now either absent or infinitesimal, and previously blaring ones like sirens and car alarms a distant and thudding dullness. Almost heaven. Almost.

He worried a bit about his income, as he had no real fallback position after quitting his critic gig. For now, he reassured himself that at least he retained a sizable savings, since he had managed to save all that cash he had planned to use on Doctor Rhyndelboume. He could survive for a while before he had to come up with a plan B.

In the meantime, there were many works of literature lying around for him to read as he healed, in his now preternaturally quiet abode.

His sewn-up ear holes were healing up nicely by the time the Oscar telecast rolled around, though he had not yet received his prosthetics and so had not yet ventured back into the city. But he had removed his stitches and the scars did not really look *too* horrid.

He fixed a large bowl of mac-and-cheese into which he stirred some canned tuna, and sat down to watch the show, which he had done every year religiously since he was five years old, but never before with the sound switched, as it were, totally off.

As with everything else in his life, he found the Oscars without sound a massive improvement. On the red carpet, all the stars were asked what they were wearing, but Rick would never know how they responded, and who the hell cared, anyway? The opening number and the monologue by the host trundled on in blissful silence. Rick allowed the closed captioning to run along the bottom, but the A.I. translator was getting so much of it wrong that for once it was pure comedy. It was easy to follow who was nominated and of course who won. With the first acting award, Rick decided to nix the subtitles, because the acceptance speeches were too annoying, and it had been a great mistake to read along. Greatly improved simply to watch them drone on without sound and without visible text.

But when they got to the awards for sounds effects and sound-effects editing, Rick felt a crisis looming. The producers had lined up a pair of young rising stars, some guy and some girl, to present. They were reading their teleprompter with snide smirks on their faces, clearly believing this category was beneath them, and they looked like they had put back a couple of martinis before waltzing out onto the stage. As they went on and on, bantering and looking helplessly at one another, Rick realized they were bringing back that old chestnut of explaining ad infinitum how sound effects work and who Foley had been. *Well, why don't we just stop talking like a couple of idiots and show you how it's done, as if you couldn't figure it out for yourselves?*

Cut to a canned segment of footage interviewing various Oscar-winning Foley artists and sound engineers. As they demonstrate how they create the magical sounds you hear on the silver screen. Such as banging a hammer down on a tautly pulled cable to creating a *sproing* that would be altered into the *pew-pew* of blasters in the latest *Star Wars*. Such as playfully splashing water onto each other's faces to create the uncanny effect of water splashing onto the face of Best Actress nominee Mamie Maddox as young Miss Lucy Darley in *Sanderton*. And that old crowd-pleaser, chopping a watermelon in half with a machete to accompany the guillotine blade falling onto Beryl

Staines's neck in this year's Best Picture contender *Robespierre and I.*

Rick turned it off. He could never watch the rest of it, and he knew now he could never watch another Oscars show again.

He began concocting elaborate fantasies of traveling to Hollywood and knocking off all the Foley artists one by one in clever ways.

During the weeks of his convalescence, he had grown his hair out a bit longish, and with his new prosthetic ears now arrived and glued into place was able at last to go outside.

It was a lovely spring day. Exiting his building, he was delighted to feel the warmth of the sun on his face. Cars flew past on the street, but he felt their rumble beneath his feet better than he could hear them. He knew the noises they must be making rather than the cottony muffle in his head, but he was trying to train his brain not to make up for their loss. He thought it might be nice to go for a walk in the park, so he descended the stairs into the subway, joined the jostling crowd on the platforms and in the train cars, and finally emerged at the entrance to the grand park.

No one had given him a second glance. He was happy that his fake ears were doing their job. He was determined to avoid running into some young woman or small child who might bat at his face and knock them off, exposing his deformity, though such an event seemed highly unlikely, as it might only happen in a movie.

The trouble began again as he passed the famous carousel. He had lived in the city all his life and was walking his typical route. The music of the carousel had never changed in all these years. As he came abreast of it, watching the children and their parents rising and falling effortlessly on the gaudy painted horses, the music seemed to flood his brain. As the children opened their mouths, he could hear their high-pitched laughing and squealing. He could hear the mumbly chatter of passersby who had stopped, like Rick, to watch. When the carousel came to a stop, he could hear the screech of the apparatus and the yells of the operator busking for new victims.

Rick ran away and fled under a footbridge, and found himself breathing heavily. He could hear his own breathing and heart beating madly. He clutched at his head, holding his hands over his ears, and felt them slipping from their perch. He put them back into place, hoping they looked all right. He could hear the soft tread of other park-goers crossing the footbridge above. He heard the rustling of the leaves swirling in a tiny vortex across from him in the underpass. He heard the grunting and groaning of the homeless man waking up in a pile of garbage just next to him, and saw the look of shock on the man's face as he watched Rick fixing his ears back into place.

He moved on. He couldn't stay here. It had been a mistake to go out so soon. If he had spent a few more weeks in the safety of his apartment, perhaps he could have better trained his brain to leave well enough alone. He wanted to run, but the faster he went the louder his footsteps sounded, even if perhaps it was just the reverberation caused by his feet smacking the paved walkways.

A rollerskater rolled by with a boom box, skating figure-eights to a disco beat.

A cluster of cyclists sped past with a loud whine of their tires as if they thought they were in the Tour de France.

A horsedrawn carriage came clip-clopping toward him—a beautiful white mare pulling a polished white coach with a top-hatted driver on the seat and a couple of lovebirds in the plush red seats. Rick could swear he heard a pair of coconut halves in his head as the horse trotted nearer, being expertly manipulated by a prize-winning Foley artist, and as the couple rolled past he heard every slurpy, wet, smacking move of their lips and tongue as they kissed. And when the driver lit up a cigarette, Rick heard the crackle of the dry tobacco as it came alight.

When Rick showed Doctor Rhyndelboume what he had done, he was aghast. The doctor spoke in a mwah-mwah-mwah miasma of mumbling such that Rick had no idea what he was saying, but his highly stylized facial expressions were worthy of Emil Jannings. Rick removed his prosthetics and showed him how well they worked to ensure his outward appearance wouldn't elicit similar reactions among the lay folk.

"But it didn't work," he explained to the doctor. "In an ironic twist, to coin a phrase! Because you were right, it's not a problem with my ears at all. It's my brain." He couldn't hear himself talk, not really, yet of course he knew what he was saying, and he knew how he sounded, and he knew full well he would be understood.

Doctor Rhyndelboume clasped Rick firmly by both of his shoulders and began imploring him, one might suppose, to visit a psychiatrist. Since the intertitles were missing, Rick couldn't tell what this mad-scientist-haired silent-movie actor was actually trying to say.

"I'll give you all my savings if you'll take care of it for me."

Rhyndelboume looked at him perplexedly. *Oh, what ever could he mean?* the intertitle might have said.

"You're an ears, nose, and throat guy, right? So my first thought was that you could just slit my throat. But that's no good, obviously. If it's not the right job for you, just give me a referral to a brain surgeon. But if you're game, doc, I want you to cut open my skull and start poking around until we find the magic spot. Then cut it out. Just cut all that noise right out of my head. I'm sure you can do it..."

Rhyndelboume tore at his hair, looked deeply into his own conscience, tallied up his own bank account in his head, looked up to the ceiling, and implored to the heavens above, *Why me, O Lord?*

Rick looked at him in breathless anticipation. He could see in the mirror what the shot looked like, of himself as Erik the Phantom, hoping against hope for release from his personal hell.

Finally, from Rhyndelboume, a hideously faint but obvious *"NO!"*

It was not the kind of response for which an intertitle was even required.

Rick returned to his apartment. It had indeed been premature for him to go outside. Thank goodness you could purchase anything you wanted online, and all of it delivered right to your door. And since money was no object, it only took a few days for him to complete his preparations. He received in the post a case of Scotch, a supply of rubbing alcohol, some antiseptic, a gross of sterile bandages, a starter scalpel set, a power drill, a hobbyist's diamond-dust-encrusted circular saw drill bit, a couple of different types of bone saw, a stainless-steel icepick, and several highly absorbent Egyptian cotton beach towels. Although he was mildly apprehensive about the imaginary sound the power drill would make once it was turned on, he was pretty sure based on his previous experience that he could go through with it. And once he found the magic spot and scrambled it with the icepick, all the noise would be switched off forever.

That was the thing, the ultimate truism, the final trite cliché: *If you wanted a job done right, sometimes you just had to do it yourself.* ⅗

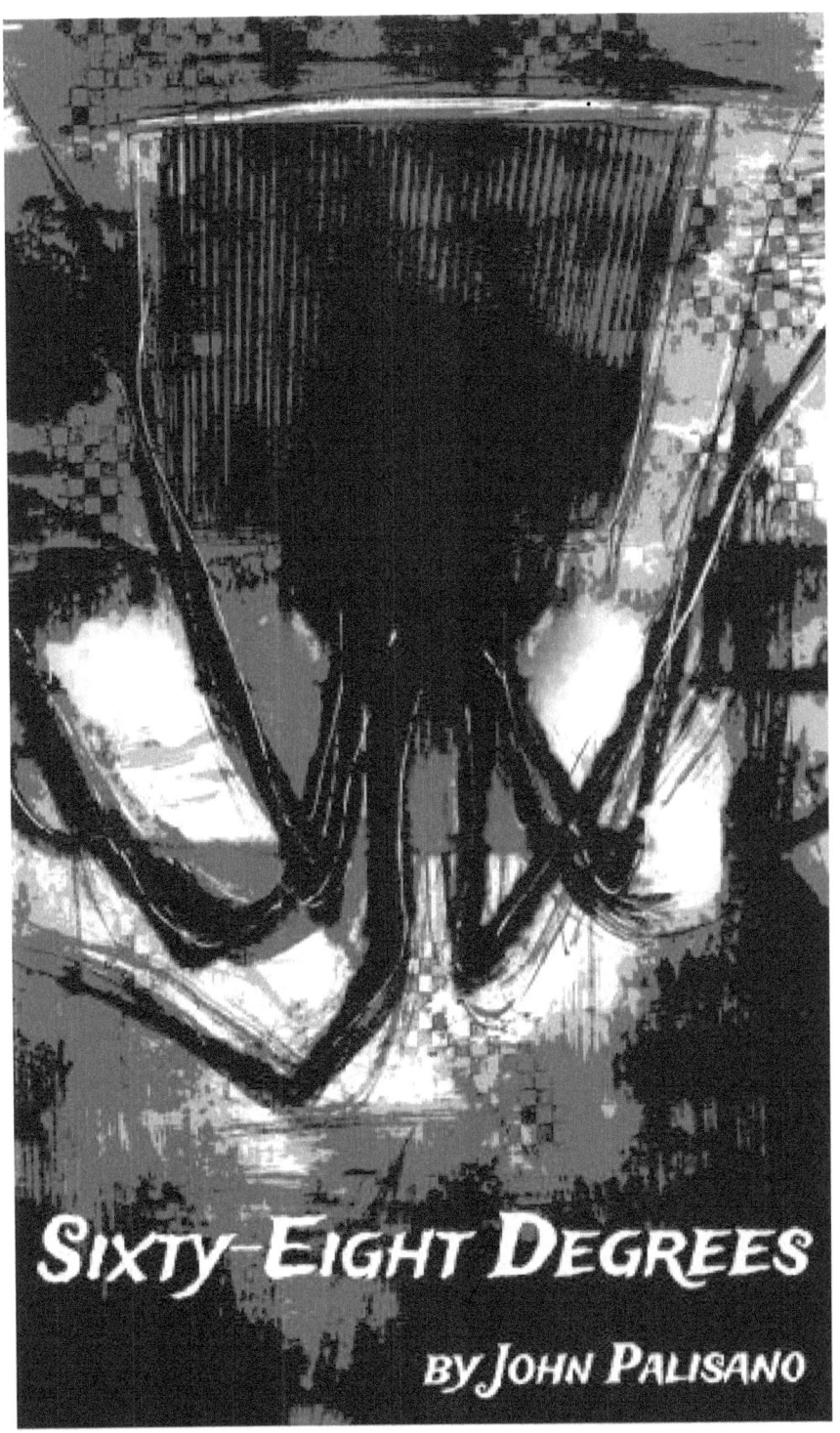

SIXTY-EIGHT DEGREES

BY JOHN PALISANO

SIXTY-EIGHT DEGREES

BY JOHN PALISANO

THE SERVICE GUY TOLD us none of the air conditioning pipes were connected. Now we know that's not true. Everything's connected. What happens in one room affects every other room. Ain't no one going to convince me different.

"Always keep the temperature at sixty-eight degrees." That was the other thing he'd claimed. "No matter what, if the house is cooler than that, it'll heat up. If it's hotter than that, it'll cool down. The system is optimized at that temperature. It's what all the research says is optimal."

The smart thermometer made the hallway glow blue. "It's like what if they made Hanukkah themed Christmas lights," Chris said. "Imagine that?" It delighted him. Calmed him. My cousin could be easily amused.

Kept me up. "Kinda reminds me of those black lights they use to look for body fluids at crime scenes and motel rooms," I said.

"You're always so negative," he said. "Why do you always have to go right to thinking about the bad stuff about everything?"

"Don't know," I said. "Probably because that's what the world has earned."

Chris was right. Everyone was always trying to pull a fast one. Get the money and run. Tell you what you wanted to hear. Get the check. Get gone.

Then there was the stench. A mix of mildew and rot, the service claimed it was only the initial blast of cleaning chemicals working itself out and that in no time at all, we'd be breathing in what they claimed would be hospital grade air. Yeah. If that hospital was built inside a meat processing plant.

Every time Chris turned the air conditioning on, my room filled with the foul smell. I swear it went directly inside my lungs and made me feel like I had a chest cold. I tasted it in my throat even after I took a shower. It was even stuck in my nose. No amount of blowing erased it. Worst of all? When the air conditioning was turned on, it felt like I couldn't breathe. Every time I heard the compressor kick in, my nerves jumped because I knew what was coming.

"What the hell is in this thing?" I asked.

Chris got mad. "There's no way this is as bad as you're saying. All you do is complain. Every damn day. Why don't you do something about it instead of bitching about it?"

"What can I do?" I asked.

"Shut up about it."

We bickered like an old couple instead of the cousins we were. I chalked it up to that. He needed help with his COPD. He couldn't drive himself anymore on account of needing an oxygen tank. I was his live-in caregiver. In exchange? Cheap rent in a big house in Austin. Not bad. Pretty fair. Most the time, we got on just fine.

The next time he turned on the air conditioning, I cracked my door to the outside. I didn't want to be stuck breathing that mess in again.

It helped.

I fell asleep and made it halfway through the night before feeling suffocated. When I got up, I realized that not only did the air smell its usual, awful self, but there was a fine white powder blowing out from the ceiling vent, as well. Plainly visible, the powder coated everything in my room. It looked like it hadn't been dusted in a decade.

"Now what?" I ran my finger across my bureau and picked up some of the powder. The stuff was sticky. I smelled it—as rank as the air, maybe more so. "Where is this stuff coming from?"

I went right to my door and opened it. Bad air was one thing, but dust was worst.

Checking my room for something to block the vent, I saw nothing immediate. I texted Chris.

Please turn off the AC. Powder is coming out of the vents. 911.

Chris didn't reply, but I heard his phone ding from inside his room. A moment later, I heard him cursing me. The air conditioning went off. I heard something slam from inside Chris's room. He didn't text back. He didn't come to see what was wrong. He just went back to sleep. *Freaking family.*

I found a roll of electrical tape under my sink, took it, stood on a chair, and used it to seal off the ceiling vent.

"You're going to destroy the unit," Chris said. "It's going to make it work too hard and fry it out. That's what they said happened last time."

"But none of the vents were shut," I said.

"You always have an answer for everything, don't you?"

"It's not that," I said. "It's just that it doesn't make any sense."

"They said all the rooms were separated. None of them are connected. So, whatever is happening in your room is on you."

"How could it possibly be on me?" I asked.

"Figure it out," he said. "And take that damn tape off."

I took it upon myself to investigate, waiting until Chris dragged his oxygen machine and his cables back inside his room for a late morning nap the next day.

In the hallway, I pulled down the ladder door that led to the attic. Careful to step lightly so as not to wake Chris and clue him in to what I was up to, I made it to the top and clicked the light switch on the floor.

Stacked in neat piles, storage boxes looked clean and unbroken. The rat traps had not been triggered. Spotting the huge air conditioning unit to my left, I used the light on my phone to scan it. The entire thing was sealed. There were no signs of leakage. It looked right as rain. Cylindrical metallic tubes snaked from the main unit and connected to the vents in our rooms. I noticed my room was split off from the main vent. As were the guest room and Chris's room. *They most certainly are connected.* I snapped a shot to show Chris. *How is the stuff only coming through to my room, then?*

Chris must have sensed me up there because the damn unit fired up. As loud as a jet engine, I instinctively jumped backward. Putting my hands to my ears did little to lower the deafening sound.

I found the light switch and clicked it off. I hurried down the ladder as fast as possible. The unit blasted me the same as if I'd stuck my head against a concert speaker or the engine of a plane.

Using the stick to push up the ladder, my ears rang. That may seem like an exaggeration, but ring they did.

Making it to my room, I put myself down and stared at the ceiling.

The entire house seemed to shake. Not only did my ears ring, but my head felt pummelled. The tape on the vent ballooned out a little bit. I'd put it back up when Chris was out of the room because he rarely ever came inside on account of all his machines.

Organic colors crept into the side of my sight. That meant a migraine was likely on deck and ready to knock one over the bleachers. Damn it.

The tape on the vent flapped off halfway. It hung down like a paralysed tongue. The vent steamed out bad air, followed again by the sticky, nasty powder.

I sighed. Shut my eyes. It was all so overwhelming, after all, and my head felt as though a vice were ratcheting up inside. I took some painkillers, but the migraine snuck inside before the door shut.

Metallic red and green colors floated behind my eyelids. Speckles of white and black washed over the colors for a moment, only to have the colors return again. My brain felt squished as though inside a large hand; every blood vessel and nerve stretched to the point of breaking. Pain flooded through my skull, finding purchase in my sinuses, back teeth, and especially behind my eyes and temples. *If only I had a drill, I could bore a hole in the side of my head to let the pressure out. Didn't doctors used to do that? Once upon a time?*

The humming sound of the air conditioning unit seemed to move through the air. At first, it was only heard through the ceiling and walls, but I swear the sound travelled until stopping inches from my throbbing skull.

I hate you.

I felt like I was falling, despite lying down on my bed. Turning over and over, my body tumbled aimlessly into a multi-colored tunnel. The humming sound increased in volume until it was as loud as being inside a tornado. Faces appeared inside the colors. Most human, some strange and nearly formless. Maybe one can catch me? Pull me out from this? But there were no hands. Only eyes, watching with no pity or care, only gross fascination.

The powder came, too, like a spinning dust devil. Reaching toward me with branch-like arms, the powder coated me and stuck to me. Soon, my fingers stuck together. It went up my nose and down my throat. It clumped and I couldn't catch my breath. Before it sealed my eyes, I saw a being below me, no larger than an adult, seemingly lifeless. The powder emanated from the being and I thought it was being burned and the powder had to be its flesh, cooked and breaking apart, bit by bit, as though cremated.

I fell faster and closer to the being until it turned. Its face had almost disappeared, turned to dust. Then my eyes were sealed and I was left drifting in darkness, suspended in unimaginable pain. I was sure my head would explode from the inside. And then I felt nothing for a time.

I must have blacked out.

When I woke in the middle of the night, I realized I'd lost several hours. My head still ached, but not as bad. I found water. I found a snack. I washed up. I returned to bed, anxious and disappointed in the episode. *A lot of people with migraines get auras. See things. Hallucinate. Not a big deal. Don't let it shake you.*

I realized something else. The air conditioning was off. Chris must have shut it. That was likely what'd woken me.

Checking my phone, I scrolled my notifications. When looking at the news, I couldn't believe what I read.

SECOND MISSING PERSON FOUND INSIDE AIR CONDITIONING UNIT

My thoughts raced. Scenes from my vision played out. The person, decomposing, turning to dust. Could that be what was happening at our house? Could it be the installer was a serial killer who'd been hiding the bodies in the huge air conditioning units? Maybe, somehow, he knew the coils would cremate the bodies over time, the crime perfectly hidden.

Oh, my God. This can't be happening to us. Not our house.

Every one of my pores froze. I just knew it had to be true. We'd have a third missing person in our unit, and that is what I'd been smelling and breathing in. *But how could I have seen that in my migraine hallucination? That'd require me to be psychic, or for some supernatural thing to have haunted me. Neither of those are really me, are they? I'm just a regular guy.*

My thoughts went to how to figure out what to do.

Do I even mention this to Chris?

The dull ache persisted.

Go back to sleep. Figure it out tomorrow.

When I put my head back down and shut my eyes, the dull ache increased once more. *Don't let the migraine come back. Let me rest. Let me get through this.*

As I drifted back to sleep, the dust came. *You sure you want to breathe this in now that you know it's a dead person?* The other half of my mind answered. *Forget it. You've already been breathing it in for a while. What's another few hours?*

I was just too tired to rouse.

Returned to a dreaming state, the edges of my head hurt once more. How could it hurt even while I slept?

Finding myself approaching a home on a dark, wooded street, I spotted my sister Andrea and her husband Adam. They busied themselves with a hose, which I couldn't understand the reason behind. "You've got to turn it off," Adam said. "All water needs to be shut. We need to go inside and do the same." They didn't even acknowledge me. They hurried inside as the sky darkened. Rain fell, only it was not rain, but dust. The powder. Blowing around me, I felt I couldn't breath once more.

My tongue felt swollen near the back of my throat. I vaguely recalled Chris telling me that I snored very loudly, and that he was sure I had sleep apnea. I brushed it off, but the choking feeling made me second guess his theory. Clenching my throat with my hand, I knew I had to get inside their house or risk the powder overtaking me. *Maybe it's already too late.*

Was it?

As I crossed their door, an unfamiliar dog shivered on their couch. It must have known something very bad was coming.

Then I saw Adam and Andrea working under their kitchen sink, attending to the plumbing. "It's already started," she said. "It's all going to get inside."

The powder? How could it get into the plumbing? Wouldn't they need water to wash it off? Wouldn't I?

A loud cracking sound ripped through the air. The house shook. They screamed. I would have, too, but my throat was so swollen, breathing even a single breath was taking all I had.

I collapsed. I heard voices around me—Andrea and Adam. They'd finally noticed me.

I rolled onto my back and saw the sky outside their huge window. Blue had given way to shades of red and orange. Clouds moved quickly before vanishing from sight completely. I saw the darkness beyond, then stars of many colors.

The air around me thinned, I was sure.

Where is Andrea? Adam?

They'd gone, too, left me to suffocating on their living room floor. Or maybe, I thought, they'd collapsed and were struggling to stay alive, too.

Powder blew inside.

Impossible.

The doors and windows were closed.

Gathering like sticky embers, the powder coated my skin and face. It blotted out my sight, but not before I saw strange, enormous shadows in the sky. What could be causing them, I wondered? I made out what appeared to be insect-like appendages moving toward the ground. *You've seen too many movies.* It all went black.

And I heard voices once more, after a few moments.

I can breath.

Beep. Beep. Beep.

I felt no pain.

"Cousin?" I heard. "Cousin?" Chris loomed over me, his face painted in concern and relief. "You're back with us. Oh, thank god."

His was one voice, the other belonged to a doctor who watched over my cousin's shoulder.

My blood turned to ice. The sound had followed me. Low, humming and persistent, the hospital's air conditioning kept me trapped. I looked for the vent, but didn't see one.

"I have to see the vent," I said, my voice cracking and sore. "The powder. The scent."

"Mister Feldmar," the doctor said. "You're suffering a serious amount of exposure to a neurotoxin."

"What?"

Chris nodded. "You were on to something with the air conditioning," he said. "But it wasn't a dead body in there. They hid a plastic bag of Westbite inside. Probably forgot. Or thought they'd be coming back for it another time."

"Seems the coils cooked it and sent it inside your room," the doctor said. "You're lucky to be alive. It's been touch and go."

"What?" I couldn't believe my ears. Westbite was bad news. People were dying after one dose. How much had I had? The powder.

Taking my vitals, the doctor said, "I'm pretty sure the anti-toxins worked."

"My God. Is this real?" I asked. "How'd I get here?"

"You didn't answer your phone," Chris said. "You were non-responsive. Do you know how hard it is dragging my damn oxygen machine up and out all by myself?"

"I'm sorry," I said.

He laughed. "Me, too. I should have believed you. I can be so thick."

I just smiled.

He said, "I'm just glad you're here now. Getting treatment."

"But, how did you know to check?" I asked.

"Your whole room was covered in powder when I went inside. So were you. It was all over your face. I had to clean you."

"You're pretty lucky," said the doctor. He put a hand on Chris's shoulder. I noticed he wore long sleeves, even though it was summer. Of course he did. They kept the place slightly above refrigerated. "Let's allow him some rest."

Chris nodded. "Okay," he said. "Don't worry, cuz. They gave me one of the family rooms to stay in. No one is using them. And I have my oxygen with me. I'll check on you in the morning."

"All right," I said. "Sounds good."

"A nurse will be checking on you periodically. Don't worry. We won't leave you all alone."

"Great," I said.

As they walked out the door, Chris gave me a last wave and was gone ahead of the doctor.

The doctor stopped at the thermostat. "Just making sure this is set to sixty-eight for you."

68.

"We need to set each individually. Each of these rooms is on their own system in case we have a patient with something transferable. None of the rooms are connected," he said.

But I knew better. Everything's connected.

Just as he slipped away, the cuff of the doctor's sleeve caught on the edge of the door jamb. Two small points glistened from within, then moved. Something was inside his sleeve. My memory pictured the huge shadow creatures descending toward earth in my nightmare.

Could it be one of them? A small one? Infiltrated us? Already? How could that be?

But before I could look again and reaffirm what I saw, the doctor was gone.

I watched the hall for a few moments, sure the insect thing would skitter around the corner, anxious to take me out, anxious to preamble any chance of my telling anyone I'd seen it. Anxious to exterminate me.

I blinked. *No. Don't think like that. You're going to drive yourself crazy. It was just a very bad hallucination brought on by the drugs. That's all. Nothing more. Don't let it take root inside you.*

My line of sight settled just above the door, where I spotted the air conditioning vent. *That's where it's been. Finally.*

As I looked at the over-painted white blades, the humming sound increased. My heart clenched. My body went colder still. Impossibly cold. From the middle, a small bit of dust blew out from the vent, rocketing out before settling into a smooth, rockabye descent. But it wasn't dust at all. Where it fell, it stuck. Where what followed stuck again in clumps. I recognised the rank, earthy smell. I'd know it anywhere. I put my hands to my ears to try and block the sound, but it was inside my head—inside my very body. I tried to call out. Tried to yell. Tried to scream. But the powder was inside me, too. Inside my throat. Swelling my tongue. Suffocating me once again, choking me until I saw nothing at all, but heard only the omnipresent sound of the air conditioning, humming. Humming. Humming.)(

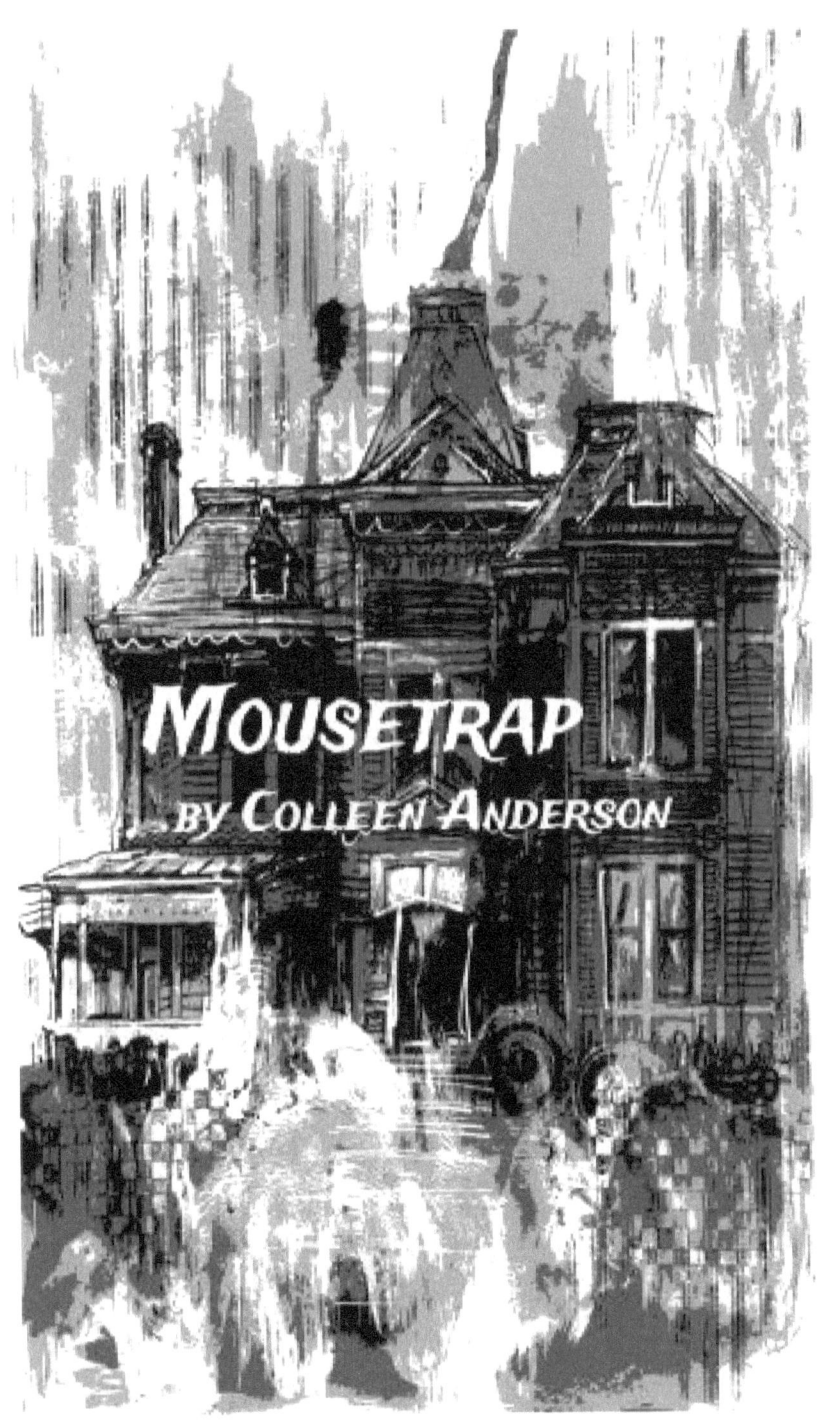

MOUSETRAP

BY COLLEEN ANDERSON

MOUSETRAP

BY COLLEEN ANDERSON

A SOFT WHISPER, muffled scratching on wood. Then the silence punctuated with slow breaths of sleep. Another scratch, a scrape, faint as if coming from a distance, as if against paper, or cardboard, or plaster. The sound floated, indistinct yet pressing against the quiet.

The placid drifting of slumber dissipated and Min-jun's eyes snapped open. He listened hard, ears straining to grasp that shadow of a sound. The dark allowed only faint grey shapes of the dresser, the corners of the room insubstantial, the curtains like wraiths hung to dry. A faint glow from the hall nightlight shyly peeked in the open door.

Min-jun tensed, searching for that noise that had pulled him from dreamland. They'd only been in the house two months, the house with good old bones, as Gerhard put it. Those bones had their way of absorbing sounds, creaking in the wind, settling as October's cold breath swirled hungrily. But this wasn't the house groaning and complaining, he was sure of it. An invader; that's what it was.

Muscles rigid, he tried to settle his breathing to hear better. Min-jun had nearly convinced himself it was a wayward dream that had pushed at the subconscious. He closed his eyes, exhaling slowly. Gerhard didn't move beside him.

The scratching came from the wall above his head. He bolted up, peering hard at the wall. Of course, nothing showed in the night.

"Gerhard," he whispered. "Gerhard, there is something in the walls." He gently shook his husband's shoulder. With no response, he pushed a little harder. "Gerhard."

Gerhard didn't move. His voice mumbled, "Probably mouse. Deal with in the morning. G'back to sleep." He rolled onto his side.

Min-jun lay back down but remained hyper alert to every scrape and creak. How could he go back to sleep when something crawled through the veins of the house? There could be rats or mice, or cockroaches or who knew what. They could be swarming across Min-jun and Gerhard, their little legs tickling, itching, leaving a trail for others to follow. Crapping and chewing and depositing who knew what diseases. There were so many things they, those unwanted things, could be doing. He rolled out of bed and grabbed a robe and slippers, then padded out of the room, closing the door softly.

He flicked on the hall light and quietly crept the house, listening, searching, but nothing appeared. His movement held *them* at bay. Surely, if there were vermin, they'd invade the kitchen first. Digging a flashlight out of the neatly ordered kitchen drawer,

Min-jun flicked off the light and sat in a chair placed before the back entrance. Ears were his organ to seek and identify. Staring into night's obscuring blanket, his eyes jiggled, trying to focus on something. He closed them... and jerked awake. The grey had lightened but no intruders had shown. He went back to bed.

Groggily, Min-jun dressed and trudged to the kitchen. The warm salty scent of toast and bacon tingled his nose. If he could smell out the creatures, he could have found them already. Yawning, he walked up behind Gerhard working at the black gas stove, noticing the shirt and tie, and Gerhard's hair pulled into a short tail. He hugged his husband about the waist and lay his cheek on the strong back, inhaling the crisp scent of clean clothes.

"Morning, love. I heard you stumbling around last night." Gerhard turned and kissed Min-jun. "Your tea is already steeping."

"Do you think we have mice?"

Gerhard scooped eggs and bacon onto two plates and dropped a piece of toast on each. They sat at the tiny table near the window, a temporary setup until the kitchen renovations were complete. "Maybe, the house is over a century old. There are bound to be some holes here and there."

Min-jun sipped the tea, warming a path to his belly. "I hate mice. And rats."

Gerhard smiled, his cheeks dimpling. "Mice are kind of cute and we're sharing space with the wildlife. Why do you hate them so much?"

Min-jun shrugged. "I—they're creepy. Those beady eyes, and the tails." He shuddered. "Those pink fleshy, creepy tails. Ugh."

"You ever seen a possum? Those things are like giant rats, with the same pink tails. And nutria." Gerhard's eyes sparkled. "They're bigger, like beavers but with rat tails, though not pink."

He glared at Gerhard. "You're not helping."

Wiping his mouth, Gerhard stood and put his dishes in the sink. "I've got to get to the office. We have a meeting on a big redevelopment downtown. I'll probably be late as we're also taking the stakeholders to dinner. You working on the house today?"

Min-jun nodded. "I have a couple hours of checking in with my crews, then I'm going to start on the kitchen."

Gerhard paused at the living room entrance. "Are you sure you want to do this? You could as easily get one of your crews in to help. It's a pretty big job to do on your own."

"I'll get them in at the end, to do the painting, but I want to put everything in, make sure it's done right and give it the personal touch. Don't forget, it's my gift to you." He smiled and stood.

"My hopeless romantic." Gerhard came over and kissed him, a hint of cinnamon and lavender on his skin. "Okay, I'll see you later. Don't overdo it!"

After the door clicked closed, Min-jun washed up the dishes in the old enamel sink pitted as if it had seen a war. He'd be tearing it out today, to make way for the wider and deeper two-basin sink.

Min-jun made a few calls, checked that his construction crews were on track and then carried in crowbar and saw and toolkit. The kitchen's entries lead to the living room, a short hall to the back door where once had been a pantry/mudroom and the hall entry to their bedroom. The fridge butted up close to the sink with barely any counter. Big paned windows started over the sink, over to the next wall between sink and stove where small cupboards bordered the gas range. He had already knocked out the pantry wall between the back entrance and the hallway.

As he tugged the fridge away from the wall, a panorama of dirt, crumbs, insect casings, elastics and a fork constellated the black and white hexagonal tiles. "Disgusting." He reached behind the fridge and unplugged the dusty cord, then pushed it to the other corner, plugging it into the extension cord. Turning back, a perfect cartoon-style mousehole stood revealed in the wall. A trail of tiny brown pellets polka dotted the area. A fusty, moldering acrid taint wafted from the area.

Min-jun swept everything, then mopped the floor twice. He peered at the floor, then mopped it a third time. With flashlight, he knelt and peered into the small hole with chewed edges. Of course, nothing stared out at him.

He turned off the water, then crowbarred the counter loose. Below, where pipes snaked out of the wall, more holes appeared, sinister spots to the unknown denizens that scuttled and scurried through the house's flesh, and a trail of droppings. Gritting his teeth, Min-jun sawed and cut and removed a whole section of wall, replacing it with new drywall. Much of the kitchen had the long, vertically slatted wood of the Victorian era but wherever piping or wiring had been added, new entries for mice. He mudded the cracks, then set the lower cupboard in, but not before he sealed everything with a silicon base. No mice would penetrate those barriers.

The front door clicked shut, and Gerhard appeared at the living room entrance. "What are you doing still working? It's ten-thirty!"

Min-jun ran a hand across his gritty, face, wiping grime away. "I found the mouse holes, patched 'em all."

Gerhard squinted, surveying the kitchen, tools piled in the center, orange extension cords worming across the floor, fridge sitting askew, bins and pots piled beside the stove, and the half-finished counter. He sighed. "Well, they say renos always take longer than planned. Come to bed. The kitchen's a disaster and tomorrow Asal and Cory invited us to a little cocktail and dinner party they're having, which looks like it's good time for us, since we can't cook in this."

The next day, after Gerhard left for the office, Min-jun finished installing the lower cupboards and the sink, though he didn't have time to connect the pipes. He was satisfied though; the holes were gone. No more mice. He tried for a nap before going for dinner but he could only think of mice, their mangy bodies scraping against walls and pipes, depositing festering piles of disease.

Later, at Asal's and Cory's, the three couples chatted, eventually coming around to home renos.

"Mice! The worst," Cory shook his head, curls bobbing. "You ever see those rat movies? *Willard*, I think it was. Some misanthrope has them kill for him." He scrunched his mouth, his front teeth framed by his lips.

Asal rolled her eyes. "Nothing like Hollywood to put the fear in you. And that was rats, not mice."

"Still," Gena sipped a beer and added, "they can carry diseases like henta virus, or whatever it's called."

Zed, her partner, nodded, leaning back. "Oh, yeah. It wasn't mice per se, but rats were a direct cause of the Black Plague, carrying fleas that had been infected. Mice can be as bad."

Min-jun said nothing, his lips pressed tightly against an outburst. Gerhard glanced over and changed the subject.

All he said when they returned home was, "See there's a reason not to like them."

Gerhard said nothing.

The wine they had drunk sapped Min-jun's energy. He fell asleep immediately... until someone scraped fingernails over wood. A sibilant sawing, gnawing along the wall, just out of reach, of something working its way into the flesh of the house. Insidious, nails dragging, clawing through the barriers to chew into Min-jun's dreams. But the holes were blocked!

This time sleep could not reassert its hold. In the gray pitch of an early fall morning, Min-jun dressed. Starting far from the bedroom, he surveyed the living and dining rooms but no openings showed.

Sun painted the walls by the time Gerhard found Min-jun rooted to the computer on the living room couch.

"Did you know they can spread not just hanta virus, but Lyme disease, salmonella and some neurological thing that inflames the brain, besides other diseases. It's terrifying."

Gerhard sat beside Min-jun on the couch, putting an arm around his shoulders. "You shouldn't let last night's talk bother you. They were yanking your chain."

Min-jun didn't look up as he bookmarked several sites. "Yank away. It's the truth. They're unhygienic. But it's not just that. I heard them again last night, in the walls."

Gerhard stretched. "Just because you blocked the holes, it doesn't mean that they aren't already inside. You just blocked the inner entry. We might have to get pest control in."

Min-jun scribbled onto a piece of paper. "When you go shopping today, pick these up."

Gerhard read over the list. "Mousetraps, rat poison, steel wool, glue traps... Those are inhumane! The mouse gets stuck and suffers a slow, painful death."

"Fine. Whatever, just get the other stuff and the spray foam."

Gerhard left—Min-jun finished installing the sink but kept stopping—was that scratching? Silence pulsed the air when he stood motionless. Nothing. He grabbed a flashlight and started at one corner of the house, carrying a pad and pen, noting every potential mousehole. Shadows jittered in the small spaces.

The house's radiant heating had thrilled them, but every metal foot could conceal a small gap. A mouse freeway started from such pencil-sized holes. Digusting vermin chewing into things, invaders scampering uncontrolled, a virus within their home's flesh—he shuddered. But it was more than that. Min-jun didn't like to think of that time, that dark time when he'd been helpless. He shook himself.

When Gerhard returned, Min-jun set the old-fashioned snap traps with peanut butter or cheese at the most likely spots. He started to push steel wool into the holes and spray the foam but Gerhard's gentle yet firm grip on his arm stopped him.

"Love, leave off for now. We need dinner and you won't get rid of them all in one day. And... I wanted to say how lovely the new sink and counter are." He kissed Min-jun, smiling. "We can move the pots into these cupboards—so much more spacious than the Victorian ones!" He swept his hand to encompass the new side. "I absolutely love the enamelled sink and the molded marble countertop."

Min-jun refocused on the sleek veined marble. The damn rodents had eaten into his daily routine. Looking at the glistening sink and countertop, he remembered they were creating their dream home. It would be beautiful and there were always hurdles in home reno.

He drew Gerhard into a deep kiss, savoring the cinnamon and smoke flavor of him. "And *this* is why I love you. You keep me balanced."

On Sunday morning, he checked all the traps. Nothing. As he whipped up pancakes for breakfast the tacking of claws on hardwood pattered through the living room. When he peeked in, nothing. Min-jun drummed his knife as they ate. Gerhard convinced him that a brisk fall walk among sunset-colored trees would be just the thing. Wind blustered, tossing up leaves, but the fresh air cleared his head as they strolled along the river, reconnecting. The resonance of nature settled into Min-jun's bones. This was what it was all about; being with family, connected to the world, at peace.

As they walked back to the house, Gerhard stopped them on the sidewalk. Arm in arm, they looked up at the French vanilla and chocolate brown trimming of the Victorian home. "She is a grand old lady, isn't she?"

Min-jun nodded. "I love the shape, with the bay window and the muntin paned glass. You're right. She has great bones and I'll get her ready for her coming out."

They laughed and wandered inside. They settled into the "drawing room" as they had chosen to call it, the smaller alcove where gentlemen had once smoked cigars. A glass of port for Gerhard and scotch for Min-jun. They sipped and chatted curled on the couch. The smoky drink warmed Min-jun. Spending time with Gerhard laced his veins with love for this patient man.

The mousetrap near the fireplace pulled his gaze. Something was different.

"Wait." He leaned forward. "Look at that. See the trap. It's not sprung but the peanut butter is all gone! Those little bastards!"

Gerhard didn't quite suppress his sigh. "Why don't we just get in exterminators? Then we can seal up the holes."

Min-jun waved away Gerhard's comment. "No, I'll do it. I'm halfway there." He had to show he could conquer this.

"You realize that with the weather growing colder, more will try to come in."

"Not once I get the holes closed up." Min-jun always completed his projects and sneaky rodents would not win.

On Monday, Min-jun checked the traps again. The peanut butter and cheese had been devoured from almost every unsprung trap. The little buggers had feasted. Scratching again! Min-jun stilled. Nothing. He shook his head. It was like expecting to be tickled; the nerves fired even without anything there.

He should have been fixing the new alcove for the fridge and putting in the upper cupboard beside the sink. Instead he sawed at the nest of steel wool with a serrated knife. Pliers and clippers didn't work. His fingers stung from the lacerations. Bandaged from numerous metal nips, Min-jun left off his attack and started preparing supper. As he opened the cupboard and pulled out a bag of quinoa, it left a trail like gunpowder to a keg.

"Shit!" He tilted the bag up and carried it to the new porcelain sink. A raw hole through the bottom of the thick plastic was big enough to insert three fingers. "Goddamn mice!" Fury surged and he wanted to throw cans, knives, dishes at the invisible monsters. Searching the older cabinets by the stove, he discovered a crack in the back cupboard, the telltale rice-sized trail confirming the secret passage. He jammed more steel wool in, using a chopstick to push it farther.

He picked up the quinoa, debating if the three-quarters-full bag could be salvaged. Then he remembered the articles about feces and urine and the diseases from mice. More hidden things; bacteria, infection, viruses. His flesh twitched as if mice crawled on him. Tossing the bag in the garbage pail, he took it out. Min-jun carefully searched every cupboard, running his fingers along ever corner, prodding with a chopstick. Pulling out the pots beside the stove, he stuck his head in and listened. Was that gnawing coming from the corner? He shone the light at the base and then traveled up the cupboard to the second shelf. Red pin dot lights glittered back.

Min-jun jerked and smacked his head on the counter, dropping the flashlight. He grabbed his head as he tumbled backward. Strobes flashed behind his eyes and blackness wriggled at the edges.

"Babe! Are you okay!"

Gerhard's arms held him until the pain subsided enough to talk. "God. Damn. Mice!"

"What?"

He kept his eyes shut and waved toward the cupboard. Would Gerhard see those malicious eyes?

"Huh, yeah I see it. That's not a big hole but I guess that's all it takes."

Min-jun finished making supper in silence, unable to talk to Gerhard between his throbbing skull and listening for telltale sounds.

Their dinner consisted of salad with salmon. Min-jun didn't want to tell Gerhard that he'd spent most of the day hunting mice.

Gerhard left for an overnight business trip and Min-jun took the opportunity to buy the adhesive glue strips and pattern the floors with them. He also tried the next style of trap; a homemade contraption with a bucket and a rod through the top spearing an empty water bottle smeared with peanut butter, with a ramp made of wood. The mice would run up, try to walk on the bottle for the peanut butter, and fall into the water and drown.

Mice chomped and chewed at his sleep all night. Min-jun woke fretfully to see shadows pulsing as he strained to listen. Even when he slept, Min-jun was unsure if the scraping and wood gnawing were in his dreams or burrowing in from outside.

At 5:00 am it was still dark. Gerhard wouldn't be home until late. Min-jun dressed and ate a dry bun with butter caulked on as he checked all the traps. Nothing—peanut butter and cheese gone and not one trap sprung. The bucket remained untouched. He inspected every glue trap. A centipede, a couple of spiders, one beetle. Of the twenty he had placed, one pad held a few strands of brown fur and that was all.

Min-jun clenched his fists, his teeth grinding. He screamed, stomping. The fucking mice! "God damn you! I will kill you all!"

When he'd finally calmed down, his throat raw, shaking and sweating from spent fury, Min-jun planned. They would not win, not again. He would maintain control.

Min-jun worked through the morning, into the afternoon, only pausing to drink some water, then continuing.

"My god! Min-jun, what have you done!"

He hadn't heard the door open as he concentrated on sealing another hole. The high pitch of Gerhard's voice broke through his routine.

Min-jun looked down from the ladder, night's pitch pressing in around his flashlight; the glow from the living room light limned his husband. Still, Gerhard's eyes shone large, with too much white.

His breathing came in short, quick gasps. "Min-jun, honey, please come down from there." He flicked on the kitchen light, staring at the walls, his mouth open.

Min-jun scrubbed at his eyes, trying to clear the fog away. Lassitude flooded his limbs and he glanced at the stove clock as he descended. Eleven-thirty! In the morning? But Gerhard wasn't back till evening. Eleven-thirty in the evening!

Gerhard grasped his shoulders, waiting for Min-jun to focus on him. "Babe, are you okay?"

"Yes, I've just been working all day. Time got away from me." He stood on his toes to kiss Gerhard, but he turned away so Min-jun's lips only brushed Gerhard's cheek.

"But, babe, have you seen what you've done?" Gerhard's trembling finger pointed up.

Frowning, Min-jun didn't know what he meant but turned in the soft kitchen light and looked. Caterpillar like blobs crawled along every seam where the walls joined and at the ceiling, a strange undulant trail of cream-colored foam.

"Oh my god, I—" Words failed him. He'd only thought of ridding the house of mice.

Gerhard drew him into the living room, onto the couch. "Min-jun, I'm worried. You've become obsessed with this mouse thing. The kitchen hasn't changed in days and have you even checked on your crews?"

Min-jun sagged into the cushions, rubbing his eyes. "I—no. No, I haven't. I don't know what's come over me."

Gerhard's blue eyes darkened with worry. "I think you need a break. Get out of the house, see the doctor, then go check your crews. Please."

His stomach growled. He hadn't eaten since that bun, hadn't shaved, hadn't looked up. "I've made a mess of the kitchen."

Gerhard's hands clasped his face. "I love you. The kitchen can wait. Please, please stop for now."

Min-jun paused. But the mice. Then he realized Gerhard was right. "Okay, I promise. Tomorrow, I'll take a day off. We can go for dinner somewhere since I've left the kitchen in this state."

It was as if the house's shadows pulled back; they'd been pressing in, blinding him. Gerhard smiled, his brow still creased. They hugged and Gerhard kissed his eyes, his head, murmuring. I'll call Dr. Saeedi and make an appointment tomorrow, okay?"

Min-jun just nodded into Gerhard's shoulder, suddenly too tired to do more.

He kept his promise, checking on the crews, seeing the doctor. She scheduled a few blood tests, saying, "Stress can cause us to lose focus on some things while becoming hyper focused on others. Take some time to do other things; put it in your phone so you don't forget. Go for a walk, sit and eat a meal. Is there anything in your past that could be bringing out this obsessive behavior?"

Min-jun froze for a brief micro-second. He wouldn't mention it, would not give it more space. No, it would not control him again, when he had lived on the streets, a short time in the scheme of his life, but long enough fighting rats and mice, dogs and cats, other children and monstrous adults for a place to sleep, enough food for his belly and freedom from the kicking, the slaps and narrowly avoiding more harrowing ordeals. He shook his head.

He thanked the doctor and left. And stayed true to his promise. There turned out to be some issues with one of the crews and bookkeeping to update. After spending half the day out, he set his alarm before he entered the house. It was 3:00 pm. He would work for two hours, removing the foam he'd sprayed in the kitchen and then meet Gerhard for dinner.

Entering the hallway, he ignored the traps, and did not search for mouse turds. He scraped and chiselled at the foam, cursing, never looking down. The tenacious substance would require sanding every corner before painting. Not to mention the work that he still needed to be do on the alcove and replacing the other counter. He sighed. His phone rang.

In two hours, he had only removed three-quarters of one ceiling seam. He forced himself to stop and wash up. Meeting Gerhard at the café, relief relaxed his husband's creases. They talked only briefly about the doctor and moved on. Min-jun felt like he hadn't talked to Gerhard for a week, but it hadn't been that long at all. Peace settled in and he smiled, finally easing into enjoying the evening.

After a few glasses of wine, they ambled back to the house, wrapped against the frosty air. Min-jun focused on Gerhard, ignoring anything to do with mice. Falling into a deep slumber after lovemaking, Min-jun did not remember his dreams.

For the next three days he followed the doctor's order, going for walks, varying his routine, wearing earplugs at night, and cleaning up the damage he'd done to the kitchen. He removed the traps that remained empty, vowing to bring in exterminators after he finished the renos. An equilibrium returned, but after the second night his sleep grew restless; red-eyed mice treaded his sleep, quickly chewing through to nightmares where his toes smarted from sharp bites. Awake, he tried slowing his breathing, calming his heart but he was sure he heard gnawing in the walls, that slow sawing through wood, the soft grating along drywall.

He said nothing to Gerhard.

The alcove had been completed; drywall done, baseboards waiting for the final paint job, and the fridge connected properly. The foam had been sanded away, although the trail had left its mark. Min-jun felt good. Now he could move ahead, replace the rest of the cupboards.

His phone chimed and he looked away, glancing toward the living room, seeing fresh turds near the couch. They were insinuating themselves. But no, they were only mice, dumb animals just trying to live, oblivious to anyone unless they presented a danger. A cat would have been great, but Gerhard was allergic.

Min-jun's hand ached. He'd been gripping the phone. Exhaling deeply, he pocketed the phone. Part of the routine; maintain the balance. He had to pick up the rest of the materials for the kitchen; drop cloths and plastic to protect the new fixtures and keep the particulates out of the dishes, the other raw materials, the last countertop.

Glancing into the living room as he walked to the front door, a brown figure boldly sat in the middle of the floor. Min-jun froze. The mouse's red eyes balefully stared at him, unafraid.

He closed his eyes and swallowed. There was no mouse. Their eyes weren't red unless they were albinos. Just hallucinating. Opening his eyes slowly, the floor showed nothing but carpet.

He met Gerhard for tea. As they chatted about the next step for the renos, a familiar voice said, "Oh hey, so nice to see you both."

Zed, her hair cropped short and tinged red at the tips, smiled down at them. "How goes the renos? You get rid of the mice?"

Gerhard tensed, looking at Min-jun.

Min-jun shrugged. "Working at it. We've sealed a lot of holes, but we'll probably have to get exterminators in."

She shook her head, large brass hoops swinging in her ears. "It's sort of impossible to keep wildlife out, ya know. You might just have to accept that mice will be part of your life. You know, every winter, they'll come in. You'll never get rid of them all."

Min-jun's laugh came out more as a cough. "Yeah, well, maybe we can at least tame them."

"You're sure you're going to be okay?"

"Yes, yes, stop worrying."

Gerhard zipped his suitcase, looking up. "I can always cancel if you need me to."

Min-jun laughed. "Hon, I'll be fine. You know this is too important a trip for the company."

"Well, I could shorten it and skip the conference."

How he loved that man. "I'm fine, really. I've been going for walks, and I'm ready to do the final push on the kitchen. You being gone for five days means I can work uninterrupted and you get to come back to our dream kitchen."

He walked Gerhard toward the front door. Gerhard turned and wrapped his arms around Min-jun's waist.

"You will take breaks, right? You'll still go out and talk to other people? I don't want you obsessing."

Min-jun cocked his head. "You mean like you're doing right now?"

"Touché." Gerhard exhaled. "All right, but I'll call you in the evening, once we're done."

Min-jun devoured Gerhard's kiss and gently pushed him out the door with a few more assurances.

Min-jun taped thick sheets of plastic over the new cupboards, the sink and the three entrances, carving a slit so he could get to the bathroom. The windows were covered as well, and the room sealed well. Before he started tearing out the cupboards by the stove, he noticed a black rice-shaped crumb. He stared, then wiped it up—just a piece of toast or food. He expected dirt and the shells of bugs to speckle the floor and was not disappointed. Using crowbar and brute force, he pried and pulled at the old wood. Some splintered into jagged auburn teeth showing small chewed holes in the wood. Other slats stubbornly hung on, reluctant to leave their home, but by 10:00 am Min-jun had pulled all the old wood away.

Wiping tears of sweat from his face, he poured and drank down a glass of cool water. As he leaned against the sink, he surveyed the kitchen. Halloween lurked around the corner and the trees' twiggy fingers scratched at the sky, trying to pull the sun closer and allow the weak sunlight through the windows, painting the kitchen, especially the wood he'd pushed to one side.

On that pile of broken wood, cracked planks and countertop pieces sat a hunched brown furry thing. It nibbled some little nugget between its pinkish paws, its eyes flashing red as it eyed Min-jun.

His heart hammered, trying to leap from his chest, burst through his ears, shoot from his head. The throb drowned out the heart, the drumbeat became the war song. Rage heated him. It would not win; he had put this all behind him. He had escaped. The streets would not come back into his life—he would not let them! Cleanse it all!

Moving slowly, Min-jun bent and grabbed a piece of wood, raising it in incremental pauses. The mouse didn't move. He raised the wooden club—smashing it down on the mouse. It leapt and scampered toward the living room. Min-jun scrambled over the pile, skidding on a few loose pieces and raced after the mouse.

And stopped abruptly. Mice scampered everywhere, brown ones, grey ones, a couple of white. When Min-jun entered, they all stopped, eyes shining, watching, red lights in the shadows under the couch, near the fireplace, on the bookcase. Min-jun stared, then screamed, smashing left and right, leaping at fleeing figures. "You will not win! You will not take me back!"

Panting, Min-jun searched the floor. Books had toppled, the carpet rucked like a storm had passed, coffee table jammed into the couch. Not one mouse carcass anywhere.

Min-jun's stomach clenched and dropped. Living like a rat, he'd had to fight the monsters for scraps of food, cringing in the rain as they fought back, biting and scratching his little fingers. They had infested him with fear and terror so that he woke screaming every night. He'd been rescued but not before they had shown him who had won. He could not lose to them again.

You might just have to accept that mice will be part of your life. Zed's words mocked him. He couldn't accept them. Eventually they would gnaw through all that was good. Calm, like that after a blizzard has spent itself, settled over Min-jun.

He dropped the wood and returned to the kitchen, digging through the food and the fridge until he pulled out their best cheeses and the peanut butter. But he laid no traps. Using duct tape, he sealed the slits in the plastic leading to the back entry and the bedroom. He taped down every corner, up to the sealing and across the floor. Pushing the woodpile into the living room, he then put the smallest crumbs of cheddar and gouda outside the doorway, leading to the center of the kitchen. More tape sealed most of the living room entry except for one small hole.

The room looked like a sterile zone in a science fiction movie. Patience and time were all he needed. Min-jun grabbed a couple of pots and container, and then sat with his back to the new cupboards. And he waited. And waited.

Five days passed and Min-jun hummed as he worked. Accepting them had been the way to conquer the monsters, conquer his past. He didn't know what he hummed but it didn't matter. The mice would no longer bother him.

The front door open and shut. "Hey babe, I'm home! Wow something smells good."

Gerhard scratched at the plastic at the living room entry. "Min-jun? Are you there?"

"I am," he called back. "I'm just cooking."

More crinkling of the plastic and the tape being pulled away. "You have it sealed well. I guess the kitchen's not done." Gerhard's head poked in and he worked at widening the gap in the plastic. "How's it going?"

Min-jun took the frying pan off the stove, scooping the food into the white porcelain bowl. A blue china dish held hot sauce. "Good. I finally conquered the mouse problem."

"Oh good." Gerhard finally pulled himself through the opening and stopped, staring at Min-jun.

He picked up a torpedo shape. The tail was nice and crispy, the little paws folded into crunchy bits. He'd seared off the fur before sliding it into beaten egg and lightly coating it with garlic seasoned panko flour. "I couldn't battle them, so I accepted them." Holding the mouse by the tail, he dipped it in the hot sauce and held it above his mouth. As he bit into the still warm body, the hot juices squirted into his mouth, coating his tongue and paving the way for more.

He smiled at Gerhard. "They're really quite tasty." As he swallowed the rest of the mouse, there was the lightest pinching in his stomach, as if claws grasped for purchase. ✕

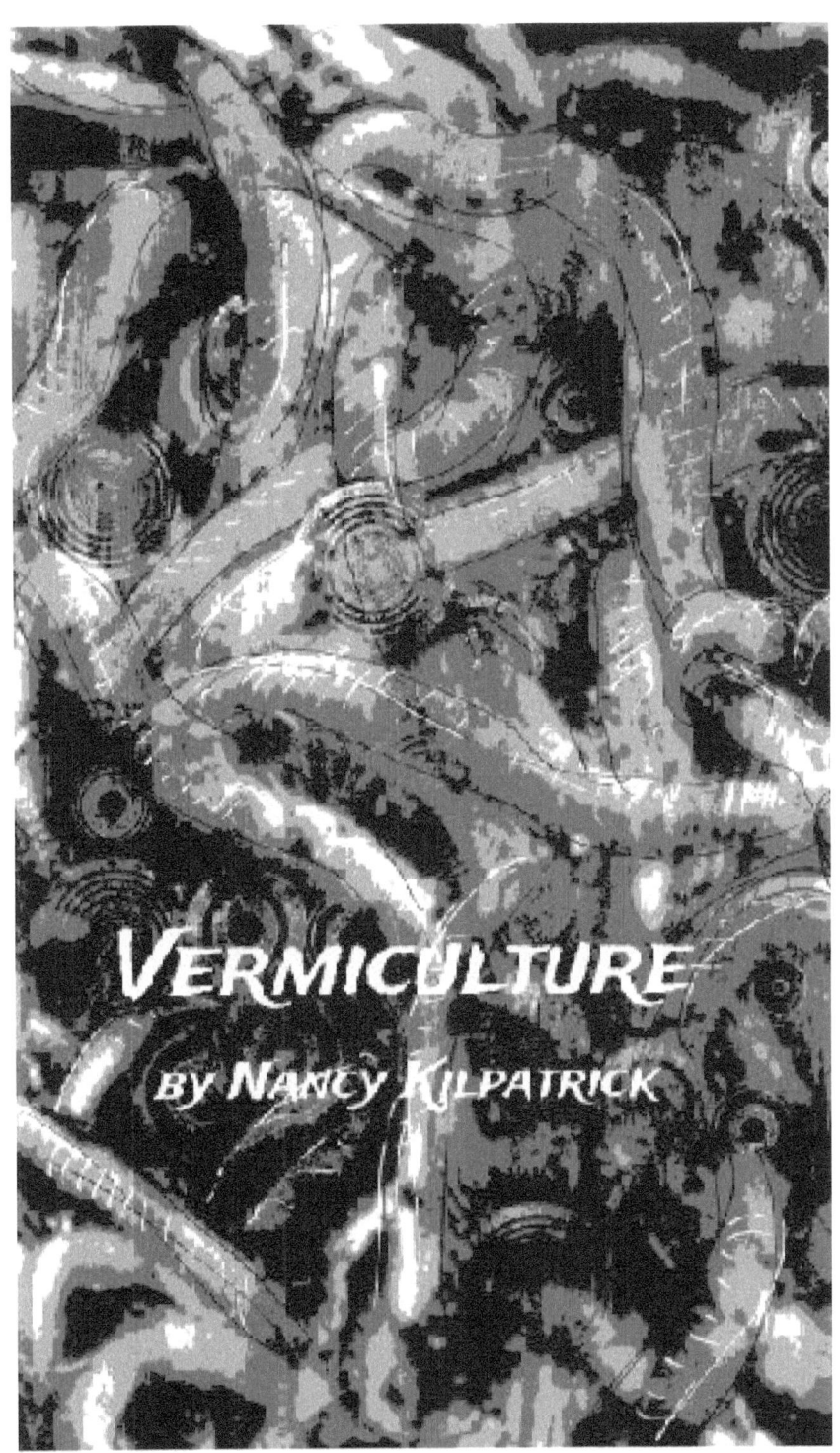

VERMICULTURE

BY NANCY KILPATRICK

VERMICULTURE

BY NANCY KILPATRICK

IT STANK. ROTTING BROCCOLI stalks and tomato ends. Rancid orange peels. Sickeningly-sweet overripe banana skins. Harsh and bitter coffee grounds. Francis picked through the reeking garbage with the blade of a paring knife. He'd been proven right again. Like most new ideas, this one wasn't working. The worms weren't doing their job.

He dug under the remains of a week's worth of meals, down past the newly formed rich topsoil. They should have been there. Ten starter worms. Dull red-brown. Four inchers. Squiggling up through the dirt to gobble the putrid mess through one indistinguishable end and excreting something that leads to new earth through the other.

The knife blade flipped over a lemon half. Three fat-bellied creatures slithered along the edge of the yellow-brown citrus fruit, slinking away from the kitchen light. Francis felt his stomach churn. One burrowed under a discarded romaine leaf that wasn't quite long enough to hide it. An end of the worm lifted up into the air slightly as if that were the head and it was looking at Francis. The thing gave him the creeps.

Why was Monica always changing things? After forty years of marriage, he should be used to it, but he wasn't. If she hadn't been such a nut on recycling, they'd still be tossing food scraps in the compost recycle bin for pickup like normal people. But oh no, she'd wanted a home composter—the latest toy on the market. He thought they were a waste of money. Besides, they needed to be kept outdoors, and the condo had no yard or lawn, only a small deck. One of those cone-shaped plastic bins would have used up a quarter of it and Francis had put his foot down. Kitchen composting was the answer, Monica assured him. Earth worms. In the cabinet. Under the sink. Clean. Out of sight. But not out of mind.

Francis hated creatures that not only failed to resemble human beings but might actively be involved in their decomposition. Insects and reptiles in general. Any kind of worm in particular. Earth worms especially. Blind, dumb, soft-bodied creepers. Driven by instinct. They'd swallow anything, the worst garbage, even rotting flesh. The plumper they were, the more elongated the body, the more detestable.

It was only Monica's promise to be responsible for the whole enterprise that swayed him. All he had to do was empty food scraps into the bin occasionally, instead of into the city's compost bin. The worms would do the rest.

"Eat up," Francis ordered harshly, "or you're fired."

The exposed end of the worm seemed to quiver and Francis blinked. Just looking at it made him nauseous. He had an urge to attack it with the knife but then remembered that when you slice a worm in half you end up with two. He slammed the home composter lid shut as well as the cabinet door and started dinner.

"Fabulous meal." Monica dabbed her lips with the napkin, stood and carried only her own plate away from the table. He sighed at her laziness.

Through the doorway he watched her open the grey cabinet door and dump the remains from the plate into the compost. "They're doing a great job," she called.

Francis got up and went to have a look. The mound of rotting food that had been sitting near the top of the bin not two hours before had turned into fertile silt. "Impossible!" He could hardly believe his eyes.

"You old curmudgeon. *You* didn't think it would work." Monica nipped him on the ear lobe gently and at the same time tried to close the cupboard door with her knee, and failed—Francis had to do it. She turned to rinse one glass under the faucet and place it in the dishwasher.

"Why can't you do all of them, or none of them?" he said, rinsing the rest of the china and cutlery, but she'd already left the room.

They watched a little TV, crawled into bed early, watched a bit more TV and after, an aborted attempt at lovemaking,

Monica was snoring. Francis, though, lay wide awake. He should have been reviewing the figures for tomorrow's meeting but instead his brain was busy trying to comprehend how the worms had processed so much waste in so short a time. Eventually it got the better of him.

The kitchen tiles felt cool against his bare soles. He flipped the light switch but the environmentally-correct bulb choose that moment to blow. "Wonderful," he mumbled, thinking he really should be asleep. Tomorrow was the big meeting, first thing, and he had to report on the company's profits for the quarter. They were down and it would be tricky and he'd need to be wide awake to use the most conservative wording or be eaten alive by the ravenous up-and-comers, who were pushing for change.

There were no spare bulbs in the storage closet— Monica had forgotten to buy them. He wrote *LIGHT BULBS* in large letters and underlined the words on the shopping list attached to the refrigerator with a magnet shaped like a briefcase. The light from the dining room would have to be enough. A quick peek, that's all he needed. His curiosity might or might not be satisfied, but he'd be off to bed getting the sleep he needed.

The moment he opened the cabinet door he thought he heard a low rumble, and held his breath. Nothing. The building had been constructed the year he was born; things creaked. He lifted the lid of the compost bin.

Francis had to rub his eyes. The scraps from dinner —quiche, carrot tops and skin, bits of fettuccini, Earl Grey tea leaves, whole wheat pie crust—all of it had vanished. He got the flashlight from the tool drawer.

The added light just confirmed reality. The clock on the stove read eleven. The nightcrawlers had devoured everything in what? Three hours?

He was confused, upset in a way he couldn't explain, about to turn away and try to repress awareness of the whole thing, when a sudden movement caught his eye. From the rich new earth a glistening pale dot surfaced. The head, or the tail, of an albino worm. It lurched up and plopped itself onto the topsoil in jerky movements. Francis had no idea a worm could move so fast and it rattled him. Once the worm was still, it lifted one end straight up in the air. There was something abject in its position, as if it were the leader appealing on behalf of the others. Francis knew he was thinking irrationally, but he couldn't help feeling stared at. And he sensed that the worm was waiting. "You get a reprieve. But it's temporary. Until your performance can be reassessed," he said nervously, wondering what on earth kept prompting him to talk to these disgusting invertebrates.

The plump rusty nib facing him seemed to relax. It's body went flaccid. Francis gagged and reached the bathroom in time to throw up dinner in shades of orange, tan and brown.

The meeting did not go well. Francis, half asleep, stumbled verbally. The newest, youngest vice president was on his case the whole time. He left work early, claiming to be exhausted—which he was.

All the way home he berated himself. Two new factors that had gouged into profits—the recycling program the local government had forced the company by law to set up, and the union's demands for changes in the working conditions—had eluded him completely during the meeting. No wonder the CEO and the other vice presidents had looked at him as though he were incompetent. The loss didn't make sense because he hadn't fully explained the unorthodox expenses. And now it was too late.

Given the current cost-cutting agenda, he'd be lucky if the Board didn't dismiss him. Of course, he could float a memo to each of the brass, in other words, grovel. Might get him off the hook. He'd have to come up with a legitimate-sounding reason as to why he hadn't mentioned the anomalies responsible for such major disbursements.

Damn those worms! If it wasn't for their insatiable hunger, he'd have slept the night before and been wide awake for the meeting.

As Francis pulled into the driveway, anger severed rational thought. He made a decision. Like a man possessed, he tore open the cupboard doors and lifted the bin out. He snapped a jumbo extra-strength Glad Bag open and deposited the entire recycling bin inside. After he double tied the bag shut, he took it to the trash disposal room and dropped it down the chute.

As he re-entered the apartment, Francis brushed invisible dirt off his hands and sighed in relief. Monica would just have to adapt; they would do what they did before—bag the garbage in the small compost bags and send it down the shoot for the city's weekly compost pickup. He poured himself a glass of Chivas and, toasted to the adage, "The old ways are the best way."

"You did what?" Monica stood in the kitchen, arms crossed over her chest, lips downturned.

"Calm down. We'll get one of those cone things you wanted in the first place and put it on the deck, all right?" He kept his voice even, his tone rational.

"No, it's not all right. What was wrong with the worms? They were doing the job."

He didn't know how to tell her. And, since having a nap and a decent meal, his earlier actions seemed a bit ill-considered, not that he'd admit it to Monica. "Worms aren't meant to live under kitchen sinks. It's unnatural. They should be outside, in the ground, where they belong. You didn't want a dog for that reason."

Monica stared at him with suspicion. "I don't believe this," she said, shaking her head. "You're afraid of them."

"Don't be ridiculous." Francis picked up his cup of Columbian coffee and headed for the living room, but she was on his heels.

"You're afraid of a few earth worms. That's it, isn't it? They scare the pants off you because they're something new and therefore terrifying."

"I refuse to indulge in this inane argument. They don't *scare* me at all. It's simply a matter of a humane approach to another life form."

"Bullshit!" Monica stalked from the room. He heard the apartment door open.

"What are you doing?" he called. There was no answer. A few minutes later, the door closed. He heard plastic being rustled, and hurried to the kitchen.

She had retrieved the bag he'd disposed of and was reinstalling the bin under the sink. "Since it's just a question of humane treatment," she said, scraping leftover salad onto the dirt, "it seems reasonable to keep the worms another day or so, until we get the new recycler. Then we can release them into the park, which is much more compassionate than suffocating them in a non-porous garbage bag while they starve to death, don't you think."

Monica left Francis staring at the closed cupboard door. She'd beaten him at his own game. His temples throbbed. He touched one with a shaking hand; the skin felt clammy.

First thing the next morning, Francis was at the local hardware store. The cones were popular—the store had sold out. The clerk said they expected more next week. It was the same at the other three smaller stores he stopped at on his way to work, and at the two department stores, which he had his secretary phone later.

Damn!, he thought, pulling into his driveway that night. He'd been so preoccupied all day that he completely forgot about sending the memo. Now he was stuck in a circular train of thought: he had to find a compost bin; the entire city had gone crazy for the latest fad; maybe he should instruct his broker to buy stock in one of the companies—obviously a blue chip of the future. But beneath that track bubbled fear—the worms were under his sink. Waiting.

As Francis walked into the kitchen, he saw a note on the table: call the CEO at home, and a reminder from Monica that tonight was her first pottery class—she'd be in late. He hated changes in their routine.

Although Monica detested cooking, she'd prepared a seafood casserole before she left for work that morning to placate him. It was in the freezer. And there was an amaretto cheesecake—his long-time favorite "...to keep you from eating garbage while I'm away," she wrote. The worms will like that, Francis caught himself thinking, and shuddered.

He picked up the phone, about to dial his boss at home, anxious about what could be important enough to warrant a call on a Friday night, when out of the corner of his eye he noticed the cupboard door beneath the sink was open a crack. He hung up and hurried over to close it.

That same rumbling sound came from inside the cupboard, like a trash compactor, grinding. A machine that just won't quit processing. He shook his head, trying to clear it of nonsense.

Francis opened the door slowly. The lid of the bin was ajar. Just like Monica to leave it that way; she did everything half-assed.

He reached in and gripped the lid to straighten it. The churning became a physical sensation. The plastic hummed in his hand. The vibration crawled up his arm. Francis shoved the lid away from him. It clattered to the floor, leaving the interior of the bin exposed.

"Oh my God," he whispered. The remains of breakfast had vanished. There were no scraps from the preparation of the casserole in sight. Rich black soil nearly overflowed the bin. Soil that writhed and undulated from some force just below the surface.

Francis stepped back. He couldn't believe his eyes. Whatever was happening here was abnormal. Perhaps he should get help. But logic intercepted that thought. He hadn't read up on the process, Monica had. Maybe this was part of the composting. It stood to reason there'd be more soil. *But this soon, and this much?* a little voice in his brain warned. And the movement. What about the rumbling?

While Francis struggled as to what to do or not do, a hole spiraled downward into the dark earth. He stared, transfixed, as a white fleshy form nudged its way to the surface. The legless elongated body slithered across the black dirt. Francis was repulsed but relieved. It was still a worm, disgusting to be sure, half the length of a pencil, but thicker. Reality was intact. But tension prompted him to be sterner than he felt. "Don't overproduce," he warned. "You'll flood the market." The worm seemed to shrink back.

The bizarre thought flashed into Francis's mind that the thing was ashamed. He was about to castigate himself for personifying a non-human creature when awareness hit: *the damn thing's pissed at me!* he thought. *It wants praise for its efforts.* But Francis felt too stubborn to give any. It was enough that he was even talking to a sub-species, talking reasonably, as one intelligent form to another, but to acquiesce to cheap emotional ploys, real or imagined? He had to draw the line somewhere and this was the line.

"Shape up or ship out!" He grabbed the lid and smashed it down onto the bin, slammed the cupboard door shut, then raced from the room. He ripped the clothing from his body, crawled into bed naked, burrowing under the covers, shivering, hiding his head beneath the pillow.

He woke in a cold sweat. Groggy. Not himself. The clock radio read eleven.

Francis's eyes felt glued shut, his stomach an empty pouch. He staggered blindly into the kitchen and to the freezer, instinctively drawn toward nourishment.

The casserole was at the top, the transparent lid of the baking dish frosted from condensation. He lifted the dish out and slid it into the microwave, setting the dial to defrost. While waiting for his meal, Francis rubbed his eyes open then located the course catalogue for the art college. *Claywork: Advanced*, ran from 7:30 to 10:30. Monica should be in soon. It was too late to call the CEO.

When the timer rang, he yanked out the serving dish. The food was still cold on the surface but he couldn't wait any longer. He took a large slotted spoon from the cooking utensils rack, about to scoop casserole onto a plate, but changed his mind. Instead he used the spoon to eat right from the dish. Chunks of frozen tuna, icy shrimp hardly warm at the center, broccoli imbedded with frost, teeth-chilling noodles; he gnawed through it all. Everything tasted the same, but

Francis was starving. When he looked down he was surprised to see that the serving dish was empty, but for a few onion bits and half a slice of carrot.

He shoved the dish away and went to the refrigerator for the cheesecake, then to the flatware tray for a fork. The plate he had been going to use for the casserole was still on the table. But when he sat down and opened the baker's box, the sight of the familiar swirling brown and creamy texture triggered an unforeseen instinct that overwhelmed him. The next thing he knew he was licking cheesecake coated hands and staring at a circular cardboard tray littered with crumbs.

He sat for a few moments feeling blank mentally and bloated physically. Then he took the few bits of food that remained to the composter. The lid had fallen off. Earth overflowed the bin and was piled at least an inch deep on the cupboard floor. The soil pulsed and raged hungrily. Within moments the fat white worm surfaced. "Contemptible glutton! Overconsuming. Underproducing. Well, you'll get nothing more!" Francis snapped. He felt savage.

The worm reared like a cobra about to spit venom and Francis ducked. He grabbed the slotted spoon and used the convex side to bash its head-tail in. But the hole swallowed up the worm.

Francis dumped the bin's contents onto the kitchen floor. Down on all fours, he grabbed handfuls of dirt and frantically sifted through the soft clods, using his feet to etch trenches in the soil. Finally he found it.

The gross form squiggled in his grip, but not for long. Francis tore it to pieces. At least half a dozen.

Then he used the edge of the spoon to chop the warm chunks of flesh as fine as chopped garlic. "Try to recoup *those* losses!" he shouted.

Fists on hips and breathing heavily, Francis paused. He surveyed the destruction at his feet like a man who'd put in a distasteful but productive day's work. He was just about to congratulate himself when he heard the rumbling. The soil began to move. Fast.

He couldn't believe what he was seeing and rubbed grimy fists into his eyes. Suddenly he became aware of earth packing itself tightly between his toes, spreading them wide, then along his arches, circled his heels and sliding up his ankles. By the time he reacted, his calves were confined by the dense, hard soil. He struggled to shake his legs free but couldn't budge them. Arms flailing, he dug at the dirt cast that now imprisoned his thighs and groin. The frenetic motion resulted in only outer particles falling to the floor; the dirt had hardened like baked clay.

As the earth pack reached his chest and constricted his rib cage, Francis feared he was being buried alive. The putrid stench of decay lit into his olfactory nerve. "There are options!" he screamed. Humid dirt crawled along his shoulders and up his neck. "You've proven an asset. Invaluable. You've still got a bright future ahead—"

Compost squished between his compressed lips. Warm wet life slithered over his tongue, along the roof of his mouth and down Francis's throat. Simultaneously, he gagged on and eagerly swallowed that life. And when the soil blinded him, his heart outpaced itself.

Time stopped.

In the metamorphosis of that eternal moment, old, dead matter transmuted into fertile new life. Although he hated to do it, Francis had to accept the change. ✕

COMPULSION

BY JILL HAND

COMPULSION

by Jill Hand

THE FIRST TIME I USED kitchen shears. The blades were serrated and had a notch for cutting through joints and poultry bones. I thought they'd be perfect for cutting off my finger.

I had used the shears many times for cutting through chicken bones, especially when I made Poulet Vallée d'Auge, James' favorite dinner. It's a chicken casserole from Normandy. In addition to chicken, it's made with herbs, apples, crème fraiche, and mushrooms, served flambé with apple brandy.

It was time-consuming to shop for all the ingredients then cut up the chicken and carefully core and peel the apples and trim the mushrooms. I was tired from working all day and would have preferred sending out for pizza or Chinese food, but James said that was a waste of money. He said it was better to cook meals at home. Looking back on it, I should have told him to make his own dinner, if it meant so much to him.

Getting back to the shears, I thought they'd cut through my finger, but it turned out that human finger bones are thicker than chicken bones. I'm not a petite woman, but I wouldn't say I'm big-boned. Average is the best way to describe me.

When I knew I couldn't put it off any longer I got the shears out of the drawer in the kitchen where I keep them, along with things like corn on the cob holders, and shish-kebob skewers and extra batteries for the smoke detectors. Having considered which finger would cause me the least inconvenience to lose, I stuck out my left pinkie. (I'm right-handed, so it had to be a finger on my left hand.)

The instructions weren't specific about which finger had to come off, only that I had to cut off one of my fingers or else something very bad would happen, either to me, or to Lacey, my golden retriever. I love Lacey. I was terrified of the thought of something bad happening to her.

Opening the blades I positioned my finger in the bone notch. Then I took a deep breath and brought the handles together as hard as I could.

I'd hoped to get it over with quickly, but all that happened was the blades broke the skin and bounced off the bone. I tried again, and again, desperately hacking at it, but it was no good. If my finger was going to come off I'd have to use something stronger than kitchen shears.

Lacey padded up, whining with anxiety, her claws clicking on the kitchen floor tiles.

"It's okay, girl," I told her. "Go lie down."

She looked at my bleeding finger then up at me. I could tell by her expression that she was worried.

"It's okay," I repeated. "Really. Everything will be fine just as soon as I get this finger off. Go get your bunny, go on!"

Her tail drooping, she went to get her stuffed bunny.

My finger throbbed, the pain pulsing in my palm and zinging all the way to my elbow. I wished I'd thought to take a couple of aspirin first. I also wished I had a power saw, but I didn't. James took it with him when he left, as well as the good laptop computer and most of the money in our joint checking account.

Then I remembered the lopping shears. We used them to trim tree branches. I went outside to the shed where we kept the lawn mower and the garden hose and the cages for tomato plants. The lopping shears were lying on top of a bag of mulch. I carried them to the stone wall which runs along one side of driveway by the mimosa tree. Some of the lower branches of the tree needed trimming. I thought about doing that before I cut off my finger but decided not to. I wanted to get it over with.

Positioning my finger between the blades I brought the handles together. There was a *crunch* that sounded like it did when I cut through branches.

It hurt. I had expected it would, but the pain was like nothing I'd ever experienced before. I shrieked. Inside the house Lacey howled.

My screams brought white-haired Mrs. Gruber from the house next door. She looked at my bleeding hand then at the lopping shears lying in the driveway where I'd dropped them. Her eyes grew huge behind the thick lenses of her eyeglasses.

"You cut off your finger," she said.

"Yes," I said.

Black spots bloomed before my eyes. I wondered if I was going to faint. I'd never fainted before, but it seemed like if anything would make me faint this would be it. I sat down on the wall.

"Hold your hand above your head," Mrs. Gruber said. "I'll go call an ambulance." With that, she tottered back to her house. Mrs. Gruber was around ninety. She used to be a nurse, so there could have been a sound medical reason for her telling me to raise my hand over my head. However I wasn't convinced she would remember to call 9-1-1. Once she got inside she was likely to forget about me and go watch TV or take a nap.

I held my hand up and let the blood run down my arm. Lacey had stopped howling and was barking the way she does when she's annoyed that I went outside without her. That was good. Maybe everything would be all right now that my finger was gone.

To my surprise Mrs. Gruber didn't forget about me. She came out of her house carrying a dishtowel with an elastic bandage and an ice pack bundled in it.

"I called the police. The ambulance is on its way," she said. She bent down, smelling like L'Air du Temps and mothballs. Her snowy curls bobbed as she wrapped the bandage around the stump of my finger. Blood immediately soaked through the bandage.

The finger had rolled to the end of the driveway. It no longer looked like something that was part of my body. Mrs. Gruber tottered over and creakily bent down to pick it up. She placed it on the ice pack and wrapped the dish towel around it.

"Take deep breaths and try to stay calm. The doctors may be able to reattach it. Then you'll be as good as new," she said.

She looked up at the tree. Its fernlike leaves and feathery pink blossoms swayed in the breeze. "Mimosas are so pretty, aren't they? I believe they came from the Far East originally," she said.

We could hear the whoop of sirens approaching.

"That's the ambulance," Mrs. Gruber said. "Do you want me to telephone your husband? He'll be upset to hear you had an accident."

"No thanks," I said. I wasn't sure if she knew James didn't live here anymore. I didn't feel like going into it at the moment, or telling her it wasn't an accident.

The ambulance pulled up in front of the house, followed by a police car. Mrs. Gruber went to meet them carrying my finger.

I was in the hospital for three days. They couldn't reattach my finger. The surgeon came to see me afterwards when I'd recovered from the anesthetic. A nineteen-eighties sitcom about the zany antics of a group of high school students was playing on the TV. I couldn't believe how bad the hairstyles were in the eighties. My roommate, a woman named Karen who'd had gall bladder surgery, was watching it while talking on the phone to someone named Sandra who was about to go on a cruise.

"You're going to have an amazing time," Karen kept saying. "It's going to be absolutely amazing."

The surgeon apologized for his failure to put my finger back on.

"The tendons were too damaged. I'm sorry. We had hoped for a better outcome," he said.

I started to tell him it was all right, but he interrupted me.

"It's not all right," he said angrily. "Those clippers for trimming tree branches are dangerous. They shouldn't be allowed to sell them. I won't go near them. I won't let my wife go near them either. One wrong move and... well..." He grimaced and shook his head. "I've seen too many tragic accidents like yours."

I didn't tell him it wasn't an accident.

Despite the pain in my hand, which the drugs dulled but didn't eliminate, I enjoyed being in the hospital. My supervisor at work was horrified when I called and explained why I wouldn't be there for a few days. She told me not to worry, just concentrate on getting better. Guilt-free, I watched TV, and chatted with Karen and enjoyed the novelty of choosing what I wanted to eat by circling items on a menu then having it brought to my bedside.

In addition I had plenty of time to think. I'd lie awake late at night, after the pain medication wore off and before a nurse came with a paper cup with more pills in it. I started to wonder if I'd been imagining things and I'd cut my finger off for nothing, but then I dismissed that idea. It wasn't my imagination. I was certain of it.

The question was what should I do now? Cutting off my finger had been bad, but poking one of my eyes out would be worse. I suspected I'd soon be ordered to do something like that or maybe even something worse. I needed to make a plan.

Mrs. Gruber sent an arrangement of carnations and daisies. She called to say I shouldn't worry about Lacey; her sixteen-year-old great-granddaughter Nikki was walking her and feeding her and filling her water bowl. She said Nikki was also collecting my mail and leaving it on the kitchen counter.

"Thank you, and thank Nikki for me. Tell her I'll pay her when I get out of the hospital," I said, adding, "The weather's nice. Maybe she could take Lacey to the dog park. Lacey loves the dog park."

It would be better for Nikki to spend time with Lacey at the dog park instead of inside my house. I'd rather she wasn't in my house any longer than was absolutely necessary. I didn't want the clock to start talking to her the way it talked to me.

James had bought the clock home about a year ago, saying he'd found it at an estate sale. He carried it into the house and sat it down on the coffee table in the living room, shoving the papers I'd brought home from work and the library book I was reading onto the floor to make room.

"Look! Isn't it great? I always wanted one," he said. "They're collector's items. They cost a lot of money, some of them."

"How much did you pay for it?" I asked. I was appalled by how ugly it was. I wanted to say that whatever he paid, it was too much, but I didn't. James was easily offended. He tended to pout, closing his mouth and blowing out his cheeks like a puffer fish when he was angry. He'd sulk, holding a grudge for days. It was behavior he didn't begin to display until after we were married.

I didn't like the looks of the clock at all. It gave me the creeps. Besides, we didn't need it. We already had two alarm clocks. There was a clock on the microwave, and a retro-style gold sunburst clock on the living room wall that we got for a wedding present. We have iPhones that tell us the time, and James has an Apple watch. We didn't need this ugly thing.

"Forty-five dollars," James said, after a guilty pause. I suspected he was lying and it had been much more. Money was tight, what with the mortgage and our car payments and our other expenses. We'd agreed that any purchase over fifty dollars had to be approved by both of us first. I'd been good about it but James frequently transgressed, as I discovered from going over the credit card bills.

"I can buy things if I want to," James said, nettled by my silence. "I earn money. I have a right to buy things."

When I didn't reply, he fumed. "There you go, giving me the silent treatment again. I was happy and then you had to go and spoil everything."

He picked up the clock. Hugging it protectively to his chest, he stalked off. I could hear him rooting around in the hall closet where we keep the tool box, followed by the sound of hammering. He hadn't bothered to ask me where I thought the clock should go. I could feel a headache coming on. James would be in a foul mood for hours. No matter what I did or said he'd be sullen, all because of the damn clock.

It was a cuckoo clock, the kind that comes from the Black Forest in Germany. It was big, almost two feet high, carved from dark-brown wood. On top was a wooden deer's head with spreading antlers. Below it was a chalet with a pointed shingled roof flanked by pine trees. These were painted dark green, with dabs of white paint at the tips, representing snow. Beneath a circular dial with Roman numerals two little men sawed wood, swaying back and forth. Little wooden figures would pop out from behind doors, seemingly at random. Their painted face wore sly expressions. There was a hunter with a gun, a woman carrying a baby, a man wearing lederhosen holding a stein, a girl with blonde braids, and a red-haired boy in a pointed green hat like Robin Hood's.

The pendulum swings, going *snee snee snee*. It chimes once on the half-hour. Every hour a door at the peak of the roof opens and a bird pops out. It opens its pointed red beak and makes a high-pitched whistling scream, like a teakettle. Underneath, two metal weights shaped like pinecones hang from metal chains.

Describing it, the clock doesn't sound so bad, but it gave off waves of malevolence that made me feel physically ill.

James later explained that the clock had an eight-day movement, meaning that about once a week it had to be wound by pulling the chains down.

The clock didn't go with the rest of our décor. It was too big, too dark, too old, too frightening, the way one of its doors would suddenly fly open and a little figure would pop out. It may have been intended to be whimsical, but it didn't seem that way to me. It was uncanny the way a door always seemed to open with a loud snap just as I was walking past. It was as if the clock waited for me to appear so it could startle me. I never saw it do that when James was there; it only seemed to happen when I was by myself.

It got so I dreaded going near it. I'd sometimes go out the back door and walk completely around the outside of the house, coming in the front door in order to avoid it.

The clock didn't talk at first. That came later. At first it was content to simply loom there, its pendulum swinging, throwing its spiky shadow onto the polished floorboards and scaring me by popping its doors open. One time, all the doors flew open at once. I cried out and backed away.

"What's going on?" James called from the spare room he'd fitted up as a home office. He spent a lot of time in there, playing computer games and doing other things that I didn't find out about until after he left. To my astonishment I discovered he had several different identities on dating websites, including one in which he claimed to be a wealthy businessman called Esteban Moldovano.

"It's the cuckoo clock," I said, my voice shaking. "All the doors came open."

James came out and examined it, frowning.

"They're closed now," he said, looking at me strangely.

"They were open a minute ago," I told him.

"Did you bump against it? If you jostled it you could have made the doors come open," he said. "You should be more careful with it; it's an antique."

Amplified shouts and thunderous explosions came from the spare room.

"Shit," James said, dashing back in there. "My platoon is supposed to be launching an attack on a castle full of Nazi vampires. I'm missing it."

The clock had a nasty habit of gathering spider webs, gray sticky ones that engulfed it overnight. James demanded to know why I didn't dust it.

"I do," I said. "I dust everything."

It's true. Although I hated the cuckoo clock I still flicked the feather duster over it at least once a week, just like I did everything else in the house.

"Dust it more often," James said. "It can't be that hard. When I go to other people's houses I don't see spider webs everywhere."

There weren't spider webs everywhere, only on the clock.

Then it started talking, ordering me to do things.

At first they were innocuous things.

"Spin around," it would say when I approached with an armful of laundry. "Put that down. Spin around. Spin."

There'd be feeling of gathering menace if I hesitated. The atmosphere brooded and grew darker. It felt like something was creeping up on me, something that wouldn't hesitate to do me harm.

"You'd better do it," the clock would hiss. "Spin. Spin now."

I'd spin until I was dizzy. I didn't want to find out what would happen if I didn't. I learned it was a bad idea to refuse to obey the clock's commands after I resisted its demand that I eat a centipede that was crawling in the bathtub.

"Eat it," the clock ticked gleefully. "Eat it! Go on, eat it!"

Shuddering, I scooped the wiggling thing up in a wad of toilet paper and flushed it down the toilet.

There was a furious silence. Then Lacey yelped. She'd cut her paw on a piece of glass and was limping and moaning in distress. Somehow a glass pitcher had fallen from the top of the breakfront in the dining room and shattered. There was no reason for it to fall; it was at least six inches from the edge, but it had.

Lacey needed stitches. The clock had made its point clear: disobey and one of us would get hurt.

I tried resisting its commands. I put Lacey in the boarding kennel to make sure she'd be safe and then I resolutely refused to do what it told me. But I couldn't hold out. The feeling of panic built to the point that it was overwhelming. I had to give in.

"Cut yourself!" the clock would say. "Slap yourself!" "Bite your lip! Harder! Make it bleed!"

It got so I was covered with bruises. The marks on my arms were still there a month later, when I went to the hospital after I'd cut my finger off.

"Did a cat do that?" asked a nurse, noticing the long red scars.

"Yes. It was a stray I took in. I had to give it away," I said.

"It's a good thing you did. It really tore you up," she said.

There was no cat. I'd done it myself, with a fork.

I didn't tell anyone the clock was making me do things. They'd think I was crazy, or at the very least that I'd developed an obsessive-compulsive disorder. It wasn't that. I had no compulsion to check and re-check to make sure I'd locked the back door, or that the burners on the stove were turned off, or to do any of the other kinds of things that compulsive people do. It was the clock. I was fine before James brought it into the house.

I'd never liked cuckoo clocks. My grandparents had one that had dead birds carved on it. The birds hung upside-down by their curled claws beneath a pair of crossed rifles. I disliked staying at their house because of it, but bad as my grandparents' clock had been, this one was a hundred times worse. This was the cuckoo clock from Hell.

Then James left, saying he needed some time to himself. He'd done it before, leaving for a day or two and then coming back. This time a week went by. I called his cell phone. It rang and rang. I thought he wouldn't answer but eventually he did.

"What?" he said.

I could hear voices talking and laughing in the background.

"Are you coming home?" I asked.

"I need a break. I told you that. Weren't you listening? Sometimes people need to take a break," he said. The noise in the background grew louder. It sounded like a party. "Just a minute, I'll be right there," he said to someone.

Gathering my courage I blurted, "Most of your clothes are still here, and that cuckoo clock. You need to come and get the clock."

"Don't tell me what I need to do," he said. His voice grew colder. "Don't touch any of my things. I'll know if you do and you'll be sorry." With that he ended the call.

I tried to call back but it rang and rang before going to voice mail. I left a message saying it was important that he call me, but he didn't. The next time I called I got a recorded message saying his voicemail was full.

That was on a Sunday. When I tried to call him at work the next day the woman who answered the phone said nobody named James Harris worked there.

"Yes he does," I said. "Check again, please. He's my husband. I know he works there."

"We have a Rachael Harris in accounting, but no James," she said. I could hear the keys on a keyboard clicking. She must have been consulting a list of personnel. "Wait a minute. I see we have a James Hannon in building and grounds, is that who you want?"

"No. His name is James Harris. He works in marketing. He's tall and has fair hair. He usually wears a blue suit," I said.

"Doesn't ring a bell, but let me check again," she said. Keys clicked. "No, there's nobody by that name in marketing. Maybe you should try over at MCS, that's Meridian Cost Solutions. They're in the building next door. People are always getting us mixed up with them."

That was two days before the clock told me to cut off my finger. Afterwards, in the hospital, I tried to think what I should do next. I thought the clock would know what I was up to if I took it down off the wall to throw it away. If I loaded it into the trunk of my car, intending to toss it in a dumpster, I thought there was a good chance the brakes would fail and I'd have an accident.

If I tried to smash it with a hammer I was afraid it would make me turn the hammer on myself. I even had the wild idea of burning the house down, but I had no idea how to do that and not be sure the fire wouldn't spread to the houses nearby.

I could hope James would return and I could manage to persuade him to get rid of it, but that seemed unlikely. I thought I'd seen the last of James Harris. The few people who attended our wedding were my friends, not his. He'd told me he had no living relatives, and that all of his friends had other plans for that day. It came as a shock to realize I'd never met any of his friends. I knew almost nothing about him, not where he was from, or where he'd gone to school or what he'd been doing before we met.

In an effort to recall more about him I looked through the pictures on my phone. He wasn't in many, and in those he was only a back of a head, or a bit of profile, just an ear and a hint of jawline and neatly trimmed sideburn. Whenever I tried to take his picture he'd pretend to cooperate, solemnly facing me and waiting for me to press the button and then turning away at the last second. I'd feel frustrated but then I'd join him in laughing at how quick he was. It had seemed playful at the time, just a harmless bit of teasing, but what was the point?

We'd been together two years. We furnished a home, made love, did all the things couples do, but there was something strangely elusive about him. What was James, really?

That's what I wondered as I laid awake, waiting for the nurse to bring me more pills. ✗

ANOTHER DOOR OPENS

BY SÈPHERA GIRÓN

ANOTHER DOOR OPENS

BY SÈPHERA GIRÓN

I BLAME THOSE DAMN KIDS' movies and their crazy images. You know the ones, like the nightmare Pink Elephants in the original *Dumbo*, hell even the ones in the remake, or the creepy Parrot Umbrella in *Mary Poppins* or the angry talking trees in the *Wizard of OZ*. The worst though are the doorknobs, like in *Alice in Wonderland* where they mock her. Stupid doorknobs for noses, weird shaped keyholes for puckered mouth and screws or other embellishments creating eyes. Stupid movies play like puppets in my mind and they tell me things.

When I moved into my latest apartment, I didn't really have a choice where to go. I had arrived in Toronto from small town Lucan with a suitcase in hand and a smile on my face. I figured that I could waitress in any number of places with ten years experience at Flo's Food Emporium, highlight of Lucan. Although Lucan was a sleepy town, it did have its charm and was a hub of traffic to and from London, Toronto and Stratford. There was huge interest in Lucan for true crime and horror buffs. It was the home of the Black Donnellys.

Although for years, the owners rarely let the curious walk the Donnellys' land, many still wanted to drive by and see where the historic residence had burned down. And maybe even see a ghost!

So, I knew from tourists, and the mad rush of bus tours. Good experience for the big city.

But wow, rent was pretty horrific in Toronto, but I couldn't stay forever in the Air BnB I had found while I job hunted and apartment hunted.

I didn't have a steady gig, but I did get work now and again through a hospitality app. Like Uber for servers. I got pretty good at the huge banquet hall and museum party gigs, but still, work was sporadic when I first arrived in the spring. And I only ever got about one in five jobs that I applied for. If you don't hear the ding from the app when a new gig goes up, you might not even have a chance to apply for it, there are hundreds of hungry servers vying for the same gigs!

At any rate, I had enough for a tiny room, well, a city apartment, I guess. In Lucan, this room might be the pantry, and perhaps it once was, it was a big huge old house on a street of big old huge houses, and they all were boarding houses.

When I first walked towards the house for my appointment many months ago to meet the property manager, the house's sad droopy eyes haunted me from halfway down the block. Without even glancing at my phone for verification, I knew that house knew that I was going to be its latest tenant.

The cars on the street were old and broken down, except for one shiny fancy-ass silver car parked in front of the house.

The cracks in the sidewalk muttered and twittered, taunting me, waiting for me to step on them. But I never did. They could spread out as far and wide as they like, and I would still know how to jump over their leering maws. The path leading up to the house was old-fashioned cobblestone. Why it was so curvy like a snake was beyond me, the other houses had proper sidewalks that led straight to the steps. But this one was windy and those cobblestones jutted out like pimples ready to pop. Didn't quite like that so I walked quickly over them, hoping my Doc Martens would protect me from any splatter. The old wooden stairs groaned as I walked up them and though I'm not a Skinny Minnie, I'm not sure I've ever been afraid of falling through stairs before in a place I was about to call home.

The landlord startled me as he was sitting in one of the old overstuffed sofas on the porch, waiting. The pillar had hidden him, of course, and so when he spoke, I jumped.

"Hey, no need to be so jumpy," he grinned. He was young, like me, perhaps in his late twenties, with a broad smile and twinkling dark eyes. He wore an expensive blazer and shirt with designer jeans. I know the type. Quick to charm the pants off of you and just as quick to leave. But boy oh boy the time in-between.

"I didn't see you there," I confessed. "Name's Kay."

"Yes, Katherine Morris," he said holding out his hand. I stared at the hand and he waved it. "Shall we?"

I walked ahead a couple of steps and reached for the

door. He was quick to grasp the handle.

"Allow me," he said.

I looked down at the hand on the knob, his large strong hand, I bet he knew how to use those fingers. His fingers turned that knob and the door cried out as he swung it open. The smell of cat piss and dusty old thrift stores hit me like a fist. I put a hand to my nose.

"Gotta oil that thing, those hinges," he said as he leaned down to look at the bottom of the door. "I'll get that done before I leave. Don't want everyone complaining."

We stood in a tiny narrow hallway, stuffed in with not many options. There was a door on each side of us and steep narrow stairs leading straight up.

"I'll go first, in case there's anyone around," he said. He mounted the stairs that creaked and groaned under his black shiny boots. I followed him up and we reached a narrow landing where there were four more doors.

"I'm showing you the third floor," he said as he led me up another flight of squeaky stairs. The smell wasn't as bad up here and there were only two doors on this landing.

"The penthouse," he joked.

I rubbed my forehead with my hand. I was sweating. It must be ten degrees hotter up here than below.

His forehead glistened as well, creating soft curls that dropped from his carefully coiffed hair.

He took a ring of keys from his jeans and sorted through them until he found an old-fashioned key. A skeleton key. He pushed it into the keyhole. He had to rattle it several times.

"Seems to be stuck," he half grinned. I could tell by his sweat that he was trying not to scream in frustration as the door kept pushing him away. I knew his type. All charm and sweetness, and then next thing you know, they are screaming at you because something fucked up somewhere else. I knew it all too well. So, I had to maybe give him credit that he wasn't screaming. Yet.

He chose another key and then another until at last, the door yielded.

"I need to get a better key made."

The door swung open to reveal a tiny attic room with a sloped wooden roof and a tiny window. Ugly wood paneling lined the walls. I walked the short length of the room towards the window, it reminded me of the circle windows in a submarine. Or a big O of surprise on a cartoon character. Or those damn trees in *Wizard of Oz.*

The room was dark save the limited light from the window. A tall weeping willow somewhat blocked the street view. Funny I hadn't really noticed the tree from the outside when I was navigating the cobblestones. Or at least how old and angry it was as it seemed to huff in disdain, leaves brushing the screen on the window. The trunk was huge; no doubts the roots were responsible for the unevenness of the cobblestones. The cobblestones gleamed below in the sunlight, shiny like wasps' eggs in a honeycomb. I thought I saw one shift, but the dude was speaking. I turned around and noticed that though the room was small; it seemed to have everything. Certainly, more than most rooms or apartments in this price range that I'd seen so far.

"The stove is gas, a small unit to be sure, but you have two burners and a small oven. Some of the downstairs units only have hot plates so you're in the deluxe suite," the landlord chuckled. There was a small sink and even overhead cupboards. "You'll need to get your own bed. Most tenants seem to prefer futons as they are easier to get up the stairs."

"The ad said a thousand a month..." I said.

"Yes, a thousand a month. I have a couple of offers already, but, one's a family and you and I both know this room isn't big enough for four people."

I nodded. Big enough for one but no more.

"Is it just you?" he asked. "How many are you planning to have here."

"Just me."

"Pets?"

"I have none right now. Is there a rule?"

"No rule about cats. A few of the other tenants have them."

"I figured as much."

"You probably wouldn't want a dog in here." He said. I shrugged.

"No interest in a dog. Three flights up and then this tiny room... not my style." I said, pretending to be lofty and disinterested. He nodded.

"You can see the place is empty. You can move in the first. Three days from now. We'll do one last spray for bugs before you move in."

"Just like that."

"Well, might as well get you moved in before I change my mind or that family comes back. You got the money now?"

"Cash, check, draft?"

"Do you have the cash for first and last?"

"Yes."

And just like that, the house made me its newest tenant.

After I moved in, work was good for a while; I was barely home during the summer tourist season. I ended up working so much as a temp server that I didn't think to look for a job until things began to slow down in the fall. Suddenly, work was slow. A week went by with no work. And then two.

I woke one day, my head throbbing. It was one of those hot, windy fall days and the attic was a million degrees. The wind whistled through cracks in the windowpane and caused the door to rattle. I stared at the door, the knob twitching, the screwy eyes staring back as the keyhole gasped with its O mouth.

"What am I going to do?" I flopped back on my futon and wept towards the ceiling. Tears leaked from my eyes, hot and salty, dripping into my ears.

The cracks in the ceiling swam the more I stared at them. My tears blurred them into faces that ranged from concern to laughter. Outside, the willow tree scratched at the roof. Tears flowing into my ears made the world sound like it was underwater. The doorknob rattled. No, you can't come in.

The dragging of branches against the roof in the wind was insistent. I flopped over onto my stomach and pulled my pillow over my head. I sobbed into the mattress, hoping no one heard me, I didn't want them to know I was weak.

"I'm going to be homeless..." I sputtered to no one. The house seemed to sway in the growing wind. How I yearned for a comforting pat on the back or a warm hug. Instead, my phone dinged, the special notification ding that meant a job had been posted. I jumped up and found my phone then stared in disbelief at the listing. Five days in a row for museum parties. I clicked "apply" and then the wonderful ding of acceptance echoed in the room. I got it! The holiday season had begun!

Again, the money flowed, and I even got a few tips, although you weren't supposed to get tipped through the service. But once in a while, those money sponsors at the museum fundraisers would slip me a fifty or even a hundred. Good times indeed!

New Year's Eve was a blurry spin of glitter and lights, aching back from hauling endless trays of dishes and glasses, throbbing feet, my app said I walked twenty-three miles that night, and a thousand-dollar tip from some wealthy bazillionaire.

A brand-new year and by the time we had run the last of the glassware through the dishwasher and had all the chairs returned to their rightful spots around the tables we rolled, the dawning sun was sparkling through the windows.

And boy was it cold. There had been freezing icerain all night and the roads glistened like boiled sugar. I slipped as I stepped out of the building and nearly fell. Luckily the railing was suddenly under my fingers and I was able to steady myself.

"Not sure I'm going to make it to the streetcar..." I

stared with dismay down the sidewalk as did several other temp staff who also were ready to face the morning.

"Huh..." said Sharon. "That looks pretty deadly."

"I guess we should call an Uber."

Even when I got out of the Uber at my building, I dreaded going home. The house looked awake and angry, tongue glistening, eyes dark and menacing. The cobblestones were covered with ice but there were also patches of snow and their unevenness actually made it easier to walk on than the city sidewalks had been. I carefully balanced, my parka rustling, my heavy boots squeaking in the stillness, my knapsack so heavy on my back.

"Just gotta make it to the door and then I can pass out. "

I made it to the stairs, also slick with the fresh ice. I grabbed the rickety rail and slowly half crawled up the steps. I'll be damned if I break a leg after all the work I did that night.

I looked around. The willow tree was smirking, and I know the house across the street was laughing at me too but as long as no one else saw me, all would be well.

But it wasn't.

The new year brought strange things. 2020 was more than a news show. It was a raging cauldron of fury, from environmental issues, to political feuds to the pandemic.

As the new year unfolded, I waited for job

opportunities but there were none except a short blip around lavish Chinese New Year parties. The Year of the Rat; clever and agile, and again, I was rewarded for my work above and beyond the thirty dollar an hour wage that temp work brought.

However, by late January, it was becoming apparent that the world was shifting, as the house moaned under the frosty winds, the roof creaking with each new layer of snow. Something was in the air. Even the door agreed; its doorknob face shifting from a state of astonishment to one of wariness.

Every once in a while, I'd pull out a sock from my dresser, one stuffed with bills, loonies and toonies. I looked around the room, careful to note who might be eavesdropping. No one at this point. Even the guitarist next door hadn't made a peep.

As I sorted and counted my money, gentle strums followed with some of the worst folk singing I'd ever heard. I knew that he wasn't a good singer but holy socks, that was the worst.

It was becoming a habit, rustling through the money, stacking it and counting it. The neighbour had changed songs, still trying to sing. And oh boy, I don't know if he had on headphones, I think he must have, but he was trying to rap Eminem's Godzilla challenge about fifty times in a row. But at least he drowned out the sound of the money rattling around. One sound you need to hide in a boarding house is the sound of money.

I still had enough for another month of rent and some groceries, thanks to the bazillionaire. And I still had a month of rent in the bank. I could relax... for a minute. I had planned for the slow times; it wasn't my first time in the hospitality business. I rebooted my phone in case the work app had glitched out and I wasn't getting the notifications.

The door still stared at me and I turned my back to it.

Scrolling through my phone, waiting for more work, it was becoming apparent that the world was still shifting. There had been some kind of illness, an outbreak in China in December... and despite that seeming so far away, it was becoming a concern to certain bloggers and YouTubers. I switched from my phone to my tablet, studying charts and scrolling through feeds. At first, I had written it all off as silly conspiracy theories from the tinfoil brigade, but slowly, it seemed something else was going on.

As the days went by, there were more videos, more theories, and soon, more actual news from the big news places.

Wash your hands.

Wear gloves.

Wear a mask.

Don't wear a mask.

Use sanitizer.

Don't use sanitizer.

So many theories and advice. I stood up and reached for my work knapsack. One thing about being a server, you're always wearing disposable gloves, and I had a bad habit of taking a pile when I'd begin a shift and shoving them into my apron to use as I went instead of always taking from the boxes in the kitchen. You never knew if a box was going to chomp down on your hand, so it was always best to just grab a bunch of gloves at the beginning to be safe. As I dumped my knapsack out, and really went through the shoes, uniforms and aprons, I saw that I had amassed quite a pile of gloves over the past few months. And that wasn't even including the ones I had stashed in one of the plastic storage boxes I used as a dresser.

Did I need to wear the gloves?

I stared at the pile. I went to my little submarine window and looked out at the world. It looked the same, the arrogant willow tree, the half-covered cobblestones hatching wasp eggs, the sidewalk reaching down the street, daring someone to step on its cracks.

As I looked, I saw someone walking down the street, wearing a hospital mask. And then I saw another... crazy!

I pulled out a few twenties and my empty knapsack and strapped on my winter boots. I needed to go get supplies. Needed to go out there before something more happened.

I reached for the doorknob, but he scowled at me.

"I need to go out and get some food...I think there's something wrong." I told him. I reached for the door again, and it rattled. My vinyl-covered hand grabbed the knob. It was hot!

"Ow!" I called out and tried to pull my hand away. The glove was melting onto it. The neighbour was still trying to rap the Godzilla chorus. I pulled my hand out of the glove as it melted completely and then dripped to the floor.

"What the hell!" I said. I found an oven mitt and

reached for the door again. At last, I was successful in getting that door opened. I put on more gloves.

While I was out in the world, it was obvious that things had shifted a bit. I hadn't really gone out in a few days. The air felt anxious, thick and pregnant with anticipation. And not a good one. The sidewalk was really going out of its way to entice me into the cracks, but I wasn't going to fall for that. I went into the corner grocery store and bought a mountain of canned goods, as if a tornado was coming and I'd be holed up for a month with nothing but a can opener. I also bought candy, some cleaning stuff like Lysol spray and wipes as recommended by many YouTubers and of course, a few bags of my favourite coffee. I also stopped at the beer store for a two-four and the dispensary for a couple of bags of weed.

As I approached the house with my purchases, it seemed almost pleased, its eyes raised in relief, and the cobblestones didn't give me any trouble as I climbed the stairs. The key even worked the first time I tried!

I lugged my bags up the creaky stairs, the smell of cat and mold stronger than ever. I passed all the doors, so many doors, doors that presumably had people behind them that I'd never seen or heard, or maybe the cats had eaten them all.

My neighbour was home, still trying to rap Godzilla. Good lord, dude, give it up!

I shoved the key into the O but the door spit it back out.

"Oh, come on. These bags weigh a ton!" I told it. It smirked and stuck its tongue out at me. I crammed the key in and didn't let it come out again until that door was jiggled open.

I dragged all the bags inside and before I could turn around, the door swung shut.

The door spit the key out at me, as if it was sticking out its tongue. I picked the key up from the floor and studied it. How did that happen?

I realized I still had gloves on from the outside world and went into the little bathroom to wash my hands in them and then I took them off and washed them again.

The news reports all said to wash hands. That there may be an outbreak. That there may be some kind pandemic beginning...

In my lifetime...

I put the gloves into the little wastebasket in the bathroom and then I went to one of my bags and found the spray. I went back and sprayed the basket with the gloves. That was a lot of spray and it made me cough.

I went to the window to open it. It was resistant as it often was when it was cold out.

"Come on, window... open up. You know we can't breathe all that spray..."

The window sighed and opened. I pressed my face against the screen, sucking in fresh air. Mr. Rap Star was still struggling with the lyrics. Holy crap, you're not going to win, dude. The contest is over...

I turned back and thought about the gloves in the wastebasket. They had been touching everything in the outside world. Maybe I needed to throw them out.

Sighing, I put on another pair of gloves, and grabbed a plastic bag from my stash of bags in another box that I used for storage and returned to the bathroom. I scooped up the dirty gloves from the trash with the bag and tied up the bag. I grabbed the can of disinfectant and sprayed the doorknob with it. He puckered up his face angrily. Then I took a sheet of wipes and wiped the door.

"It's for your own good," I told him as I tried the door again. I saw the key on the shelf and went back to get it. I wiped it with the wipe and shoved it in my pocket.

I finally got the door open and went down the three flights to put the bag in the trash, wiping every door along the way with the wipes.

Man, it was COLD out there.

I ran back into the house and up the stairs. I wiped the door again with the wipe and shoved the key into the O.

This time, he let me back in without a complaint.

I went back inside and realized that now I had to wash my glove hands again to take off the gloves and throw the gloves into the trash and spray the trash and...

UGH!

I went and got another bag from the bag pile and put the gloves into it, touching them with a fresh wipe.

"Oh my god! Now what!" I tucked the bag into a corner by the door.

The door smirked at me, creaking slightly open.

"NO!" I slammed it shut. The noise must have startled Mr. Rap Star as he stopped for a moment, but only a moment to clear his throat, and then he started up again.

I locked the door, twisting that knob so hard that there was no way it was coming open again without my knowledge.

I put away my goods and settled in to watching TV. I didn't have cable so I could only get whatever my HD TV antenna that I got at Factory Direct could pick up. Of course, it was frustrating that just when I'd start to watch something, the tree would sway in the wind and the channel would go to static.

And even when it worked, it seemed like there was only news, news, news... horrible news from Canada, the States, from around the world.

It was almost a joke, really. Where were the sitcoms?

I turned off the TV and resorted to watching movies from YouTube on my tablet.

Days passed and judging by the cold and snow on the outside, the dire news on the inside, and the lack of pings for jobs, I sat on my bed, eating soup and crackers, aiming for distraction. It was too cold to go for an aimless walk. I saw the boiled sugar ice had returned, and the heavy tree limbs scratching my roof did nothing for my sleep. But at least I had booze and weed to knock me out. At least until they were gone.

Twice, I heard the creak of the door as Mr. Rapper came and went but it seemed like he was as housebound as I was. At least he got off the Godzilla train and was working on old Eminem and even some rock songs. He wasn't too bad when he was playing good ol rock and roll, that was his forte. Sometimes I'd just lie on my bed smoking weed and listen to him.

The wall between us seemed to like the rock songs better as well. The wall glowed, almost yellow when he'd play. Yet if he rapped or fell silent, it was back to old dark wood paneling.

One day I looked outside and saw that spring had come. The snow had melted, the sun was shining. Of course, this is Canada. You can begin the day with summer and end with a blizzard, so I didn't fall for nature's tricks. There weren't many people walking around and those who did wore hospital or dust masks.

A walk would be so nice, even if the sidewalk would try to trick me.

I pulled on my coat and gloves. I put a couple of wipes into my coat pocket. I grabbed a twenty from my stash and went to the door.

But the door wouldn't open.

I pulled the knob, I even put the key in the hole though it was the wrong side. The tree scrapped angrily against the roof and the floorboards rippled under my feet. The air grew thick and hot, heat rolling into the key and knob, burning my hand through the glove, leaving the glove melting on the door once more.

What the hell!

I didn't have the energy to fight with the door, so I resigned myself to taking off my coat and gloves and going back to my bed cocoon. I listened to the neighbour sing a Who song, "Won't Get Fooled Again." He began coughing during one of the screams that he used to do so well.

A short time later, I heard the neighbour door open and then a knock on my door.

I froze. No one had ever knocked on my door before.

"Hello?" I asked.

"Hey... it's your neighbour. I was wondering, since it's like, so hard to get to the store... well, you know what I mean... do you by any chance have a roll of toilet paper I can buy from you?"

"Toilet paper?" I laughed.

"Yeah, man... there's none anywhere in the city from what I've heard." He said and then coughed.

"Um... sure?" I raised my eyebrows and went into my bathroom where I still had several rolls. But then I thought, if I open the door, and yet... he coughed... and yet...

I went to put on my gloves and took the toilet paper. I even wrapped my winter scarf around my face so that I looked like the mummy. I went to open the door, but it wouldn't open.

"Damn door is stuck again," I shouted.

"Let me try," he said through his coughing. He rattled from his side, but the door resisted.

We both pushed and pulled for a while.

"Never mind. I know how stubborn this house can be," he said. I heard the door to his unit slam shut.

And I never heard him sing again.

It's been a long time now, since I last heard the neighbour. I still have never been able to open the door and I haven't tried in many days. The news is worse all the time. There is death everywhere even in Toronto. And the smells that come through the walls are worse than cat and mothballs. And there hasn't been a job ping in months. At least the landlord hasn't been by for his rent either. Or at least, I don't think he has.

I thought about my growing up years in Lucan and when I used to work at Flo's which lead to meandering thoughts about the Black Donnellys. How they had come from Ireland and ultimately been murdered by the town vigilantes, how their house had been burned to the ground and yet people still came to see the spot where their home had once stood over a hundred years later. Sure, they hadn't been goody-two-shoe citizens of the world, but they likely weren't any worse than any of the other townsfolk. That's what made their story so compelling. And of course, why the ghost - hunters were always looking for answers.

People are weird. They say they want love, peace and happiness. But it's all lies. So much hate. So much bitterness. So much racism. It was no wonder that everything was falling apart, that the Year of the Rat began with a purging.

It's really hot up in this attic and I guess at some point, I should come out for air. But the world has gone mad out there. Those who haven't died in the pandemic are running in the streets, packs of people looting and murdering. The news, what news there is, grows worse daily.

It makes me sad, so sad that instead of pulling together to save the world, to save each other, man did what man does best. Be assholes. Just like the town was to the Black Donnellys.

I want to go outside. It's so hot. So fucking hot up here.

I heard the downstairs front door scream, much like

it had when I first saw the place. It was weird to hear it screaming all the way up here. I guess it was time to get oiled again.

I wipe my hair away from my face, sweat dripping and stinging my eyes. I put on a clean t-shirt and shorts. I've been doing my laundry in the bathtub so that I don't stink even if the house does. I take a pair of gloves from the box and slip them on, not so easy when you're sweating to death. I put some money and wipes in my pocket and grab the key.

The door puckers up, the O snapping shut.

"I need to leave. I'm going to lose my mind in this heat!" I tell it.

It refuses to accept my key so I know trying to get out from unlocking on the inside isn't going to work. I keep fiddling with the handle, the door is angrier. I can see its face, I can feel it.

At last, I give up. I don't have the energy to argue. I go to sit on the bed, the fan blowing hot air on me. I stare at the door.

"Let me out."

The branches of the tree scrape the roof angrily, one branch seems to almost burst through the little submarine screen. I go to look out the window. I thought I saw the fancy ass car of my landlord glint from behind the willow, pulling away.

There's another smell, now. It seems familiar. Then a puff of smoke blows into the window.

I try to look down, but the window is so small that I can't even get my head out.

Is this place on fire?

The door slowly swings opens, and I see the hallway

is thick with smoke.

Holy fuck!

I run out, smoke stinging my eyes. I feel for the neighbour's door. The knob is in my hand and I bang on it.

"Fire!" I yelled. "Get out, there's fire!"

The flames are licking the stairs and there's no way I can get down. I go back to my room and shut the door.

I call 9-1-1 and hope to hear sirens soon.

The smoke is so thick, I can barely breathe.

I'm coughing, my eyes watering, tears rolling down my cheeks.

"Help!" I yell out the window. "Fire!"

As I scream, I see the door open again. But this time, there's no fire. This time, the hallway is full of tall green grass and bright green trees framed by a cloudless blue sky. There are birds singing. The willow tree doesn't scrape angrily on the roof anymore. The grass rustles invitingly.

I step out into the soft green carpet, and the door swings shut behind me with a smile as the house embraces me.)(

ABOUT THE CONTRIBUTORS

~ COLLEEN ANDERSON ~

Colleen Anderson is a Canadian editor and writer of fiction and poetry whose work has appeared in over 200 publications. Her collection *A Body of Work* was published in 2018. She recently edited the anthology *Alice Unbound: Beyond Wonderland*, co-edited two other anthologies, and was long-listed for a Stoker in short fiction. www.colleenanderson.wordpress.com

~ MICHAEL BAILEY ~

Michael Bailey is a freelance writer, editor, book designer, and a resident of forever-burning California. He is the recipient of the Bram Stoker Award (and 7-time nominee), Benjamin Franklin Award, a few dozen independent accolades, and a Shirley Jackson Award nominee. More at www.nettirw.com.

~ KEALAN PATRICK BURKE ~

Kealan Patrick Burke is the Bram Stoker Award-winning author of six novels and seven collections, including *Sour Candy*, *Kin*, and *Master of the Moors*. His most recent release is the collection *We Live Inside Your Eyes*. Visit him at www.kealanpatrickburke.com or on Twitter @kealanburke.

~ STEVE CARR ~

Steve Carr, who lives in Richmond, Virginia, has had over 320 short stories published internationally in print and online magazines, literary journals and anthologies since June 2016. Four collections of his short stories, *Sand, Rain, Heat* and *The Tales of Talker Knock*, have been published. His plays have been produced in several states in the U.S. and he has been nominated for a Pushcart Prize twice. His Twitter is @carrsteven960. https://www.stevecarr960.com

~ JOHN PEYTON COOKE ~

John Peyton Cooke has written several novels in the horror and crime genres. His queer vampire novel *Out For Blood* has recently been reissued by Valancourt Books. *Torsos* was a finalist for the Lambda Literary Award for Best Gay Men's Mystery. Other novels include *The Chimney Sweeper*, *The Rape of Ganymede*, *The Fall of Lucifer*, *Haven*, and *The Lake*. His short fiction has appeared in Christopher Street, Weird Tales, The Magazine of Fantasy & Science Fiction, and Best American Mystery Stories 2003. www.johnpeytoncooke.com.

~ JG FAHERTY ~

A life-long resident of New York's haunted Hudson Valley, JG Faherty has been a finalist for both the Bram Stoker Award (*The Cure, Ghosts of Coronado Bay*) and ITW Thriller Award (*The Burning Time*), and he is the author of 7 novels, 10 novellas, and more than 75 short stories. He writes adult and YA horror/sci-fi/fantasy. You can follow him at www.twitter.com/jgfaherty, www.facebook.com/jgfaherty, and http://jgfaherty-blog.blogspot.com/

~ SÈPHERA GIRÓN ~

Sèphera Girón was in the first Pulp Book of Phobias with one of her magician stories, *Five in the Six*. Other magician stories appear in anthologies *Intersections: Six Tales of Ouija Horror* and *The Abandon Anthology*. She also has work in *Dark Rainbow* and *Amazing Monster Tales*. For more information:http://sepheragiron.ca

~ JILL HAND ~

Jill Hand is the author of "Too Hot in Boilertown," in *The Pulp Fiction Book of Phobias, Volume I*. Her work has appeared in many anthologies. She is the author of the gonzo noir thriller, *White Oaks*, from Black Rose Writing.

~ NANCY KILPATRICK ~

Nancy Kilpatrick is an award-winning author of 23 novels, over 220 short stories, six collections, editor of fifteen anthologies, plus graphic novels and stories, one non-fiction book, one stage play, one radio play, and lots of non-fiction.

~ STEPHEN KING ~

Stephen King is the author of more than sixty books, all of them worldwide bestsellers, most recently *The Institute*, *The Outsider*, and *Elevation*. His novellas and short stories have been collected in ten volumes, and another, *If It Bleeds*, is due for publication in 2020.

~ DONNA JW MUNRO ~

Donna JW Munro has an MA in writing popular fiction from Seton Hill University. Her pieces are published in Dark Moon Digest # 34, Sirens Ezine, the Haunted Traveler, Flash Fiction Magazine, Astounding Outpost, Nothing's Sacred Magazine IV and V, Corvid Queen, *Hazard Yet Forward* (2012), *Enter the Apocalypse* (2017), *Killing It Softly 2* (2017), *Beautiful Lies, Painful Truths II* (2018), *Terror Politico* (2019), and Thirteen O'Clock Press anthologies. Contact her at https://www.donnajwmunro.com

~ JOHN PALISANO ~

Bram Stoker Award-winning author John Palisano is the author of many short stories, several novels, poetry, and non-fiction. He lives in Los Angeles. www.johnpalisano.com

~ MEHITOBEL WILSON ~

Mehitobel Wilson lives in Kentucky. Recent short stories have appeared in *The Pulp Horror Book of Phobias*, *Apex #75*, *Forbidden Futures #4*, and *Zombies: Encounters with the Hungry Dead*. Her dark fantasy novella, *Last Night at the Blue Alice*, is available from Bedlam Press. Selected stories have been collected in *Dangerous Red*. Visit her at mehitobel.com.

ALSO FROM LVP PUBLICATIONS:

Subliminal Reality

Simple Things

Revisiting the Undead

Darkling's Beasts & Brews:
Poetry with a Drink on the Side

Final Masquerade

Dark Voices

Available at Amazon, Barnes & Noble and
LycanValley.com

www.ingramcontent.com/pod-product-compliance
Lightning Source LLC
Chambersburg PA
CBHW031643100726
47898CB00006B/1961